The Journey of Aurora Starr

Marla Kay Houghteling

The JOURNEY *of* AURORA STARR

SECOND GROWTH PRESS

Photo credits: Photos taken by Evander L. Cole in 1898-99.
Cover photo: "Cripples from scurvy and freezing."
Frontpiece photo: "Junction of Tahltan and Stickeen Rivers."
Original negatives of Evander L. Cole's photos are in the
archives of the Clarke Historical Library at Central Michigan
University. Also in the collection is the account of his Klondike
Gold Rush experience.

The first draft of this book was written under a Creative Artist
Grant from ArtServe Michigan. The project was funded in part
by the Michigan Council for Arts & Cultural Affairs.

michigan
council for
&arts
cultural
affairs

To Norm, who built a hut for me so I could write this book

Contents

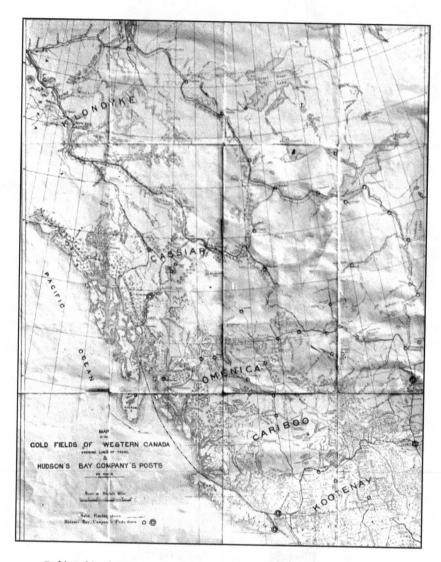

Gold Fields of Western Canada

Chapter One

To Gather Ice

Select a clear, cold day, and with ice tools—which should consist of a cross-cut saw, an axe, a pike pole, and an ice ladder—go to the scene of your operations. Cut three feet wide with the saw, and split off with the axe, by chipping out a V, or wedge-shaped hole, at each edge; then strike a few light blows in each hole until the block separates from the mass. In this manner you can get your blocks out nearly as true as with the saw.

I t was the coldest winter in any living person's memory. All of Michigan hunkered down, stunned by the unrelenting frigidity. The air was a tangible object, so brittle it could shatter into pieces. The ice cutters had been at work since New Year's, removing two by three blocks from the frozen harbor. Now it was too cold to venture out for long. Aurora Starr did not allow herself to dwell on the even deeper cold of Canada.

One thing softened the desperate reality of the sub-zero temperatures: she was heading to where Martin was. He had been gone for a year now, and it would be months before she could reach him. Sometimes she had difficulty remembering the sound of his voice, even his face. She retained a blurry image in her mind, but it refused to come into focus. Then panicked, she'd retrieve the wedding picture and stare at Martin's black and white likeness until she was reassured. Three letters and that curious note in a whole year!

She had wanted to leave immediately after Christmas Day at the Bartek's, but there were too many matters to take care of on the homefront. The nagging unease was clarified that day: something was wrong. Not just the failure of the expedition, but something more permanent—a shift in Martin as evidenced by the cryptic note from him, not sent directly to her, but included in a letter to his parents telling of Frank King's death. She spent January making arrangements for the house, the animals, her students. A recent graduate of the county normal was going to fill in for her, and live in the house. Clyde Kleckner and his nephew Pat promised to keep an eye on her property. With some misgivings, she transferred her animals to the Kleckner farm. She would miss the steady companionship of the dog Marble and the cat, and her daily contact with the cow and horse. Pat assured her he would personally watch after them and, now that he was a confident writer, send word of how things were going at home. "You don't need to worry, Mrs. Starr," he said, "as soon as you send me a post office box number in Seattle, I'll write you a letter with all the news."

She hugged him, registering how solid, how much a man he felt. Yet he was earnest and serious in a boyish way. She knew she could trust him. "Bless you, Pat."

And then at the end of January, the package arrived. Ulrich, one of Martin's companions at the camp near old Fort Halkett, explained in a laboriously written note of rescuing a brown leather notebook as Martin attempted to burn it. He worried about Martin and thought Aurora should have it. Ulrich handed it over to a doctor who was passing through the cripple camps, and the doctor posted it to Aurora. It was a miracle—this notebook reaching her, almost like having a part of Martin with her now. There were dark, singed areas on the leather, and the edges of the pages were blackened. Why would he want to destroy the book?

Aurora did not think twice about dipping into her inheritance. The vastness of the journey was incomprehensible to her; she could only think in increments: across the Straits, through the Upper Peninsula, to Wisconsin, across and up to St. Paul, where the Great Northern would take her the breadth of the continent to Seattle. Three days to St. Paul, then three days by train to the west coast—if she was lucky. She sent off a note to Martin's parents, telling them of her plan. Thank goodness, she would be gone before they could respond.

It would be foolhardy and likely impossible to follow Martin and Frank's itinerary. Martin had not reached Dawson, had not even crossed into the Yukon Territory. She wasn't sure when Ulrich had taken possession of the notebook, but by checking an atlas in the Blackbird Reading Room, she knew the former Fort Halkett was in British Columbia on the Windy River. Would Martin be traveling now, moving through that cold, unforgiving world, now without Frank?

Once she reached Seattle, her plan was to board one of the many steamers that went up the coast. But where would she disembark? How would she find a guide to take her inland? She could not think of that now. There had as yet been no word from the provincial government in Vancouver. But what did she expect, that a letter would arrive saying, "Yes, Martin Starr is in Dawson, mining tons of gold!" She thought of the thousands of men, just like Martin, who had disappeared from their families. And what if Martin was at this time attempting to come back? What if they missed each other, passing in opposite directions?

"Take it in stages, Aurora," her mother told her when she became discouraged at completing a project. So now she was concentrating on getting to St. Paul without freezing to death. She had little energy to be sentimental about leaving her homestead and all the familiar, known people who formed her world. The farmhouse creaked and snapped in the cold, as if protesting its abandonment. Aurora glanced back once, though there was no one on the porch to bid her farewell.

" " " " "

Aurora's body operated sluggishly, controlled by a chilly core. She had crossed the frozen Straits on a sleigh with another woman from Blackbird who was going only as far as St. Ignace. The first night away from home she stayed in a drafty, creaky hotel in the Upper Peninsula. At night she barred the door with a chair because of the two drunken men in the room next to hers. She slept in her clothes, including her coat, and her shallow sleep was interrupted by bottles clanking and rolling on the slanting floor on the other side of the wall.

A smoky logging train with a passenger car attached took her on to St. Paul, where she boarded the Great Northern. On the platform, porters distributed hot bricks wrapped in burlap to keep the passengers' feet warm. She could hardly wait to find a seat and rest her feet on the lovely package. The cold seeped into her boots, forcing its way through the wool socks she wore, knitted from the same skein of yarn that had produced socks for Martin. She wore a sweater over her merino wool dress, with a cotton slip, woolen knickers underneath. Her good gray coat was accented with a red scarf; her head was buried in a huge black astrakhan hat and thick gloves made her hands clumsy. The noise of the engines, the cold-dazed crowds, the shouts of the porters and train staff, the steam hanging motionless in the cold air intimidated—and invigorated—her. For a moment she forgot about her mission, that her hopes for a settled life with a family might be over. She was off on an adventure, no daily chores, no obligations. She had never traveled by train—and had never been out of Michigan.

In splurging for a sleeper compartment, Aurora felt the thrill of treating herself in a first-class manner. Who knew when she would next have a decent bed or experience any comforts like those on the Great Northern? The second-class coaches were comfortable, but passengers were obliged to sleep in their upholstered seats. Never having slept in a public place, Aurora had no wish to compound her vulnerability. As a woman traveling alone, she must remain alert. Indeed, it seemed all her senses heightened: the sights, noise, odors, textures and even tastes of the journey made her pay attention as she moved through alien territory.

She stowed her satchel in the sleeper, taking in the maroon plush seats which faced each other with a table in between, all of which converted into a bed. "And if you want to sleep in the air . . ." said the porter, and as if performing a magic trick, he released a silver lever on the ceiling to lower an overhead berth, suspended by chains. Aurora was enchanted. The berth was already made up in crisp sheets as snowy white as the world beyond the damask-curtained window. The inside of her sleeper was oiled walnut, with carved flowers bordering the ceiling. A stained-glass transom glowed above the door to this space of comfort and refuge, a temporary nest.

Goodness! Suddenly it was too much luxury. She made her way to the day coach, touching each side of the narrow passage with her hands to maintain balance, trying to adjust her gait to the swaying motion. Taking a seat by the window, as the train jerked and chugged out of the station, she leaned forward from the green upholstery to look down at the confluence of the Mississippi and Minnesota Rivers. She thought of the Mississippi growing, broadening, as it made its powerful way to the Gulf of Mexico, where it was warm and people wore just one layer of clothing. She removed her boots and placed her stocking feet directly on the brick.

Aurora felt an observer, free and unconnected. Was this how men felt as they set off on their adventures? Released, liberated? Was this how Martin felt, and was it the real reason he chose to leave home on his various trips?

An older woman, about the age her mother would be, nodded and sat down beside her, her fur coat making it a tight squeeze into the seat. "I believe I got the last brick," she said gaily, placing it beneath her shiny brown boots. Aurora smiled, feeling the warmth thaw her own toes.

In less than five minutes she learned that the woman, Wilma Thompkins, was going to Montana to help out her daughter who was due with her first child. After the birth, she planned to stay on for a couple months. Her husband, a banker right here in St. Paul, would be looked after by his spinster sister, who lived next door to them. Wilma hoped for a grandson, but you couldn't control these things, now could you?

No, Aurora replied, you could not.

Keeping her eyes on Aurora's wedding band, which had been put on for the trip (it usually resided in an abalone box on the dresser, so she did not lose it while doing chores), Wilma launched a series of questions. Aurora found the falsehoods slip from her lips. It was so easy, so freeing, to invent a history. It didn't really seem like lying, more like giving voice to an impromptu fantasy.

"My husband is out in Seattle, establishing his medical practice. More doctors are needed with all the Klondikers returning. I'm to look for a suitable house for our family." Yes, she had two children, a boy and a girl, who were being watched after by Aurora's parents in Minneapolis in a spacious house with a large yard. After several minutes, Aurora nearly believed this fiction.

She thought of Starrvation Corner, her warm kitchen, now inhabited by a stranger. The lilac buried in snow (would it survive this winter?); the smokehouse, the cow and horse, Marble and the cat, and Pat. The young man possessed an instinctive kindness towards animals, and she hoped he could convince his uncle that the cat and dog would do no harm in the house. While the barn with its hay and animal warmth provided shelter, they were used to being inside with humans. And she smiled thinking of Marisa and her active household. How she would like to have Marisa along on this journey! At least for part of the way.

Like her animals, Aurora was out of her element. She wasn't afraid; she was too intent on her goal to let the unfamiliar make her fearful. Even the two drunks, with their red-lidded leers and whisky-swollen faces had not really scared her. She knew the difference between caution and fear. Caution let you go ahead; fear held you captive.

Her seatmate went to the oak-paneled dining car for a late breakfast. Aurora declined politely. She was hungry, but it was too much work to keep up the new version of herself, and sooner or later Mrs. Wilma Thompkins would sense an inconsistency in her story. Now that her feet were warmer and her muscles, clenched against the cold since she left home, were relaxing, she was content to gaze out the window at the endless snow-covered land. Near the border with North Dakota the train ground to a stop. Men jumped down from the engine with shovels to remove the deep drifts of snow on the tracks. In a half hour, they were moving west again.

The day coach where she sat was half-full— families, people in twos, and by themselves, like her. A few were taking a short trip; others would go all the way to the coast, stretching out in the seats when night dropped, and the train moved steadily, its beam the only light in a frozen, silent world. Pipe smoke wafted forward from the rear of the car. As the steam heat warmed the interior, the smell of wet wool and leather mingled with the tobacco. The odors comforted Aurora, made her feel less alone, a part of this small portion of humanity moving across a landscape under arctic temperatures on one of the best trains in America. The fatigue of her journey thus far and the warming of her body's core made Aurora sleepy. She was just ready to leave the coach for her sleeper when her seatmate returned from eating. "They have lovely oatmeal and muffins," she announced, giving Aurora's arm a squeeze.

"Yes, I heard the food was very good on the train, much better than the station meals."

"Except for the cold, we can be grateful we're traveling in the winter," stated Mrs. Thompkins, who seemed to want to share all her knowledge of train travel.

"Why is that?" Aurora decided to accommodate the woman.

"One word: dirt. You can't wear good clothes on the train when it's warm. If you travel in the summer, wear gray or brown worsted with a linen duster over it. The dirt and soot work their way into the train and will never leave your clothing," she said.

"Well, I'll certainly remember that if I have to travel again," said Aurora.

Wilma Thompkins seized this rough spot in Aurora's story. "If, my dear? Don't you mean when? Surely you'll be coming back from Seattle by April? You will have found a house by then, I hope!"

"Yes, of course, I hope so, too," she responded to the annoying woman. "I believe I'll go and lie down. I'm rather tired," said Aurora, then thinking Wilma Thompkins must think it odd that she was already tired having just left home. She longed to stretch out on the clean sheets of the upper berth, suspended by chains from the ceiling, above the floor and above the northern prairie.

"Perhaps you'd join me in the saloon car this afternoon. There's to be music and singing." Mrs. Thompkins made this sound more an order than a request.

Aurora forced herself to be social. Besides the woman would be ending her journey soon. "Yes, I'll look for you there." Aurora left the cooled off brick on the seat, squeezing past the ample knees of her persistent companion. How odd, she thought, as she walked through the parlor car, and observed four men playing poker at a green-felt covered table. Cards at 11 a.m. Once a person boarded a train, normal routines and schedules were abandoned, it seemed. Well, look at her, taking a nap at this hour! In this environment, one was given license to pursue more frivolous activities. One of the poker players looked up as she passed, nodding his head slightly, his deep brown eyes, almost black, holding hers a bit too long.

In her compartment she hung her coat, sweater and dress from the wooden hangers. She left her boots outside the door, as suggested by the porter, to be cleaned. Her stocking feet sank into the soft patterned carpet, the deepest pile Aurora's feet had ever experienced. She washed her face at the marble and walnut washstand, sudsing up the little embossed bar of soap, which released the smell of roses.

She climbed up using the little ladder, stored in a space in the wall and slipped between the tightly tucked sheets and blanket. The bed was comfortable, but the sway of the train made it hard to relax; if she fell into sleep she might be thrown from the berth. So she remained there, unable to enter into sleep, yet feeling protected, warm and safe, as the clacking rhythm of the moving cars over the tracks blotted out all other noises. Finally her growling stomach forced her to action. She hadn't eaten since St. Paul, and that had consisted of a tasteless biscuit and a tepid cup of tea.

As Aurora entered the dining car, she prayed to not encounter Wilma Thompkins. She was reassured to remember that the woman ate breakfast just a short time ago.

"Are you dining alone?" asked the Negro waiter.

"Yes," she answered happily. She marveled at the flowers in the vase on the linen tablecloth. Daffodils in February. Where had the flowers come from? She lifted one of the blooms to breathe in the delicate perfume. She had just started the soup, oysters in a wonderful milky broth, when a man stopped at the table, the man from the poker game. The waiter hovered a few steps back.

"I realize there are other tables available, but none have such charming women at them. I've asked this good man here to show me to your table. May I join you?" There was a swish of fabric from his silk vest, as he bowed towards Aurora.

Her first reaction was a slight annoyance. Now she'd have to make conversation when all she wanted to do was eat this delicious soup. Instead she acquiesced. "Please sit down."

The waiter moved away, yet the man remained standing. "I'm Louis DeValle." He bowed again.

"Aurora Starr. Please. You must try the soup."

"I think I'll have the croquettes. It will be easier to make conversation," he replied. He straightened his cuffs, checking the gold cufflinks, then studying Aurora.

She considered her options: stick with the story she told Wilma Thompkins, invent a new identity, or tell the truth. Her real name had come out, so she might as well be herself. The chances were slim that Wilma and this man would compare stories.

"You are going all the way across, to Seattle?" His voice had a slight accent, foreign in an appealing way.

"Yes, to Seattle." She would give no more than was necessary. A natural caution told her to not become too chatty.

"I also am going to Seattle. It's a wonderful city. Perhaps we will be able to see the mountain if it is not too rainy." She noticed the we, not you. Mr. DeValle ate the chicken croquettes holding his fork in his left hand, pinning down the food and cutting with the knife in his right. It was the way Marisa and Jory ate their food, in the European manner. Aurora had a moment to take in the black hair, curling next to his collar, the tan complexion, the glossy trimmed beard and moustache outlining full, suggestive lips, lips that seemed too pink and full for a man.

"I see your ring. Perhaps you are going to meet your husband?"

"Yes, that's right." It was true, in a way. "And you? Are you meeting your family? A wife?"

"I'm going out for business. My wife died in childbirth last year." Mr. DeValle placed his cutlery carefully on the edge of his plate and turned toward the window.

"I'm so sorry," said Aurora. Somehow the images of *wife* and *child* did not match up easily with the man across from her.

A bustling movement entered the dining car. Wilma Thompkins rustled by, her skirts brushing the edge of the tablecloth, inches from

Aurora's elbow. She took the next table, facing Aurora, pinning her with a disapproving gaze. Aurora nodded slightly and continued with her soup.

"What line of business are you in?" Aurora was curious about this man who had sought her out. She need not have anything to do with him after this meal, but it was a relief to be out of Wilma Thompkins' suffocating presence.

"Pianos. I'm hoping to open a branch for our company in Seattle." He dabbed his moustache with the large white napkin.

"And do you play yourself? Are you musical?"

"Barely. I can play a few simple songs, but I have an excellent ear for pitch. I know what a well-built, well-tuned instrument sounds like." He smiled, revealing a mouth of crooked teeth.

Although this imperfection lessened Aurora's suspicion of Mr. DeValle, she did not want to answer any of his questions about her Seattle destination, especially with Wilma Thompkins sitting within earshot. Standing as she excused herself, she said, "I hear there is to be music in the saloon car this afternoon. It might be something you'd enjoy."

He stood, rather half rose from his seat, as she moved into the aisle. "I'd enjoy that. Thank you for sharing your table."

"And, Wilma, I'll see you later," said Aurora as she passed by.

Wilma Thompkins eyed her warily, her mouth tightening. "Yes, three o'clock."

The train slowed, its whistle blowing, as it approached a tank town. Aurora went back to her compartment and bundled up, suddenly anxious to escape the confines of the train. She stepped down onto the platform, the arctic air, rushing straight down from Canada, making it hard to breathe through her nose. The station was hardly more than a shed. She stood on the freezing platform, looking down the length of the train. People climbed out of two windowless cars, long, narrow wooden boxes, which were coupled to freight cars. When she boarded in St. Paul, she had not noticed these other cars.

As these third-class passengers went into the station, Aurora walked down to the end of the platform and peered into the interior. There was an iron wood-burning stove at one end, and judging from the smell, a toilet at the other. The only seating arrangements were long narrow benches facing each other. Aurora could not imagine traveling for three days in such a space.

The cold penetrated her coat. She entered the steamy station, a cloud of pipe and cigar smoke hanging over the heads of the passengers, who were crowded around a counter where local milk, cakes and meat sandwiches were sold. Aurora felt ill at ease, yet transfixed by the activity of this parallel world existing on the same train. She enjoyed her oyster soup, the clean sheets, the Brussels carpet and certainly did not want to sit on a wooden bench all the way to Seattle. Yet she felt guilty observing these other travelers. How did they get any sleep, she wondered.

Returning to her compartment, she found her path blocked by Wilma's considerable bulk. "I'd advise you to be careful. That man looks like a charlatan, or at least a cardsharp," she whispered urgently.

"Hardly," answered Aurora. "He sells pianos."

"That's what he says. People often misrepresent themselves when they're among strangers," she said, a shrewd expression overtaking her face, an expression Aurora had not yet associated with this woman. Aurora knew Wilma did not believe her story of meeting her doctor husband. And with a jolt of joy, Aurora realized that she did not care what the woman thought.

" " " "

The saloon car was decorated in rich reds and blues and filled with soft sofas trimmed in braided fringe. Seated at an organ in the corner was the conductor, who had now assumed a new role as the afternoon's entertainment, pulling out the stops with vigor as he played "Keep the Ball A-Rolling." Wilma Thompkins sat on a sofa opposite the settee on which Mr. DeValle lounged, legs crossed, eyes closed. Her eyes fastened on him as her foot tapped out the beat. Aurora stood at the doorway, then quickly retreated before either spotted her. The next selection "You Tell Me Your Dream, I'll Tell You Mine" was one whose words she knew. Aurora sang to herself as she swayed with the train's motion, all the way back to the compartment. Enough of socializing for one day; it was more than she usually did in a month.

That night she gave up trying to sleep in the overhead berth and, with the assistance of the porter, converted the seats into a more stable bed. Sleep came immediately and with it images of a thinner, bearded Martin. Before midnight, someone knocked softly on her door. She heard it, the sound too discreet to be urgent, but the effort to arise and deal with whoever it was—Wilma Thompkins? Mr. DeValle?—seemed too much. The vast expanse of the Dakotas surrounded the train as it steamed through the darkness, and the thought of all that wild, black space now made sleep impossible. She reached for the brown leather notebook. Back in Blackbird preparing for her journey, she could not bring herself to read it. She needed time and freedom from her chores to face its pages. It would be her companion, one to teach her about her husband. Her hands trembled as she opened the cover.

February 1898

It has taken us six days from Pelican to Calgary, and this morning we joined the crowds jamming the businesses to outfit for the Klondike. We purchased 5 horses, harness and toboggans, tents, mining implements, boat-building tools. We put in stock provisions and clothing for a year. A year! Extra cash for Mackinaw coats and pants—even leopard seal waterproof mittens and German knit and shrunk stockings with leather heels! Foodstuffs are mostly beans, flour, bacon, dehydrated fruits and vegetables. Frank and I each bought a new .30-30 Winchester . . .

Chapter Two

February 1898

Martin Starr and Frank King stayed in a poor excuse for a boarding house when they finally reached Calgary. The floors were streaked with mud, the rooms sour-smelling. The evening meal at a table crowded with Klondikers was rabbit stew with precious little rabbit, and bread so rock hard even soaking it in the stew did little for softening. "No drinking or fighting in my rooms," ordered the owner as the men dispersed. She was collecting cracked bowls from the table, wearing a long coat and thick boots as if she were swilling pigs in a barnyard.

"More like no *sleeping* in my rooms," muttered Frank, surveying the hammock-like cots. "I feel like I've been rode hard and put away wet," he said before submitting himself to the drooping mattress. After the six day journey from Pelican Rapids, Minnesota, they were exhausted. Frank was soon snoring, while Martin lay alert with worry about getting all their provisions up to Edmonton.

Frank had persuaded Martin to join the Klondike Gold Rush. These two were boyhood friends, sons of Pelican Rapids, Minnesota. Frank wanted adventure, while Martin was hoping to find enough gold to start his dream enterprise, exporting fruit from Michigan to the western states. Frank detected Aurora had not been in favor of this expedition to the Klondike. It meant she was in charge of the farm, as well as teaching school. And it meant being without her husband for one or two years. He had never met her, but he envied Martin finding such a remarkable wife, educated, with striking looks, judging by the picture Martin carried.

Before leaving Pelican, the men had made lists of necessities after talking to a townsman just returned from the Yukon. He had found little gold, enough to keep himself fed and outfitted, but the *hell-hole* conditions had driven him home. He seemed unwilling to talk much, so they didn't pester him. Martin and Frank had youth on their side and were confident they were up to overcoming any obstacles. Hadn't they spent most of their boyhoods out-of-doors, even in the winter with ice-fishing, snowshoeing, camping? Their Minnesota lives were training for this trip through Canada. Besides the old fellow left in 1897, and everything in the brochures touted better trails and an increased number of Hudson's Bay Company trading posts.

They spent a hefty sum getting outfitted: five horses, harness, toboggans, and food—mostly flour, beans, bacon, dehydrated fruit and vegetables. Then they added tools for mining and boat-building and a new .30-30 Winchester for each of the sons of Pelican.

They decided to team up with four men from South Dakota, who were staying at the boarding house. They seemed like reliable fellows, all from the same town. This newly formed group of six set out together on the one-day trip to Edmonton.

They set up camp on the north side of the Saskatchewan River, and immediately built a corral for the horses. Edmonton was a wild west town with Klondikers trying to break in their horses in a few days. Many of the men had no experience in handling horses, much less wild Indian ponies. The streets were full of bucking cayuses, out of the control of their new owners. Edmonton's citizens feared to be out on the streets, and probably wished that, in spite of all the money flowing into the town's commerce, the gold-seekers would move on. The townspeople called the invading horde "the stampeders."

Edmonton was a feast for the eyes, a huge noisy circus. Martin and Frank had never seen such contraptions and bizarre inventions.

They watched a team of horses drag a boat of galvanized iron down the street. Its inventor had fashioned a keel for the rivers and runners for the snow. There was a monstrosity resembling a lawn mower, a sixteen-foot axle sticking out on each side, covered with sheet steel. These oddities plowed down the main street, pushing wagons, horses, men out of the way.

Their little party waited for the rest of their supplies to come through from Calgary. Other larger parties and their horses were strung out along the river. Frank came up with a clever way to identify their animals. He combined letters from the two states: MI and SD. MISD was how they were all regarded by their loved ones, Frank explained. It helped to diminish homesickness to see this "word" cut into the long hair on the horses' flanks. One of the South Dakota fellows had done barbering and brought along the tools of his trade to make some income on the trail. "Make sure you wash those clippers before they touch my head," said Frank. The barber came back with: "After a couple of days on this trail, the horses will smell better than you." They all laughed, feeling they were lucky to have hooked up with one another—a swell bunch of stampeders.

The supplies all came in on the 26th, so the 27th was spent packing everything on the toboggans, then lashing canvas over the load. They set out the morning of the 28th, the horses hooked up singly to toboggans. Scarcely had they left camp than they ran into trouble. Two of the beasts headed off into the scrub. Several more balked, stubborn as mules. After countless attempts at getting all twenty-one horses back on the trail and moving, the group was worn out and the day was ending. They had traveled only four miles out! So went the first day on the Edmonton Trail, but they consoled themselves with the knowledge they were ahead of the fellow who left Edmonton in a device with wooden wine barrels for wheels and a sleeping platform on top. They passed him two miles out of town. The hoops had come off the barrels, and then the whole assemblage collapsed.

They had all read the "Klondike Bulletins," which assured them of reaching Dawson in ninety days. There was the all-water route, which required freighting the loads to Athabasca Landing, ninety miles away. Then the trip would require taking a boat or canoe down the Athabasca and Slave Rivers, across the Great Slave Lake, down the MacKenzie to the Liard, up the Liard to its headwaters. From there it would be necessary to portage to the Pelly, the river that would deliver them to the Yukon and Dawson.

Considering themselves practical men, they decided on the overland route, by trail to the Slave Lake Post, across to Peace River Crossing. They had been told that anyone with good health, outdoor skills in boating and camping and an adequate cache of provisions could make it by June. At Peace River, the route went across to Fort Nelson and the Nelson River. Then the journey followed the courses of the Nelson, Liard and Pelly Rivers to the Yukon and Dawson. One brochure called this "the back door to the Yukon."

Although the consensus was to go overland, Martin couldn't shake the nagging suspicion that the brochures were untrue. They seemed full on promises and empty on evidence.

Packed along, not visible but just as heavy, was his guilt at leaving Rory. The morning he left home, they kissed and clung to each other in the warm kitchen. She followed him onto the porch, wrapped in two shawls. He turned back once as he headed out onto Sawyersville Road to catch a ride to the Straits. Her auburn hair caught no sun, no fire in the morning gray. She pressed her lips together in a tight smile to keep from crying. Then, "Wait." She ran to him, slipping on the bottom step. She grabbed his gloved hand and laid his watch in the palm. He hadn't seen it for days and thought it lost. The chain was interwoven with Rory's hair wrapped in fine wire.

"For good luck and safety." She turned quickly before he could see the tears. He did not look back again.

Chapter Three

Camphor—For Chapped Hands, etc.

Lard, wax and almond or olive oil, equal parts, with a little powdered camphor. Used to rub over the hands after washing to prevent chaps.

After two days in Seattle, Aurora had nearly forgotten Wilma Thompkins, who had pointedly avoided her until the older woman disembarked at her stop in Montana. She obviously disapproved of Aurora's behavior. Mr. DeValle, before disappearing into the misty racket of the city, had given Aurora the name of a tourist home which "catered to women."

Seattle was overcast with a freezing drizzle coating the streets, yet legions of bicyclists skidded around the city going to their jobs and attending to business. She had never seen so many bicycles. The tourist home, a new building with intricate mauve and maroon wood trim, even a porte cochere for delivery carriages, was impressive. She checked the number several times to make sure this was the place. Yes, a small brass plaque beside the bell pull discreetly announced *Mountain View Tourist Home for Ladies.*

Later, sitting at the window in her sumptuous room, she watched the clouds lift and Mount Rainier loom up, seeming to rise from the streets of Seattle. She could not stop looking at it; it absorbed her so she could no longer discern where she ended and the mountain began. Then as if someone had drawn heavy drapes across the scene, the mountain disappeared behind a bank of clouds. Aurora took this as a good omen: she would find Martin, thin but in good health. He and his party would have found gold somewhere along the Liard, enough so that he could return home with a sense of accomplishment.

Martin badly needed to have a success. He was not a farmer; he hated the endless chores of caring for animals and crops and being at the mercy of the weather. When his Uncle Ethan left him the farm, he developed grand plans for putting in orchards—apple, cherry, plum trees—and starting a fruit export business. He would pay someone else to do the field work. "Just think of it, Rory," he said, "people in Nebraska, even California, eating Michigan apples." She married him in 1895, full of eager anticipation at helping him with his dreams, their dreams. When he went downstate to take a horticulture course, Aurora had taken care of their animals, their garden and taught school. The farm, bounded on the north by Sawyersville Road, formerly Indian Trail when Uncle Ethan homesteaded it after the Civil War, and on the west by Starr Lane, was dubbed *Starrvation Corner* by Martin soon after they moved into the farmhouse. He remarked that if they relied on his farming skills, they would surely starve.

When Frank King, Martin's boyhood friend from Minnesota, had written to Martin, touting the golden promises of the Klondike, her husband could not refuse. He did not ask for her permission, only her understanding in regarding this as an opportunity for both of them and their children—still in the future. At first she tried to talk him out of it. Their separation would be too long. They could try for a loan. The bank? Perhaps his parents . . .? Surely there must be another way to finance the orchards.

Her calm logic was no match for his determination to become a Klondiker. He read excerpts from brochures Frank had sent about small-town men from all over the U.S. who had returned home rich and set for life. "I have to do this, Rory. I won't make you sorry you married me."

The next morning as she prepared to go out she noticed her hands, which after days of not doing chores had lost their redness and cracks. The nightly applications of hand treatment in a jar, lent to her by the woman in the room next door, were healing her skin. She walked down to the wharf area, slipping once on the slick boardwalk, but catching herself. After checking the shipping schedules, it was evident that it would be foolhardy to go all the way to St. Michael at the mouth of the Yukon. It would be a long, arduous trip, and an unnecessary one, she felt. She'd then have to travel the vast length of the Yukon River to Dawson. Her intuition and common sense told her Martin had not made it to Dawson. He was somewhere in British Columbia, maybe near the border with the Yukon Territory. There was a ship going to the Alaskan port of Wrangell to pick up returning stampeders. That's where she would go: to Wrangell and then go by boat up the Stikine to look for Martin. She studied the map in the office of the shipping line. The route from Seattle passed through clusters of little islands, staying close to the coast for the most part. The nearest town of any note was Juneau, further up the narrow land projection, hugging the border with British Columbia. Her eyes moved up to the vast areas outlined as British Columbia and the Yukon.

Wrangell, a former army post, had been the point of entrance for insignificant gold rushes back in the 1870s. But it was superseded when gold was discovered on Gold Creek in the Silverbox Basin, 150 miles up the coast, leading to the establishment of Juneau in 1880. Aurora read all this in a brochure on sale in the shipping line office, absorbing all this information as if she were studying for an exam. It was a way for her to keep from sinking into fear and dismay.

When she questioned the ticket agent about the schedule and price, he stared at her. "Are you sure that's the place you want to head to?" the man asked, raising his eyebrows and peering at her through the bars of his window, rather like a disapproving schoolmaster. The building was chilly and smoky, the small stove in the center striving to put out heat in the pervasive wetness. When another customer opened the door, the smell of fish and brine combined with the smoke.

She hesitated, wondering why he questioned her. "Yes, Wrangell."

"Do you know much about Wrangell?" he persisted. "Not a lot of business, not like Juneau. Juneau is a better place to be heading."

"I don't care about the businesses," she replied with a chilly smile. "Wrangell is my destination."

"I think you'll find it tough going," he said.

"I don't expect it to be an easy journey," she said, a bit miffed by the man's persistent interest in her travel plans, "but thank you for your concern." She finally managed to get the price of the ticket out of him.

That night, back at the tourist home, Aurora made sense of the ticket agent's behavior. At dinner— a wonderful meal of baked fish, canned beans and tomatoes, creamy potatoes and a tart apple strudel—Aurora met the other women staying at the Mountain View. Some were heading for the Yukon, others had returned and were deciding how to go on with their lives. Mae Chesterfield, the owner of the establishment, was the widow of a Klondike King, to whom she had been married just six months. When he keeled over dead, Mae acquired all his wealth, in addition to the diamonds and gold he'd given her on their wedding day.

"It's my duty to help out other girls who are venturing north, and those who have come back, a bit worse for the wear," Mae told Aurora. "I can share my knowledge, give them sound advice without any men around to confuse matters. In fact, no men are allowed in the bedrooms. Any male visitors stay down here in the parlor." She smiled, revealing a gold tooth, which along with the beauty mark on her lip gave her an exotic, mysterious look.

Aurora realized why Louis DeValle had directed her to Mae's place, he assumed she was a woman heading up to the Yukon. He had not questioned her about her husband, because he didn't believe she was meeting a husband. She was a woman traveling alone, heading for the gold fields, so she must be seeking a living in the dance halls and poker parlors. Mae believed Aurora when she told her why she was in Seattle. Mae even promised to contact some of her "business acquaintances" who had mined on the Liard. "I'll make some inquiries with some fellows who just returned from the Yukon last week. Maybe some of them have heard of Martin Starr."

In her room Aurora looked in the large gilt-framed mirror. The days of being on the train protected from the elements had been kind to her. Her face, no longer reddened by wind, had a luminous quality. The rough chapped skin of her cheeks and lips was smooth. It seemed her hazel eyes were larger, perhaps more open. The moist air of Seattle caused her abundant red hair to curl around her face. She smiled. A woman of easy virtue. Was this how she appeared to others? What would Martin think? Would he be shocked, ashamed, or amused of the way she was perceived by strangers? She couldn't guess. Their year of separation had sowed these seeds of uncertainty. She was not sure how the Klondiker Martin would react. At least there were no more gray hairs.

Just last May at Starrvation Corner, standing before the mirror above the wash basin, she attempted to pluck a glistening white hair, defiant in the mass of auburn—the color of old copper according to Martin. Just when she thought she had separated it, it disappeared from view. Her fingers finally trapped the stiff, wiry hair. She gave it a yank and inspected it. Sudden tears filled her eyes. She was twenty-eight, would be twenty-nine—or more—when she next saw her husband. She had no children, and now no husband. Would she be gray when she next saw him? Her future seemed in limbo. Martin was pursuing his dream, well, it was his dream for both of them, of acres of fruit trees. Now they grew flint corn for the cow, hay for the horse, potatoes and vegetables for them. Aurora had planted the summer garden, though it was risky. A hard frost could surprise everyone as late as June, and then she'd be without a source of vegetables.

Back on that May morning, her tears disappeared as quickly as they came. There was much to do. She looked out the bedroom window, smiling to see the cat rolling in the grass, the dog stretched out in the sun. She took her bottle of shampoo outside to the rain barrel. The water from the well had a good taste, but it left a white powdery coating in all the cooking pots, which only came clean with boiling white vinegar. Rain water was best for washing hair, leaving it soft. When Aurora was a girl, her mother washed her daughter's hair with rain water. A sense of peace descended at the placing of a cloth over her shoulders and the ladling of soft water over her bent head. It was easy to imagine her mother's strong fingers massaging her scalp, then handing her a flannel square to place over her eyes to keep out the shampoo, made by dissolving powdered borax in water. Aurora followed her mother's method, rinsing out the lather of the borax solution, then rubbing into her hair a mixture of sweet oil and cologne water.

Her wet hair hung down her back, darkening the light blue of her dress, as she attended to an apple tree whose bough had snapped in the wind. On such a pleasant spring day, she didn't mind chopping apple wood; her hair would dry more quickly outside in the air. From her pocket she pulled a snarl of yarn, snips from her knitting. She separated the yellow, brown, blue, and red strands and tied them loosely to a branch. It made her happy to think of her yarn scraps woven with twigs and grasses into nests for the next generation of birds.

It It It It

It was easy to stay on with Mae. Although she was probably only ten years older than Aurora, she possessed a nurturing, mothering quality. Mae had married young, left her husband back in Cincinnati when he became a dedicated drinker and wife-beater. She came out to Seattle to cook, working in the kitchens of several big hotels. "I've always loved to cook for lots of people. That's what makes me happy," she said, the gold tooth sparking in the sun that swept through the window and across the breakfast table. "In '97 I decided to head up to the Yukon to start my own eating establishment, a legitimate business. I'd heard what those miners lived on, so I thought they'd appreciate a good meal." She stopped to pour herself more black tea into a cup so thin it was nearly transparent.

She and Aurora were alone at the breakfast table on another gray day. Aurora was aware of the muffled footsteps of someone coming down the carpeted steps just outside the dining room and the louder banging of pots in the kitchen. Mae had talked two seventeen-year-old twins from going up the coast to Amine the miners." She offered them jobs in her kitchen for now, and better jobs later, if they would stay in Seattle.

"And where did you start your business?"

Mae's sad smile lifted the beauty mark slightly. "My plans changed when I saw I'd be competing with big establishments. It wasn't enough to just offer food. If you're a woman among Klondikers, you have to provide more in the way of entertainment."

"Entertainment, like singing? Dancing?" Aurora mashed her fork into the remaining crumbs of peach cobbler, which was served at the sideboard buffet along with creamed salmon and shirred eggs.

"Oh, I've known a few women who have made a living doing that, but only if they have professional training. For most women, it's prostitution."

The word was like a slap—a hard, abrupt sound. Aurora continued pressing her fork into the plate, though no crumbs remained on the china. She'd never met a prostitute before, although there were rumors about a woman living near one of the logging camps beyond Sawyersville who was said to be free with her favors.

"Fortunately for me, I didn't have to do it very long. A month or so. It wasn't very hard, mostly giving comfort. Those men were so grateful. Most of them hadn't seen a woman in months." She held Aurora's gaze. "I'm afraid I've shocked you, but it's amazing how quickly you can change your habits when you're away from civilization."

But Aurora wasn't thinking of Mae's behavior. It was Martin, away from familiar surroundings. Martin, young and handsome, with a wife thousands of miles away, and who probably hungered for some softness, some "comfort."

Mae's house was located on the edge of the area destroyed by the 1889 fire, some thirty-one square blocks. Mae gave her a tour of the commercial district, told her how as the fire engulfed business after business, the mayor ordered that structures in the path of the blaze be dynamited. It had taken months to clear away the rubble, Mae said. But the city recovered and forged ahead. Drainage problems had always plagued Seattle. The sewers dumped their effluent into the Sound, but the tides blocked the outflow, causing sewers to back up. There were creative ways of dealing with this smelly, and unhealthy, ordeal. When Mae first arrived in Seattle, she rented a room in a boarding house whose outhouse was on stilts. The residents had to climb a ladder to reach the toilets, a feat only for the strong and agile. The person climbing the ladder tied a bow in a red rag on the bottom rung to let others know the toilet was in use. No bow meant the high toilet was unoccupied. Aurora laughed to hear of Mae climbing the ladder one night, Awhile holding a candle, mind you," to find a man from down the hall sitting on the toilet. "He was so engrossed in reading his newspaper with his candle that I scared him to death. On my way down, I yelled to him to tie a bow next time."

To address the drain issue and to accommodate the timber barons who owned the land on which the businesses were located, it was finally decided to build up the city, on top of its previous location. Stone retaining walls were constructed, the pre-fire city blocks were backfilled to raise streets. This meant the surviving stores were from ten to thirty feet below the new streets. The shopkeepers installed ladders leading from the street down to the wooden sidewalks and shop entrances. Soon new sidewalks appeared beside the new streets, and little by little stores built up, or gave up as the earth caved in around them. The abandoned ground levels, were filled with old fixtures, sometimes converted into basements or used as shelter by society's human cast-offs.

Mae said Aurora should have seen things while the city was being jacked up. "I'd do some shopping in a 'raised business,' then walk down the sidewalk a ways and climb down a ladder to get to the next place I wanted to shop." She laughed, shaking her head in amazement at a city whose shoppers had to climb in and out of a hole to do their shopping. "I was thinner then, I'll tell you. All that climbing. But some of the stores lost a lot of customers, those who didn't want to be going up and down ladders."

When Mae arrived in Seattle in May of 1889, just weeks before the great fire, she was penniless; nonetheless she enjoyed walking by the large homes on the edge of the business area. When she returned from Dawson, she purchased three adjoining lots, former sites of homes she had admired. They had been demolished in the aftermath of the fire. Her building filled one lot, leaving open space on either side.

Aurora could not help but admire her. Although she did not approve of the direction Mae's activities had taken up in the Yukon, still Aurora thought it remarkable the amount of control and power Mae Chesterfield had, the huge decisions she had made on her own. Mae told her about "the Swede," who soon booked up all her time, so she could take no other customers. She had liked him even before he struck it rich at one of the Eldorado claims. The fact that she had never been divorced from her abusive husband back in Cincinnati seemed to have little bearing on Mae's acceptance of a diamond and emerald engagement ring, a ring Mae still wore. When she and the Swede married, he put $30,000 in the bank for her and wrote her into his will. When his heart stopped six months later, she was a wealthy woman.

Here in this strange, beguiling city, Aurora's feelings changed as quickly as the light on Puget Sound. One hour she was filled with hope and expectation of being reunited with her husband. They would start life again, maybe not at Starrvation Corner, maybe Seattle. The next hour she was consumed with anger, her fists clenched, jaws aching with Martin's inconsiderate behavior. All the disruptions of their marriage grew from Martin's ambitions, his dreams. True, she had gone along with them, but now it seemed unfair. Only his ideas were pursued. What about her desire for a family? Martin wanted to wait. Her dreams were of living with Martin and their children on the farm. She'd never thought beyond that, had never felt the need to have a larger goal once she met Martin.

And now what was she doing? Searching for a husband who perhaps did not want to be found. He could have found a petite prostitute, perhaps one with a French accent, and forgotten all about his life back in Michigan. But Aurora did not stick with this version for long. She knew him to be loyal and honest. He would not be easily seduced, she told herself. Wherever he was, she was going to find him. One of her alternating emotions was gratitude to Martin for providing her with an opportunity to travel, to experience life beyond her small world.

Aurora spent one afternoon walking down to the Sound, and returned to Mountain View, her feet cold and aching. She felt cleansed from breathing in the salt air and energized from watching ships load and unload, vessels which would dwarf those that docked in the Blackbird harbor. She had walked through the business district, conscious of an older city that had existed a decade before thirty feet beneath her boots. A person could reach sections of the former Seattle, she'd heard, by going into the basements of some of the older establishments which had "built up" after the fire.

How awful for a city to burn! She imagined the heat, as the flames moved to gobble up more and more wooden buildings, as people fled to escape the inferno. Did they run to the Sound, the water stinky with stagnant sewage? Aurora remembered her mother's stories of the 1871 fire in Peshtigo, Wisconsin, when townspeople dove into the river. As the flames spread outside the town, farmers crawled into water troughs. The disaster, by some horrendous coincidence, occurred the same day as the Chicago fire, but was eclipsed by the larger city. The lumber boom insured that most buildings were wooden. In fact the buildings destroyed in Chicago had been built with wood shipped from Peshtigo.

Seattle seemed to have a short memory. Aurora sensed no lingering horror or reminders of the fire, or the buried city. Now the city was riding high on the Klondike Gold Rush, outfitting men, and women, who headed up the coast for greater riches, then welcoming them "and their gold" when they returned to civilization.

Up in her room, she rested her feet on a tasseled hassock; a cup of jasmine tea steamed beside her. From her window overlooking the street, she watched a familiar figure approach the front door. Louis DeValle. She waited to hear the series of bells, activated by the bell pull. The bells completed two rounds, then went quiet. After a minute or so, she heard a soft knock at her door.

"Aurora, there's a man come to call. Mr. DeValle." It was one of the seventeen year-olds, clearly excited by this male visitor.

"Tell him I'm not here, that I've gone out walking." Aurora doubted that Louis DeValle would believe the girl, but she did not want to see him.

At dinner Mae mentioned she heard Aurora had a visitor. "Just someone I met on the train. I think it best I not see him again." She looked up at Mae's concerned expression. "Do you have any news for me?"

No, no one among Mae's Yukon contacts knew of a Martin Starr, though there was news of a group of men at the Hudson's Bay post at Mud River in B.C. who had come overland all the way from Ed-monton and who had given up due to sickness and depletion of re-sources. They were waiting until May when the ice broke up so they could get to the coast and get on a steamer. At this news, Aurora felt a tightening in her breast, a certainty that Martin was with this group.

"You'd have a hell of a time getting to the interior from Wrangell at this time of year. Chances are your husband is staying put until the spring thaw. Wait here in Seattle until then. I have something in mind for you," said Mae. They were at the butcher's, where Mae was select-ing cuts of beef. Aurora swallowed the metallic taste that kept rising into her mouth. She would not let her eyes linger on the marbled thick cuts of cow flesh. This was different than the fish market, where pails were heaped with fish guts, and the glazed dead eyes looked up from bloody wooden boards. She didn't feel a visceral connection with fish. At the butcher's she thought of the warm flanks of her cow when she milked it, of the swish of its tail to keep flies off its rump. "The women need some education. There are some illiterates among the group. How would you like to be the teacher-in-residence until you go to look for Martin?"

Aurora was so full of thankfulness to Mae that she could not speak. She missed teaching, even the erratic schedule of education back in Sawyersville. Last May, with the school term near the end, her class had shrunk. Many students were needed at home for plant-ing. So she took the remaining children on picnics and walks, away from the enclosure of walls, away from the noise of the saws.

But she still had one constant student. She looked forward to her sessions with Pat on Tuesday and Thursday evenings. She waited for his respectful knock on the kitchen door, his open, expectant look as he entered the kitchen and took a chair. If she had a son, she would want one like Pat. She was learning that his shyness came from lack of exposure to the larger world, not from any sense of inferiority. After their first lesson, the boy told her that it had been his idea to be tutored, not his uncle's. It had taken weeks of persuasion on Pat's part to convince Clyde Kleckner, who himself could not read, that his nephew's work on the farm would not be hampered by lessons.

When the soft evening light moved to twilight, Aurora lit the oil lamp. The house was filled with the scent of apple blossoms. Anyone looking into the room would have been struck by the artistic nature of the setting. Their two shades of red hair, hers old copper and his mahogany, were burnished by the lamplight. Student and teacher, heads bent over the wooden table, offered a tableau of an old master painting.

Rather than using the standard primer supplied by the school, Aurora was teaching Pat to read from *Kidnapped*. Surely he would identify with the orphaned Davie and his reading would progress even faster. The fourteen year-old had learned the alphabet back in Ohio; he could make the letters on paper, but could not put the characters together to form words. At first Pat was embarrassed when Aurora made him repeat the sounds of each letter. His ears heated up and he kept his head down, but he ploughed his way through. She made a alphabet book for him using butcher paper. "A is for apples; B is for butter; C is for calf." Then Pat made his own book, using whatever words he wanted. When he finished his lesson, she handed him a vocabulary list from the section of *Kidnapped* they would be reading next. He was to practice saying and writing them. The first list included *lilacs, blackbirds, mist, dawn*—things from Davie's world and familiar to Pat in his life in Michigan. She showed him how to look up words in the hefty green dictionary on its stand in the front room. He took to reading with a rapidity that amazed her. It was as if once the wick was lit, his desire for learning grew in intensity. It was a gift to teach someone so willing and ready to learn. Her school students were not all bright, nor all happy to be attending school.

This night their session was running late. They were reading chapter four, where Davie meets his uncle. As Pat read haltingly, Aurora restrained herself from helping him.

I tried to get this out of my head; but though I took down many interesting authors, old and new, history, poetry, and story-book, this notion of my father's hand of writing stuck to me; and when at length I went back into the kitchen, and sat down once more to porridge and small beer, the first thing I said to Uncle Ebenezer was to ask him if my father had not been very quick at his book.

Aurora wondered how closely Davie and Ebenezer's relationship paralleled Pat and Clyde's. "I can tell Davie will go through a lot of trouble, but I don't think he'll be licked. He'll come through it all right," said Pat looking up, looking for confirmation that an orphan meeting up with a difficult uncle would survive.

As Aurora watched the boy head across the road to the Kleckner farm, her throat tightened with affection. For the first time in months, a few hours had passed without her thinking about Martin.

" " " " "

That night in her comfortable bed at Mae's, she picked up the brown notebook, sniffing the leather. It smelled of horses and wood fires. She stroked the cover, knowing Martin had touched it, had treasured it until it began to represent something horrible. As she read, the words and perceptions were ones she could match with the husband she'd last seen a year ago.

March 1898

It is an odd thing to come to such a wild, untamed place yet be surrounded by a swarm of humanity. The narrow trail is barely a sled's width and traverses through scrub spruce and poplar. Seldom have I been in such congested circumstances. Hundreds of men behind us, hundreds ahead. I feel we are being squeezed. We finally got around a party of twenty-two Englishmen with their 110 horses. What chaos! They had no control over their animals. Their rigs were constantly in a tangle, or one of the toboggans in the endless line broke, causing us to wait on the awful trail for hours until the sled was mended. After two days of this maddening situation, we made an extra push and traveled past them when they stopped to camp for the night. We made our own stop several miles ahead and with little sleep left at first light to be rid of them.

The Pembima River is bordered by steep banks, so our outfit had to be snubbed down by tying ropes around each sled, then looping the rope around a tree and lowering them one by one. To get up the opposite embankment we paid a fellow from Edmonton 20¢ a sled to haul us up, horses and all, by windlass. This man probably makes more money than most of the goldseekers.

Camp on hill back of Peace River Mission

Chapter Four

March, April, early May 1898

*J*t was tough going for the unshod horses as they crossed a wide expanse of hilly scrub timber country. The poor devils were required to pull loads over rough terrain, with an occasional meal of hay purchased from "entrepreneurs" at outrageous prices. Martin and Frank managed to feed their horses some hay with a bit of grain. However, the South Dakota four turned their stock loose at night to find their own food.

It took several more days to reach level ground. They crossed the Athabasca River, just below the site of old Fort Assinaboine, went through a spruce forest and came out the other side to see flat country with clumps of jack pine stands, the blue Swan Mountains in the distance. They could almost hear the horses breathe a sigh of relief. For two days they approached the rugged mountains and then three more of brutal hauling to reach the summit. The work was painstaking, especially on the steepest parts, with much rough talk and swearing as they pulled up the sleds with two horses and a double block and tackle. That night's camp was on the summit, next to two former Klondikers who were now in the business of selling hay. They charged $8 a ton! Frank and Martin bought some hay to feed the hungry horses; again the South Dakota fellows neglected their beasts.

The descent was even rougher on the horses. The larger animals pulled loads of 800 pounds, with the rest pulling around 450 pounds. The animals tried to keep ahead of the loads, which gained momentum down the steep pitches. Sometimes the horses sat down, a sadly comical sight, as the sleds pushed them down the mountain. There were few trees, and those that grew on the mountains were small, so snubbing was not possible. Several times the men dropped the loads from up high to the bottom of a hill, and then spent most of the time mending the broken sleds and harnesses.

Finally out of the mountains, the group followed a rough trail to the Swan River. Two of the South Dakota party's horses died. Martin and Frank decided to leave the South Dakotans. Back in Calgary, the group of six had agreed to stay together until it became a hardship on either group. The two sons of Pelican Rapids had foreseen the other four would pay a huge price for not caring for their animals. Now they would have to travel even more slowly because of the heavier loads the remaining horses would be pulling.

Martin's feet encased in the socks Rory knitted stayed warm inside his boots. He was saving the German knit ones with the leather heels for the following winter. They worked their way down the frozen Swan River and out onto Lesser Slave Lake, heading for the Slave Lake Post, a Hudson's Bay Company trading post. Frank named this section "Dead Horse Trail." The carcasses started appearing around Swan River. By the time they reached the trading post, they had sickened of counting the bodies, well over 150. At one spot on the lake, a group of fourteen dead horses made a strange assembly on the ice. It disgusted Martin to think of the spring thaw, when all these bodies went downriver.

With one exception, Martin's health had held up so far. It was while they crossed Lesser Slave Lake that he was struck with a curious affliction, something never mentioned in the literature from Edmonton. Days of the sun's glare on the unending white had rendered him snow-blind. The pain was intense, so Frank blindfolded him and smeared charcoal on his face, a tip they had picked up from some discouraged fellows who were turning around. They wished the two men well. Martin could not ride any of the cayuses because they were already too heavily loaded, so Frank tied a sturdy bit of rope to the last sled, and his friend hung on for seventy miles across the lake. Behind his blindfold, he visualized Rory carrying a sap bucket to the open field on the south side of the house where the huge maple stood, its trunk marked with healed-over holes from Uncle Ethan's days. Uncle had instructed him that trees in *open grounds, with spreading tops, discharge more and much sweeter liquid than those in the forest.* The warmth of the sun lay on her shoulders, coming through the wool of her coat, yet the air was brisk and long white clouds sailed in from the lake, like speeding freighters. The night temperatures would have been below freezing, the days brilliant with sun. He saw Rory set down the bucket in the skimpy snow around the tree's base. She would know to choose a spot on the opposite side of their last tapping, then bore a hole with Ethan's 5/8 inch auger. Once she inserted the spout with its attached hook, she would hang the bucket and wait for the slow liquid progress of the sap. Martin could hear the first drop as it hit the bottom of the bucket.

After crossing the lake, they arrived at the post, finding it to be in a tiny settlement with a church and a mission school for Indian children. Never had buildings, no matter how humble, looked so good. Martin's blindness subsided once he was able to be indoors. He and Frank were not on their own for long. At the post they hooked up with a large party of twelve who called themselves "The Philadelphians," an outfit seemingly in good shape. They set out from the post for the 80-mile journey to Peace River Crossing.

The materials passed out by Edmonton boosters, merchants who distributed maps and pamphlets promising a good trail all the way to Dawson, were now creased and worn from having been read again and again. One brochure promised that leaving Edmonton by March 1 was a guarantee for snow all the way.

However, there was no sense of peace as they neared Peace River Crossing. The dis-ease was a bit offset by the breathtaking scenery: from a hill overlooking the Peace River could be viewed the snow-capped Rockies thrusting massively towards the sky in the west.

Most amazing was the sight of the Peace, Smoky, and Hart Rivers flowing down like silvery ribbons from their sources. It was oddly disquieting to be faced with a constant stream of once enthusiastic Klondikers, now beaten-down men, returning home in the midst of these natural wonders. They never made it to the Yukon. Here, Martin's natural optimism took a dive, and he began to doubt their ability to reach Dawson. The hill down to the crossing was covered not with snow, but mud.

ıı ıı ıı ıı

They struggled for a day and half, hitching the horses in tandem to pull the loads, and then freeing the beasts from the deep mud. Even more discouraging than the lack of the promised snow was the ending of the trail. When they finally reached the crossing at the frozen Peace River, the trail stopped. "We've been tricked," said Frank, tracing the map's clear drawing of a trail from Edmonton to Dawson. Frank was even more discouraged than Martin, so Martin did his best to buck him up with assurances that they would make it, and return home with gold. He could see it would take little for his friend to join those heading home.

Even the local Indians advised against trying to cross the wilderness between Peace River and Fort Nelson, saying it was one big muskeg waiting to devour horses. The Edmonton boosters needed to gain some semblance of credibility. There was a steady stream of disgruntled, dispirited and angry gold-seekers returning to their town, so the businessmen had hired a half-breed to blaze a trail along the route shown on their maps as far as the head of the Pelly River. They paid this fellow $1500.

Martin and Frank, now with the Philadelphians, headed up the Peace River on the ice to Fort St. John. The plan was to reach the head of the Pelly River by way of Fort Graham. However, after only ten miles above the crossing, at the Catholic mission, the ice became unsafe. They made camp with about fifty other stampeders, forming a small town, and had a big meeting on a mild April day. Martin thought of Rory and April on the farm, with the buds forming little knobs on the old apple trees, the maple sap running—or past running by now.

There were several plans on how to proceed. A cattleman and experienced packer advocated following the new blazes as soon as green grass appeared. This meant taking the overland route and probably cutting a trail. Some opposed that as too dangerous and advocated going back down to the crossing and building boats in order to pick up the all-water route as soon as the ice went out. And then there were those men who were ready to go home.

Martin felt there were so many unknowns that tossing a coin was probably the smartest thing to do. He no longer had faith in his ability to make a good decision. Perhaps feeling a sense of safety in numbers, he and Frank associated themselves with a group of sixty-two men, which included the cattleman and his gang, the Philadelphians and several other smaller groups, who had decided to go overland. Everyone chipped in to employ an Indian guide, and agreed to take turns being in front and clearing the trail. The guide, the only Indian who had been into the wild terrain beyond Peace River, would take the Klondikers as far as Hay River for $60 and sufficient food supplies for his wife and children while he was gone.

// // // //

Taking the uncleared trail was a mistake, but even worse was Martin and Frank's affiliation with the Philadelphians. Soon after hooking up with them, Martin began to have suspicions about Mac, the leader. He claimed to have been to the Klondike back in 1896 and still had a working claim, where all in the present group could make $25 to $30 a day. This was something to hold on to, some promise, no matter that it could not be proved, in the midst of daily uncertainty and hardship.

Martin's confidence in Mac's leadership hit bottom when Mac sold off necessary provisions to purchase more horses. Martin and Frank argued that he should use the cash that the men had all paid in to buy horses. Provisions were too precious to be traded. You could not eat cash in the winter. But the two were voted down by the faithful, ask-no-questions members in Mac's original party. Martin asked where all the cash was. Mac said he'd sent it back to an Edmonton bank for deposit, claiming it was safer than carrying all that cash on him. How could they disprove him?

With herd mentality, most of the men eagerly latched onto their leader's promises and let him make the decisions. Next Martin volunteered to make an inventory of all the materials and provisions, but Mac told him it wasn't necessary and that he was in charge.

A mad-cap scheme with "go-devils," as Frank dubbed the contraptions, was the final straw. Mac, ever ready to experiment with his latest idea, presented his brilliant invention. This involved hitching a horse between two shafts, whose rear ends would be attached to a platform on which could be loaded up to 400 pounds. Mac assured them, "Any horse will have an easier time dragging the 400 pounds with this rig than carrying 100 pounds on its back." Everyone got busy building platforms for the forty-some horses to pull.

Less than three miles into the wilderness, there was a complete breakdown. Many of the shafts and platforms were kicked to pieces by the frightened horses, as the alien wooden devices crashed along on their heels. Those that did not destroy their attachments were having a tough go pulling the loads. Any fool, unless he came from Philadelphia, could see these cayuses could be trained to carry packs but not to pull loads.

With little or no explanation, or apology for the fiasco, Mac launched into his next wild scheme. The trusty pack saddles needed to be sold and replaced with some home-made canvas pouches, which would hang across the horse's back, with one pouch on each side. A blanket would be placed under, with a cinch rope to secure it. Martin and Frank stood their ground this time, refusing to use the Alapperellas." They would stick with their sawbuck saddles. Mac, considering this an insurrection, began to exclude the two from group discussions and plans. At night they set themselves a deadline for breaking free of this shady operator. At this point Frank stated he thought they should head back, not the way they came. Get out to the coast and take a boat to Seattle, then back to Minnesota. Martin listened, remembering how impulsive Frank had been as a boy— ready to embark on a new adventure until something else grabbed his attention. But this was not one of their boyhood fantasies, like paddling across the lake pretending to be pirates. They were thousands of miles from home. They had gone through so much; they should stick it out, at least for a while now that they would no longer be Mac's subjects.

A long-time paying claim

Chapter Five

April 1899

Piano—Hints About

Dampness is very injurious to a pianoforte; it ought, therefore, to be placed in a dry place, and not exposed to draughts. . . Have your piano tuned about every three months; whether it is used or not the strain is always upon it, and if it is not kept up to concert pitch it will not stand in tune when required, which it will do if it be attended to regularly.

Aurora had written to her friend Marisa in Blackbird, trying to include everything—the train trip; Seattle with its fishy, salty smells; its imposing, though often invisible, mountain; its buried city; and Mae. She didn't write to Marisa of Mae's past, or about the inhabitants of Mountain View. She wasn't sure Marisa would find it as intriguing or interesting as Aurora did. She told her friend she would most likely be at this address until May. As she posted the letter, she had a sudden thought. Could Marisa read? She had never actually seen her read anything. Of course, one of the older children could read it for her, but Aurora was reminded of how many things she often took for granted in those closest to her.

She also sent a letter to Pat, trying to make her letter as much a tale of adventure as possible. She reserved all her questions for the last page of the lengthy letter: Was the tenant taking care of her house? How had the animals, especially Marble and the cat, survived the winter? What books was he reading?

Although she did not receive a letter from Marisa, Pat replied right away. His handwriting was looping and juvenile, but the contents showed someone who loved trying out new words. He was obviously using the dictionary she'd given him on her departure. He said he had been *ministering to the animals' needs* and that the *frigidity of the weather had abated*. She smiled, picturing Pat hunched over pen and paper in the evening after chores, his hair bright in the lamplight. It had been one year ago when he had knocked on her kitchen door. When she opened it, she saw a figure with hunched shoulders, rain running down the side of his face like tears and turning his dark red hair to black. It was Clyde Kleckner's nephew. She had talked to the boy only once, and didn't even know the lad's name.

"My uncle sent me over," he said, wiping his face with his coat sleeve. The dog, dripping as well, squeezed in past the boy, and shook himself, sending a spray of water onto Aurora's apron. "Marble, go. Lie down." The dog gazed at Aurora before giving one more vigorous shake, then settled down in his place behind the wood range.

Aurora ushered the boy in, taking his soaked coat to hang on a hook behind the range. "That's a good name for the dog," said the boy.

"Yes, it's not the kind of thing folks typically name their dog. But he seems to like it." The dog resembled a calico cat with his swirls of black, white and butterscotch fur. "Marble came from a litter from your uncle's dog," she added.

"Yes, I know. He told me he selected the best of the bunch for you by using his fool-proof method."

"And what method is that?"

The boy looked uneasy. "He pretends to set fire to the bitch's bed on all sides. The one she tries to rescue first is the pick of the litter." He shifted his weight. "I don't agree with some of his ways."

A metallic taste filled Aurora's mouth. Her saliva turned watery. "That's horrible. Those poor dogs." She saw the frantic mother dog, still nursing, circling in her bed, the whimpers and yelps of the puppies.

"He says he stomps out the burning straw right away. It never touches the fur," he said, seeing she was upset and wanting to reassure her.

The all-gray cat lifted its head from the tight coil of warmth on Martin's chair, then returned to its ball shape. Aurora considered this a positive sign. The cat usually disappeared when any strange person entered her territory. Aurora, feeling a bit shaky from the boy's revelation, indicated a chair.

"I have just made some taffy. Would you like to try a piece?"

"Please." He pulled at it with his teeth. "Maple. My uncle isn't much for keeping any sweets."

"I'll give you some to take home. I've made plenty. Most will go to my husband. He's headed for the Yukon." Aurora noted that the boy was more alert and intelligent that she first thought. He had a steady way of watching her while she talked, as if he was committing her words to memory.

"My uncle told me." He perked up, sat straighter in his chair. "If I were older, that is where I would go."

"Martin will have to tell you of all his adventures when he returns."

"When is he coming home?"

Lightning tore a jagged rip in the sky, throwing the leafless trees into relief and illuminating the smokehouse. Aurora and the boy held their breaths waiting, and several seconds later a crack of thunder shook the house, sending the cat off the chair and under the sink.

Rising to look out the window to see if any trees had been hit, Aurora said, "I hope by next year, if not sooner." She said it calmly, but the words brought back the painful length of her separation from Martin. "I don't know your name," she said, turning from the window and suddenly realizing how good it felt to have another human in the house. She hadn't realized how quickly and completely she accepted loneliness.

"Pat. It's fully Patrick Kirkpatrick. You can see why I go by Pat."

"It's a wonderful name, but now you have to tell me what your uncle wants."

"For you to tutor me. I'm fourteen and had a little bit of schooling in Ohio, but..." He clasped his rough hands on the table and stared down at them as if they could give him courage. "I can't read. I'd like to know how."

"I guess your uncle can't spare you during the day so you can come down to the school?"

"No, ma'am, Mrs. Starr. He can't manage all the work on his own. Besides, I don't learn so well with a bunch of others. I'm better by myself."

"What do your parents think of you living up here with your uncle?" Another clap of thunder echoed off the hills to the west. She thought the boy hadn't heard her. When he finally spoke in a soft voice, he seemed much younger.

"My ma died two years ago and my pa took off." He looked up. "Maybe he's looking for gold, too." This thought seemed to cheer him up. It made some connection between this place and his former life in Ohio.

Aurora gave Pat a dry jacket and a cap. "You can pick up yours when you come for a lesson." They struck a deal: Pat would come over two evenings a week for tutoring; they would see how the schedule suited them both. Aurora would be paid in eggs (she did not keep chickens) and split wood.

Pat stopped at the door and took in the dog behind the range, snoring and wheezing and the cat, which had returned to the chair. "Why do your animals come in the house?"

Aurora knew this was considered an odd habit, perhaps even a suspicious one. Folks around here believed animals, even pets, lived outside. "They are creatures who appreciate warmth and shelter as much as we do. I feel a great responsibility to care for them."

"My uncle says they are dirty and bring in sickness. He calls them dumb." Pat said this in a way that suggested he didn't go along with his uncle's ideas.

"My animals are healthy. I take good care of them. I promise I won't bring the horse and cow into the kitchen." Pat smiled. Aurora respected Clyde Kleckner's knowledge of animals, but not his attitude towards them. To him they were pieces of farm machinery. She had heard the story that he once shot a horse because every time he rode it, the animal headed towards low tree boughs, either knocking Clyde to the ground or making him duck quickly. The horse was defective so he needed to be rid of it. Whenever she heard this now local legend repeated, Aurora wondered why he didn't sell or give the horse away. Why kill it?

" " " "

So now Aurora found herself a member of a new family, one that filled her days with purpose while she waited for the Alaskan spring. She grew fond of Mae's household and her role as a teacher. Mae valued Aurora's education, for Aurora told her that Michigan had two state teacher-training schools, one at Ypsilanti and the other at Mount Pleasant, her alma mater. Aurora mentioned that she was a rarity—a normal school certificate-holder who taught at a small rural county school. Most teachers in rural areas had scant training, many of them barely older than some of their students. The teachers with whom Aurora was acquainted had attended short summer institutes at Mount Pleasant, or had gone to the next county, which offered a "county normal," a summer session teaching practical skills and nothing of the arts, which Aurora thought an essential part of education. The county normal courses in Charlevoix County were free if the enrollee promised to teach at least a year in a rural school. Who could blame them? The job requirements were strict, and many young women lasted only a year. Engagement or marriage was cause for dismissal, as was attendance at any social function not sponsored by school or church. And the pay was low, although not as low as subsistence farming.

For all her credentials, Aurora had never been accused of being snooty. She'd been asked by the Charlevoix School District to instruct a county normal during the summer, and she had for two consecutive summers just before she'd married Martin. Emmet County had not dismissed her when she married. She was a shining example of what the county offered to its rural citizens: a good education. She had intended to teach until she and Martin started a family, but Martin said he wanted a firm financial base before a baby came. Sometimes Aurora wondered if Martin was afraid of having children.

Her class at Mae's was held in the afternoons Monday through Friday in the plush front room with its flocked wallpaper and thick carpets and a Knabe piano. The women sat on sofas or on huge tasseled cushions on the floor. Aurora started with the basics, just like in her school by the sawmill back home: the alphabet, printing letters, then reading.

Mae had returned from the Yukon with a mission. Most of the women she'd met were uneducated and unequipped to survive without becoming "good time girls." Although her experience in the gold fields turned out to her advantage, she knew of many sad, desperate and even tragic stories of other females. These women had been afforded less dignity than the pack horses used by miners. She felt herself fortunate in meeting "the Swede" and so was obligated to share her bounty. The young women still in their teens she discouraged from going, not always in the gentlest manner. Those women who were determined to head north, she trained in money and health matters. The madness of the Yukon, which had reached its peak in 1897 and '98, was waning. Now the word was that Nome was the place to make a killing. Then there were the women who returned broken and in need of a home.

Franny was in this latter category. Aurora had tried to not stare openly at the short, stocky woman's eye patch when the household gathered at the table for the evening meal. Mae had told her a bit of Franny's background. She was a seamstress for several dance halls in Dawson, creating and preparing costumes for the performers. Having a little capital of her own, she went into partnership with an "entertainment palace" owner, a Brit named Bert Harris. The establishment, as Franny herself later explained to Aurora, was a theater with a sturdy stage, to which was attached a saloon and gambling hall. Soon after Franny joined forces with Bert, he turned the second floor into a series of rooms for a brothel and ordered Franny to run this part of the business. When she refused, he struck her, the blow so severe to the left side of her face that her eye had "popped out of its socket." Disabled and depressed, Franny was taken in by a friendly madam, who sent her "sponsor" to deal with Bert Harris. Harris paid Franny for her half of the business, and the seamstress came to Seattle and sought out Mae, whom she had met briefly in Dawson. Now Franny was planning to open her own shop down on 3rd Street, taking on some of Mae's younger residents as her first employees. She couldn't spend hours doing fine embroidery and stitching because of headaches brought on by the strain on one eye.

Tonight the eye patch was a peach satin with a design of tiny white seed pearls. The color matched Franny's shawl worn over a soft gray wool dress. Franny's beauty was in her clothing, her face being flat-featured and unremarkable. Like Pat, she was a voracious learner once the code to reading had been cracked. At night she came to Aurora's room to talk about what she had just read. Often it was an article from that day's *Seattle Post-Intelligencer*, and more often than not it was the record of some grisly murder or shady event.

"I can hardly believe my eye," Franny gasped, causing Aurora to catch her breath at Franny's joke about her disability. "A man has been arrested for killing his wife—the night of the big fire back ten years ago! It says he claimed she died in the fire, but some city workers came across her body down in the old city when they were checking pipes. How about that?" She grinned triumphantly as if this murder was the best news she'd ever heard.

On a sunny brisk morning, seagulls wheeling and screaming overhead, Aurora accompanied Franny on a walk down to the center of the city. Franny wanted Aurora to see the building she had in mind for her dressmaking business. They were on 2nd Avenue, chatting as they passed Ramaker Music Company. Aurora stopped mid-sentence and stood before the plate glass window where Louis DeValle bent over a young woman who was placing her fingers tentatively on the keys of a shiny black baby grand piano. He looked up, taking in Aurora and Franny, gave a nearly imperceptible nod and returned his attentions to the attractive piano customer.

"What is it, Aurora?" asked Franny, stepping closer to the glass to peer in.

Aurora looped her arm through Franny's and moved on. "A man I met on the train. He assumed I was a good-time girl." She laughed. "I think I'll let him continue thinking that."

So Louis DeValle did deal in pianos. And he was probably devising a seduction of the young woman at the keys. It gave Aurora some satisfaction to have rebuffed him.

As they walked on Aurora told Franny of her encounter with Mr. DeValle on the train, of the awful Wilma Thompkins and of how she felt as a married woman on her own in Seattle. In some ways, it was easier to talk to Franny than Marisa, most likely because Franny had a wealth of experience and Aurora felt nothing she said could shock her new friend.

Later in life, Aurora would remember her months in Seattle with fondness. Her husband's whereabouts and safety were unknown, her own future uncertain, but being in Mae's house created another world for her, shielded her from the difficulties and sadness that were to come.

Mae and Franny wanted to take her to Bremerton. It was a day-trip, and they could see the battleships that were in drydock, having returned from the war down in Cuba. Back in Michigan, Aurora had heard about the war, but it was a faraway, foreign event. Seeing the huge formidable ships, some 360 feet long, with all sizes of guns (12-inch, 8-inch and 4-inch, she learned) gave her a strange feeling about being an American. She didn't like the idea of war, of human bodies being blown apart, of the orphans and widows who were the end products—but she was surprised at the seductive effects of viewing this display of power. Ships, guns, torpedos. How different than the harbor in Blackbird, where the schooners and barges moved in and out with hides, lumber and tan bark.

She wondered if Martin had known about the outbreak of war last year. From what Aurora read in the newspaper, her sympathies were with the poor Cuban people, who had been confined to camps by the Spanish, and who suffered from disease and poverty. Who would not be on the side of Cuba? Indeed, after the letter from a Spanish official in Washington was intercepted and the venomous disrespect toward President McKinley was made public, few Americans had any use for Spain. So much had happened in that brief war: the USS Maine sunk in the Havana harbor, Dewey's defeat of the Spanish fleet in the Manila harbor and the Rough Riders victorious in Cuba. Seeing the ships, looking a bit weary and scarred, revived the newspaper accounts for Aurora. Her country had been at war, and she had barely been aware of it. April of last year, when Spain declared war on the United States, what had she been doing? She smiled, remembering making taffy for Martin and giving Pat a piece when he first came to her door asking for tutoring.

At dinner on the night after the Bremerton trip, Sally wore bloomers. Sally was determined to head to Dawson to "make her fortune in the oldest profession," even after Mae's counseling. Just last Saturday Aurora had seen a group of women cyclists wearing bloomers, all in bright colors. It was as though a flock of glorious birds had flown by the house. The new garments made sense; long skirts were danger-ous, liable to become tangled in the mechanisms.

"If you're determined to wear those in Dawson, Sally," said Mae as she sat at the head of the table and served fish stew into shallow bowls, Athen expect to be arrested by the Mounties."

"What? For wearing practical clothing?" asked Sally. She was cov-ered in freckles and seemed fearless, and somewhat intimidating, to Aurora.

"A woman can advertise herself on the street or from her window, and the police will look the other way. That's business, even though it's technically illegal in Canada." She looked around the table, her gold tooth flashing. "But let a woman put on a pair of these >prac-tical' trousers, and she'll find herself in jail, or at least paying a hefty fine."

"That's ridiculous," said Aurora, already thinking about buying a pair for herself.

"Well, with the money I'll be pulling in, I can pay off those fines," said Sally, sending a defiant glance down the length of the table. She seemed to respect and resent Mae in equal portions.

"How much can you make?" Aurora wondered how it compared to a rural teacher's salary.

Aurora gasped when Sally said, "I've heard $250 a night."

"That's not an honest $250, Sally," corrected Mae. "No girl could make that unless she was rolling."

"Rolling?" Aurora looked at Mae, then at Sally.

"That's when you get a man drunk and steal his poke," explained Mae, matter-of-factly. "You might be able to clear $25 a night, that's after the madam gets her share. This is assuming you're not doing business out of some little shack, but in an established brothel."

Aurora was hoping her mother up in heaven was not eavesdrop-ping on this conversation.

"And then," Mae continued, dropping a gob of butter into the cen-ter of a steaming popover, just brought out from the kitchen in a basket by one of the seventeen-year-olds, "there's venereal disease. Last fall there was an epidemic in Dawson. I've heard the mercury treatments are brutal and long. You have to be hospitalized for months."

Several at the table had stopped eating, but not Sally, who took another mouthful of the stew. She chewed, swallowed, her freckles standing out in relief. "I know how to be careful, Mae."

Mae sighed, then drew in a long breath. "Songs around the piano in an hour. And I've heard that Franny, one of Aurora's star pupils, has something to read."

Franny beamed, her good eye sparkling, the other covered in a paisley patch.

When Aurora retired that night, she again entered the realm of the Klondikers. Reading Martin's words, she felt the insecurity and terror of the enterprise he and Frank had embarked on. The passage she began brought her to tears.

Today I shot Sweetie. The best-tempered of horses I have ever known. Her leg was broken, and I knew I had to be the one to dispatch her. What is worse than the loss of this faithful beast is that she provided our supper. This unforgiving wilderness forces a man to develop two minds to stay sane. Thus he can eat a pet— and sing its praises as a true companion at the same time.

Rescuing horse from muskeg

Chapter Six

May, June 1898

The Philadelphia party was now nineteen men and sixty horses with a low stock of provisions. Mac scoffed at Martin and Frank's concern over the amount of food. "If I were going it alone, I'd take nothing but salt and a shotgun," he boasted.

Now the nearly nonexistent trail, except for the blazings made by the half-breed hired by the Edmonton boosters, was a nightmare, a death trap for horses. The Philadelphia party, the cattle party and various other smaller groups, brought the total to sixty men and over 200 horses carving a way through. The creatures often sank up to their bellies in the muskeg. The men alternated between extricating the horses and clearing the trail, inch by inch. Already some were muttering about turning back before Fort Nelson.

The only speck of good fortune was at White Mud River. A gigantic driftwood jam formed a bridge of sorts, some of the logs being two feet in diameter. Though the timbers were slippery and half-rotted, they managed to drive or lead the pack horses over the raging current without any mishaps. But the horror of the muskeg returned as they made their way through bogs and windfalls between White Mud and Battle Rivers. Much of the trail was a jumble of fallen spruce, which the exhausted beasts had to climb or jump over. Mac's lapperellas proved to be an even bigger vexation here. As a horse would rise up to leap over fallen timber, the bags slipped back. Then as the animal went forward on the other side of the obstacle, the packs followed, sometimes falling off. The cinch was useless at keeping the pack in place. When Mac's men came upon dead horses from a previous group, they happily discarded the lapperellas and transferred abandoned pack saddles from the corpses to the backs of still living horses. Martin did not see how the animals could last much longer with the relentless struggle of wallowing in muskegs, half sinking with the load, then fighting to gain some semblance of solid ground. His guilt at subjecting faithful, hard-working animals to this hell-hole was overridden by a fear of being without them, of being stuck and dying a death much like theirs.

'' '' '' ''

He missed Rory and her cautious, intuitive nature. She would have smelled a rat within minutes of meeting Mac. It took him longer, but now he and Frank were leaving the party, along with three other men. They had not been with the Philadelphia party for as long as Martin and Frank, but they were as anxious to be away from Mac's crazy schemes. The three were a Brooklyn butcher named Harry; Ulrich, a Pennsylvania Deutsche (not Dutch, he emphasized, which is a corruption of Deutsche. He was German!); and Jim, a Swede from Wisconsin. They received their shares in horses, tools and food, but because Mac had done indiscriminate wheeling and dealing back at the Catholic mission, many necessary items had been traded. They ended up with sixteen horses, but too little food. They should have been striking out with a nine-month supply of food instead of the far lesser amount they loaded on the horses. Martin recorded the amount each man received.

167 lbs. flour
33 lbs. oatmeal
27 lbs. cornmeal
4 2 lbs. bacon
5 lbs. beans

" " " "

They forded the Battle River, and traversed a huge land area on the way to the Hay River. It was a cornucopia of wild game, the creeks crammed with trout, the banks busy with tracks of moose, bear and beaver. It was apparent that no trapping had been done here because there were numerous beaver clearings and frequent dams. Martin shot a couple of beaver for supper. Men who had never had this meat declared the flesh as sweet and tender as chicken back home.

This stretch of the journey provided them with the best eating they would have. Camped not far from the Battle River, Martin went out alone and shot six geese. He realized the folly of greed, for the birds proved too heavy when he tried carrying three over each shoulder. He had to head back to camp with only two and enlist help with the other four. But when he brought down a cow moose, the others treated him like a hero. They made a banquet of juicy moose steaks, then dried the rest on poles over a slow fire. What had been 700 pounds of fresh meat ended up as 150 pounds of dried moose.

Martin surprised himself in this role as hunter and provider. He had always preferred that someone else do the killing of animals. Back home in Michigan, many of the native wildlife had moved on to more hospitable settings after the forests had been cut down. He no longer saw the large numbers of bear and deer that Uncle Ethan had encountered when he homesteaded. Now with hunger and death dogging them, he was not hesitant to pull the trigger. Everyone was sick to death of beans and oatmeal. However, his attitude towards killing animals had changed in another way since he'd observed the

Cree. There was reverence in their practice of killing animals, almost as if the hunter and the hunted joined forces, agreeing that the animal would die. The carcass was treated with respect and when the men brought it back to camp, the women cleaned it in a dignified manner. Martin adopted their practice, and discovered a spiritual comfort in the wilds of Canada, when he had felt cut off from those things that usually sustained mind and spirit.

They crossed the Hay River and on June 5 caught up with the cattle party camped on the edge of a meadow. One of the steers from the bedraggled herd was near death. Martin cringed to see the manner in which the cattlemen slaughtered it. His own small party had been eating meat fairly regularly, but most of these men had not had fresh meat since Edmonton. They polished off the steer in no time.

The group of five left the meadow the next day and tried to discern the blaze marks made by the Hudson's Bay Company scout, but often they were chopping and hacking the brush with no clear direction. Just when they thought they had left the muskeg behind, they entered an area worse than the bogs and swamps already survived. Upon leaving the Hay River, they gained a false sense of security by the dry terrain. Suddenly they were engulfed by swamps, then dense scrub spruce forests, then fallen timber. It was too much for Martin's favorite horse Sweetie, one of the original cayuses purchased in Calgary. She was compliant and smart, and he tamed her quickly. Sweetie became enmeshed in spruce and willow roots and went down into a hole. The horse behind fell on top of her, breaking Sweetie's leg. As Martin stood above, her head twisted to look up at him, the deep, wise eyes asking for help. Before too much sentiment could overtake him, he borrowed Harry's revolver and released her from current pain and certain future hardships. He had set her on this deadly course; it was his responsibility to end her suffering.

Harry did the butchering while the others set up camp. The chiming of metal on metal as the knives were sharpened and the metallic smell of fresh blood distressed Martin. At supper, Harry silently carved a piece of flank for each man's plate. Martin's tears fell onto the meat as he raised his fork. Soon one by one, each man paid a word or two of tribute to the faithful horse.

"Sweet disposition, like her name says," offered Jim. From Harry, "A tireless worker. Worth more than gold." And Ulrich: "May she haf oats every day."

They waited for Martin. He choked out, "I'll miss you, dear companion."

That night he stayed by the fire long after the others were in their bedrolls, snoring—or too tired to snore. He wrote to Rory, announcing their break with Mac and company. He introduced the three men he and Frank were associated with now. He told how Jim, the quiet Swede, had called Mac a "madman" to his face and that Martin suspected Mac had used that insult as justification for cutting back on their fair share of provisions. He listed all the abundant wildlife and boasted a bit of his success as a hunter. He shared his sadness on losing Sweetie, although he knew it would distress her.

As well as he could recollect, he last wrote to his wife in March. It was getting harder to keep anxiety and low spirits out of his communications, so he put off writing. He knew how much she must be worrying about him. He concluded with practical matters:

When I am at a low point, I think of you and feel sure you will be all right at Starrvation Corner, with the rent for the fields coming in, and money from the hemlock bark, too. Of course, there is your teacher's pay, which I hope has been paid on time this year. Write to me of what you planted in the summer garden. I'd trade a couple of beavers to taste a real vegetable about now.

We continue working our way towards the Liard, where surely we will start to find paying gold. We've heard there's plenty to be had all along this river, so before the arctic winter sets in, I may have some new-found wealth to bring home.

He did not feel nearly as hopeful as the letter indicated. He worried that he had put too much on his wife by leaving her alone. He knew she had not envisioned their married life living apart. But if he did not succeed on this expedition, how could he return to her with nothing but tales?

Chapter Seven

A t twenty, Aurora was an intelligent young woman, yet reticent to venture beyond the radius of comfort and protection of her upbringing. Until she was ten, her mother schooled her at home. Although her mother's curriculum was superior to that of the town school, Aurora was lonely for the companionship of other children. Her mother realized this, so Aurora began attending the town school, where she was far ahead of the other students in her class. At sixteen, she graduated from Blackbird High School.

Her parents, her mother especially, had given Aurora a hunger for books. She could never have enough. It seemed a natural step that Aurora would do what all women who loved books did—she would teach. Michigan had only one normal school, all the way over on the other side of the state in Ypsilanti. It would be a distance, far from Blackbird, farther than she'd ever been from home. Her parents thought it wiser to wait a year or two before taking teacher training. She could work in the store and take over the books, her mother's job. Libby Gray had contracted a prolonged case of pleurisy during Aurora's senior year and had been less and less able to meet the demands of everyday life. By the time she was eighteen, Aurora was indispensable at the store. Her parents avoided the mention of normal school, and Aurora was not unhappy with her life in Blackbird. Yet she felt there would be more to her life, that this would not always be the pattern. She sometimes wondered how four years had passed so effortlessly, four years of her life.

"Is there nothing at which you don't excel?" asked her father, kissing her on a blushing cheek. Aurora had suggested that the store carry more in the way of farm implements. They were sold out the first week, and Aurora was ordering again from Sears and Roebuck in Chicago.

Her father left for the post office. Aurora, working at the roll-top desk in the back room, heard the bell on the door, then the shuffling of feet, the clearing of a throat. "I'll be with you in just a minute," she called. She pushed back the heavy drape that separated the store area from the back room and saw no one.

"Hello?"

A head of glossy black hair appeared from behind a stack of 100-lb. bags of flour. The head belonged to a thin, wiry body now approaching the counter cautiously. "I hear you carry shovels and hoes?"

"Next shipment—next Wednesday. The train, you know, from Chicago." Aurora was having trouble forming complete sentences. The man's eyes were startling—the color of a robin's egg captured in crystal; they seemed to have been cut and polished and set in his head like gems. His hair was black, a contrast to fair skin pink from the sun, across his nose and cheeks and forearms where his sleeves were rolled up. But surely she could not have registered all these physical details at that first meeting. They had come to her later, in an overwhelming image.

"And you," Martin would tell her much later, "you were a goddess emerging from behind a curtain. All burnished copper and lightly toasted skin."

He never referred directly to her height, which at five feet, ten inches was two inches more than Martin's. When the two of them were alone she was unaware of the difference. Martin's startling eyes grounded her and kept her focused on their doings and conversation, not on what other people might be thinking. She was oblivious to the critical glances of women at the Methodist church, and the amused stares of business owners along Main Street, sweeping off the boardwalk and nodding as they passed.

Besides being two inches taller, Aurora was also two years older than Martin, who at eighteen was spending the summer at his Great Uncle Ethan's farm, five miles north of Blackbird. His uncle's wife, his third and last, had died. "Uncle is seventy; Lenora was only thirty-five. I'm beginning to think it might be bad luck to marry Uncle Ethan."

"Don't look at me. I'm not considering it," said Aurora. Then she thought how callous that joking remark must sound. She and Martin were walking in the woods behind the farm, which Ethan refused to have timbered, though he could have received a good price from the oak and maple growing there. They had met three weeks ago, but already were comfortable with each other. "I'm sorry. That wasn't nice of me, especially with your uncle's wife so recently dead."

Martin grabbed her hand with his long-fingered one and kissed it. "I hope you're not considering marrying anyone —that is any of the men around here."

"No. Not that I've had many proposals."

"The men must be deaf, dumb and blind then." He pulled off some pine needles from a low bough and chewed on them.

"Well, there was the Canadian who was our interim minister last year. He spoke to my father, not to me, mind you, and we went out riding once. I did not encourage him. I couldn't imagine being a minister's wife." She plucked off some pine needles, too. "The men around Blackbird don't engage me in any way," she laughed.

Martin did engage and entrance her. Perhaps it was because he was from a place other than Blackbird, although as she would come to learn, Pelican Rapids, Minnesota, was not all that different from her hometown.

For the rest of her life, Aurora would retreat in memory to that summer when she and Martin met. When sadness and indecision ruled, she would go back to those hot, blueberry days when her world expanded, when Martin Starr became her first real love. She felt a whole other part of her being emerge, as if she had been only partially formed until she was twenty. She had experienced crushes, but they had been fantasies, never to develop into anything in the real world. There were a couple of boys in high-school who she thought were handsome and whom she flirted with at church socials, but she could not converse with them. They seemed so predictable, so ready to do exactly what their fathers had done. They had no interest in music or reading, which Aurora saw as necessary as food and heat. She appreciated the way her parents did not pressure her towards marriage.

Her father noticed that Ethan Starr's grand-nephew had been coming into the store almost every day. "How's your uncle getting along?" he asked the boy, whose eyes were a more intense version of Ethan's. Blackbird gossip said that Ethan hypnotized the ladies with his eyes, and that there might be a fourth Mrs. Ethan Starr before too long. Grenville Gray tried to disregard gossip, but the boy's eyes made him uneasy in regards to Aurora.

"He's been out in the fields almost everyday, doing the haying with Kleckner. As soon as I get back, that's where I will be."

"Give him my regards." Grenville looked at the door as the bell jingled and his daughter entered the store, back from checking on her mother at the house. The announcement of the bell seemed to change the very atmosphere of the room. It thickened with desire and yearning. Grenville felt out of place in his own store.

Aurora passed the counter, heading for the back room. "Hello, Father. Hello, Martin." Grenville Gray noticed that Martin's attention was riveted to Aurora's back. She turned as she pushed aside the curtain to the back room. Her eyes locked on Martin's.

Grenville saw that the two were already on more intimate footing than he'd realized. Soon they were a familiar twosome, dubbed "the copperhead and the blackhead" by Mr. Gilbert at the post office. Martin was accepted, if not with open arms, at least with reserved politeness, because he was Ethan's kin, and Ethan was a local institution, plus being a Civil War veteran. Though most of Blackbird's whites had only been here for twenty years, there was already an established social order based on pioneers and newcomers. The Odawa laughed to hear the whites brag about how long their families had been on the Little Traverse Bay. That summer Martin was regarded as a visitor, although a visitor who would probably be back.

The following week, Aurora and Martin stood shoulder to shoulder as they faced the setting sun; it was almost 10 p.m. The horizon was a pink-red-orange smear that bathed the bay and the grounds of the Methodist summer camp, just south of Blackbird, in an other-worldly glow.

"What will you do when you return to Pelican?" Aurora was already using the shortened version of the town's name the way Martin did.

"Work with my father at the mill, I guess. The business is expanding; we just opened a store in Fergus Falls, so I might manage that." His words trailed off, as if he had lost interest in talking of matters back home.

That night the Chautauqua speaker, one of several who traveled the summer circuit in the Midwest, was a French Canadian, petite and fiery, her accented voice carrying out across the lawn as she lectured on free thought. It was obvious that the directors of the summer camp were unprepared for the substance of Vivien de Claire's presentation. No doubt the publicized title of her lecture "The Evils We Must Face" threw them off the track. There was much readjusting of corpulent suited bodies and robust throat clearings as Mdme. de Claire urged the crowd to "divest themselves of the heavy cloak of rigid authority in religious matters." There was polite, sparse applause after the woman finished, and those gathered were invited to partake of lemonade and cookies on the lawn behind the stage.

Aurora and Martin took some food and strolled dreamily toward the bluff. The road to Blackbird was below and beyond was the bay and beyond that the Big Lake. Far out a freighter moved towards the setting sun. "What was your response to the talk?" Aurora's mouth puckered at the tartness of the lemonade.

"It made me want to learn more about this free thought movement. I've done my best to avoid churches, and it's nice to know others feel the same. Sometimes I feel like such an odd duck back home." He sighed.

"I admit I find some comfort in the social aspects of church, but I have trouble believing that the whole truth is being presented in the minister's sermon." She moved closer so that their sleeves were touching. "I think we're a pair of odd ducks."

In the waning light they strolled down the little lanes lined with dollhouse structures of the Methodist camp. Some of the "cottages" were modified tents with canvas roofs and sides tied to a wooden frame. These shelters even had canvas gingerbread decorating the front rooflines. Campers sat on the tiny porches, no doubt recovering from Mdme. de Claire's lecture.

"Oh, look at that one," indicated Aurora with a nod toward a tiny house with an upstairs balcony bedecked in gingerbread trim. A woman, reminding Aurora of her mother in the tilt of her head as she gazed from her perch, sat in a cushioned wicker chair on the balcony, watching the smoldering sun dip into the bay. This lane was all houses, and had a more prosperous feel with the double front doors and double balcony doors and the pink, blue, green and yellow wooden trims. Aurora thought it looked like a colony inhabited by children.

The campers came here from the cities to the south: Detroit, Lansing, Battle Creek, as well as some from Chicago. They came up by train, or across the Big Lake by steamer, to breathe the bracing air off the bay, to eat, sleep and talk among other Methodists. However, the air could become foul when the winds shifted and brought the rottenness of the holding ponds at the tannery up to the camp. Then the scent of wet sand, pines, picnic food was overwhelmed by the smell of carnage—fermenting hair and decaying blood-streaked skins. At these times, Methodist ladies held rosewater-drenched hankies to their noses and retreated to their cottages.

Steamer coming in from Alaska

Chapter Eight

May 1899

Sea-Sickness

One of the best preventives against sea-sickness is to support the abdominal walls and those of the chest with a stout firmly fixed bandage. At the same time very particular attention should be paid to the daily emptying of the bowels. Among the medicines which have been recommended for sea-sickness, and which have proved very serviceable, are—phenacetine in 5-grain doses, bromide of potassium in 30-grain doses, chloral in 15-grain doses, and other substances of less utility. The great point, however, is to endeavor to have the organs of the chest and abdomen kept as fixed as possible until the nervous system gets accustomed to the motion of the vessel.

*M*ae and Franny came down to the dock to see her off on the *Gold Runner*. Mae concurred with Aurora's feeling that Martin would head for the coast by way of Glenora in British Columbia, hoping to make it out to Wrangell to catch a ship. Newspaper accounts told of the Canadian government coming to the aid of stranded, destitute Klondikers, many of them refugees of the Edmonton Trail. So Aurora booked passage on a cleaned-up steamer, a retired mail boat from South Africa's Cape Line. In 1897, when anything that could float was put into service to carry stampeders and others surging north, this boat had steamed into the Seattle harbor, ready to take on passengers. Now in 1899 things had calmed down a bit, and overcrowding was not the problem it had been. Unlike the voyages of the previous two years, there were no horses or dogs crammed below decks, going mad with the noise of the engines, just inches from their heads. Still there were enough passengers so that Aurora, hoping for a cabin by herself, found she was assigned a cabinmate.

Now three days into the voyage, Aurora longed to be put out of her misery, out of the clutches of the wretched nausea that had seized her ever since the ship left Vancouver Island's sheltering mass in the Gulf of Georgia. Once the ship entered the Queen Charlotte Sound, a forty-mile stretch not afforded the protection of the inland passageway, it was at the mercy of the ocean's swell. Aurora lay curled on her bed in a cabin shared with a prostitute from Astoria. Her fingers ached from clutching the sides; her only goal was to stay motionless, an impossibility in the rocking vessel. The affliction had taken her by surprise. She had been in canoes and rowboats on the rivers and lakes around Blackbird and had never suffered a queasy stomach. However, this vessel was larger than any she'd been on. She lifted her head to vomit into a large metal bowl her cabinmate had tucked into the bed beside her face. The only outcome was dry retching that brought on shuddering and chills. She felt the most defenseless and vulnerable since leaving Starrvation Corner.

For the first two days on the *Gold Runner*, she spent time reading a well-thumbed book of essays by Emerson and walking the deck, spellbound by the scenery, so monumental and overpowering she felt hypnotized. The ship passed Victoria on Vancouver Island, then close to the shores of the San Juan Islands through what one of the passengers informed her was the Active Pass. When they entered the Gulf of Georgia, Aurora had the impression that the ship was no more than a toy being pulled by an invisible string down a passageway banked by immense walls: the snow-capped mountains of Vancouver Island on one side, and the Cascade Peaks on the other. She felt tiny and insignificant, yet full of awe at the wondrous intimidation of nature. Then the ship followed the route around Cape

Mudge to enter Discovery Passage, a narrow strip less than one-half mile wide.

Her cabinmate, Elisha, spent her time in the ship's social hall, chatting with the available men. Aurora walked through this area, once. A thick haze of cigar smoke formed a permanent cloud suspended from the ceiling, and she felt drunk from just breathing in the whiskey fumes. The banquettes were filled with men, a few women scattered here and there in red and blue gowns, like rubies and sapphires tossed about the smoky room. One of these "jewels" was Elisha, her arm draped around the neck of a florid man in fancy dress. She smiled as Aurora passed. Aurora nodded and avoided making eye contact with any of the men. A host of gazes clung to her as she proceeded through the hall, regally, with no intention of lingering.

Aurora struck up a conversation with two missionaries, a husband and wife, who were headed for Skagway to minister to the "rough and ready, or not so ready," joked Reverend Michaelson. They were a jolly couple, he short and round, she tall, bending over him like an energetic willow. They were quite different from Aurora's idea of missionaries, based on ones who had visited the Methodist church to recite their list of chores in delivering Christ to the heathen. None of the adventure, the excitement of living in Africa or India seemed to have rubbed off. With their dour, humorless expressions, so intent were they on the hereafter that the here-and-now was a hindrance, something to be endured.

There were other married couples besides the Michaelsons on board, but they kept a wide berth of Aurora, perhaps assuming she pursued the same goals as her cabinmate. But the Michaelsons, oblivious to the strictures of Christian behavior, invited Aurora and Elisha to eat with them the first night aboard.

"Be grateful you're traveling now, not last year," said Reverend Michaelson.

"Did you make this voyage last year?" asked Aurora, ignoring the glares and whispers of two women sitting with their husbands at the next table.

"We started it, but got off the ship at a little island at the beginning of the Queen Charlotte Strait. The captain was none too happy with us, but we thought we'd be safer on land than on that tub, didn't we, dear?"

"Oh, yes, the old salt was a bit balmy," hooted Mrs. Michaelson. When she introduced herself, she asked them to call her by her Christian name, Bathsheba. "He finished off the supply of officers' whiskey before we'd reached Vancouver Island. This was after we'd already drifted broadside into another ship. There was near mutiny, I'll tell you."

Her husband continued the narrative. "The boat was so over-booked— they had sold duplicate tickets—that it was carrying four times the allowable passenger count. We ate in shifts, with the dining saloon open round the clock. Of course, the food was nearly gone by the time we got off. A few folks were digging into the provisions set aside for the Yukon." He stopped to catch his breath and load his fork. "So, Bath and I thought we'd try again this year. The Lord is patient," he said through a mouthful of food, some of it dribbling onto the napkin he'd tucked under his shirt front.

Aurora told them she was going to look for her husband, whom she believed to be somewhere on the Liard, or else working his way toward the coast at Wrangell. "The last word I had from him directly was written last June, nearly a year ago," she said her voice trembling, her eyes filling. She tried not to think of that other strange, troubling note of last December.

"There, there, dear," said Bathsheba, covering Aurora's hand with her own firm, calloused one, "you're very brave to make this trip. I'll say a little prayer tonight that you'll find your husband straight off." Not to discount Elisha, Bathsheba added, "And one for you too, such an adventuress, that you'll stay safe and healthy." She said nothing about Elisha achieving her goal, although with the young woman's milk-glass white neck, chest and breast tops glowing above her wine-colored gown, and with the overpowering smell of lilies which battled with the aromas of the meal, there was little doubt why this woman from Astoria was heading north.

Now held hostage in her cabin by seasickness, the memory of those first meals was something Aurora could not bear to think of. The thought of food or drink made her stomach heave. She tried to sit up, but was so dizzy and nauseous she collapsed immediately. Aurora moaned with each lurch of the ship as it ploughed through the choppy waters of the sound. Elisha was unaffected, checking in on Aurora throughout the day, helping her to sit on the chamber pot. She tried to cheer up Aurora by relating the other cases of illness among the passengers. Bathsheba had been in as well, to place cool cloths on her forehead. "You'll have to get off the ship as soon as possible, if you don't improve," said the older woman. "You can't continue without food or water."

There was no doctor aboard, but after two days of being bedridden Aurora's aid arrived by way of Elisha. One of the men she had been "getting acquainted with" was an apothecary. Aurora was ashamed to be seen by any man; she hadn't washed in days, her hair was a mass of tangles. But Elisha's Charlie was all business. He told her to open her mouth, then placed two little pills on her tongue. "See if you can swallow those without water." She couldn't. So Elisha stepped in with a cup of water. "Just a sip," she advised, lifting Aurora's head from the pillow.

She managed to mumble a thank you to Charlie. When he had gone, Elisha removed the undergarments Aurora had worn for three days. "Charlie told me to wrap your torso in some cloth." She wound a long piece of flannel cotton around Aurora's chest and stomach, rather tightly. Elisha was good at this sort of thing. She would make a good nurse, Aurora thought. The soft fabric comforted her, a spreading warmth enveloping her body. She remembered the "belly blanket," a piece of flannel her mother pinned around her stomach when she was sick as a child. Now the same sense of being cared for, though by strangers, helped her sleep.

Aurora would never know how much effect the pills and flannel had on her recovery because the next morning, the steamer moved into the narrow Lama Passage, where the trees came down to the water and now and then the silent wooden presences of totem poles appeared, and the waters were calm. Aurora felt reborn, her mind and body filled with a lightness, physical and mental. She was excited at rejoining the world. Once the *Gold Runner* had crossed Millbank Sound, the shores shot up abruptly, to over a thousand feet. Aurora craned her neck, growing dizzy as she caught glimpses of snowy glaciers far above. The cliffs were dotted with promontories, jutting out over deep, measureless pools of glassy water.

After passing Fort Simpson, the steamer entered Alaskan waters. Aurora and Elisha were in their cabin. Aurora's mal de mer, as Bathsheba called it, was a thing of the past. She learned that a good number of passengers had taken to their beds during the trip across the open waters of the Sound.

"Elisha, did you ever consider training to be a nurse?"

"Oh, goodness, I'd have to wear those awful uniforms." She made a grimace as she adjusted the lace from her camisole to creep above the edge of her neckline, a very low neckline at that.

"Yes, but you could make dependable money and not have to worry about . . ." Aurora stopped. She wasn't sure what Elisha was worried about.

"You mean like disease, abuse and disapproval?" Elisha had obviously been counseled before.

"Well, yes. I mean, don't you think about those things? It seems like a hard way to lead your life. Aren't you frightened?"

"Sometimes, but I can make more money in six months as a prostitute than in years of nursing. As a percentage girl, I can make money just dancing and getting miners to buy drinks. I'll have to find a well-run establishment. I won't try to work on my own, and I'm not going all the way to Dawson. Too far and too expensive a voyage. That's why I picked Skagway." She applied a dot of rouge to each check and slowly smoothed it into her translucent skin, which brought to Aurora's mind alabaster, like in the Old Testament.

"What will you do with the money?"

"I have a two-year-old daughter. I have to take care of her; there's no one else."

"My goodness, Elisha, you can't be more than twenty?"

"I'm eighteen. My stepmother kicked me out of the house when I could no longer hide my condition. My father wouldn't stand up to her. So I went to Astoria where my older sister lives. She's taking care of my little Carrie now." Elisha reached into a small velvet purse and drew out a photo in a silver frame, gazing at it before sighing and handing it to Aurora.

"Oh," said Aurora, struck by the child's other worldly beauty—a cap of dark curly hair and dark, heavily lashed eyes. She wore a lace dress, her hands clutching a tiny bouquet of what looked like violets. "She's enchanting." She refrained from asking about the child's father.

"Sometimes I can't believe she's mine," said Elisha, eyes glistening, her jaw beginning to quiver. "I'm going to make sure she'll never have to do what I'm doing."

"I'll be honest, Elisha. I wish you would train to make money some other way. Perhaps as a nurse or a teacher? This occupation may be lucrative initially, but what of the risks? If you get sick or are injured, what good will you be to Carrie?" Aurora was thinking of some of the arguments Mae would use to persuade the young woman. "What if you become pregnant again?"

"I'll be careful. Now I know how to take of myself. I insist that the man wear a preventative." She noticed Aurora's puzzled expression. "A rubber device. Hasn't your husband worn one?"

Aurora had heard of such things, but had never seen one. "No. Aren't they used to prevent disease?" She and Martin had no worries about that. At least they hadn't back home, before Martin became a Klondiker.

"Of course, but they can also prevent a baby from starting."

"Well, I wouldn't mind starting a baby, but it hasn't happened yet." It was probably just as well that she did not have a child to care for right now. But sometimes she saw her failure to conceive after nearly three years of marriage, before Martin left for the Klondike, as her body asserting itself—going its own way. She had sewn a batch of flannel sanitary pads in preparation for her trip, but had not used them. Since leaving home, her monthlies had ceased. Since there was no chance that she was pregnant, this lack of menses mystified her.

Elisha was saying, "and I don't intend to be in Skagway longer than six months." She looked at Carrie's photo again before putting it away. Then rather defensively, she told Aurora, "I don't have time to train for a job. This is easy. I'm already prepared."

Aurora stopped arguing. "Would you consider marriage with a Klondiker?"

"I don't know. Definitely not to one who has found no gold. There's no security or future in marrying a poor man. I'll not marry for just a roof over my head; I'd be little more than an unpaid servant. That's not enough reason to trade my favors."

Compared to Elisha's worldly, practical perspective, Aurora felt herself sheltered from some hard realities. She had never considered marriage as a form of prostitution. But weren't many marriages around Blackbird just that? Poor, uneducated women marrying for shelter and basic needs in exchange for producing children and performing endless chores. But her and Martin's marriage was not like that! After all, she had options. She could have pursued a career in education, becoming more than a rural teacher. Her desire for the familiar, and yes, her fear of the unknown and untested, had brought her back home to marry Martin.

Yet why did she feel resentful, even now? Maybe she had expected too much of marriage. Her parents' union had always seemed tranquil, untroubled. Doubtless there were frictions, but perhaps being an only child, they felt compelled to shield her from their disagreements. She thought she and Martin would be a family, first a strong pair, and then expanding as children were born. But how could any of that take root and develop when Martin was absent, she staying behind to tend to home matters? She was seized by a great impatience to find Martin, to talk over these matters, to somehow gain control of her marriage. It crossed her mind that her husband might be sick, or even dead, but she squelched such a dark thought immediately. She had already come a long way, but she knew the most physically difficult part awaited her. Still, since she had left St. Paul, in spite of the days of seasickness, she felt protected by a force which gave her an inner sense of peace—and purpose. It was true she did not know the outcome of this journey, but she was sure it was what she should be doing. She felt the energies of people who cared about her—her mother and father, Marisa, Pat, Mae—feeding into this force.

"How will you manage traveling on your own?" asked Elisha. "Where will you stay?"

"As soon as we reach Wrangell, the Michaelsons are taking me to the home of a missionary. She's been in Wrangell a while and works with the Indian women, as well as some who earn money as . . ." Aurora paused.

"Prostitutes," finished Elisha. "It's all right. You can say the word."

"Yes, well, Bathsheba says these Indian women are abused by men. I gather Wrangell is a rough place. I'll stay with the missionary woman and then find a guide to take me into the interior."

"That's good. Because if they think you're a whore, they won't let you into a hotel. And usually a woman traveling alone is considered a whore." Elisha smiled at Aurora. "Your husband is a lucky man. I hope he appreciates you."

Aurora, delighted with the smooth, steady progress of the ship, walked the deck, circling it several times, breathing in the pure air. She could not help but be aware that most women strolling with their husbands jerked their men as far away as possible from her. Aurora took a perverse pleasure in nodding and calling out, "Good morning." A few of the men responded, bringing on a poke in the ribs from their partners' elbows. She wondered if wearing a sign that proclaimed I'm a married lady in search of my husband would stop the hostility? Probably not.

Just before the steamer docked in Wrangell, the passengers united spontaneously in breaking the tedium of the voyage. The day was mild and everyone was out on the deck. A couple of the Adance hall girls" as they were known, prostitute or whore being a bit too raw, began running around the deck. Some single men joined them, shouting out to recruit other passengers as they followed the brightly clothed bodies. The mood was contagious, finally taking in even the grim married women. Soon everyone formed a line, placing hands on the shoulders of the person in front, and circled the deck, laughing like children at recess.

After the rollicking, Aurora leaned against the railing gazing out at the foreign waters of Alaska as she caught her breath. Charlie appeared at her side.

"Elisha says you're getting off at Wrangell."

She nodded. "I'm in your debt for your medical advice. Thank you."

He touched the brim of his hat in response. "Wrangell is the wildest place on the Panhandle," he continued, sounding like a stern schoolmaster. "I was there a few years back, lost a big bundle to a confidence man. Don't let go of your money, no matter how good the deal sounds." Charlie drew deeply on his cigar, finally exhaled, smoke wreathing his head before a breeze carried it out over the water. "The town was a Hudson's Bay Company post until the U.S. government bought Alaska in back in '67. Then it changed to Fort Wrangell. When gold was struck up in the Cassiar, the place became a boomtown, being right on the Stikine River. I've heard stories of the winter of '77 and '78 when miners up in the Cassiar came down to spend their earnings. Hundreds of miners, out of control. What they did that winter has stuck with the town. Any kind of bad behavior— rape, stealing, murder—was carried out with no consequences. I just want to be sure you know what kind of place it is. It's a free-for-all, and as a result a lawless place. I hope things are calm while you are there. They say last year the population was up to 10,000."

"I'll take care," Aurora assured him, thinking of Elisha's advice to get a gun.

"Which way did your husband take?"

"The Edmonton Trail. The promoters misrepresented the dangers."

"You can be sure they did. Just like the merchants in Victoria and Vancouver who tout the Stikine Trail as the best and easiest way to the Klondike." He tapped an inch of ash off the cigar. "There is no easy way."

"Why are you returning?"

"I'm going to set up businesses. Some day the gold will peter out, but lots of people will stay on. They'll need drugstores."

"Don't you have a family?"

Charlie inhaled deeply on the cigar, releasing the smoke in an unhappy sigh. "I have a wife. No children. She's not interested in seeing Alaska."

"Perhaps once you are established, she'll come," said Aurora, hoping to cheer him up. He seemed like a nice, decent man.

"Perhaps." He turned from looking out at the water to face her. "Aurora, I hope you'll allow me to use your Christian name, I wish you could be a companion to Elisha. She needs guidance. If you could persuade her to stay in Wrangell with you. I've seen too many young women ruined forever when they come north." He swallowed. "I offered her money, no strings attached, if she would turn around and go back home, but she's determined to make it to Skagway."

"I've tried to talk to her about being a . . . you know, her proposed manner of making a living. I promise I'll try once more."

But Aurora was unable to change Elisha's mind, and the young woman with the alabaster skin continued on to Skagway, where at least she would be in the same place as the Michaelsons. Aurora thought of all the people she'd met on this journey. Would their paths ever cross again?

Chapter Nine

Husbands—Counsel for

Consider whether, as a husband, you are as fervent and constant as you were when a lover. Remember that the wife's claims to your unremitting regard, great before marriage, are now exalted to a much higher degree. She has left the world for you—the home of her childhood, the fireside of her parents, their watchful care and sweet intercourse have all been yielded up for you. Look, then, most jealously upon all that may tend to attract you from home, and to weaken that union upon which your temporal happiness mainly depends; and believe that in the solemn relationship of husband is to be found one of the best guarantees for man's honor and happiness.

Aurora awakened to the chaos of Wrangell—shouts, rumble and crash of wagons lurching over the rutted streets, horses snorting and whinnying in protest of their heavy loads. She tried to reenter the dream where she and Martin were lying on a bed of pine boughs, naked, a rich potpourri of odors around them—sun-warmed skin, sweat, pine needles, the hot spice of ripe huckleberries, but the sensations floated away, dissolved. She stretched, still relishing the bath from last night in the big galvanized tub, her first bath since leaving Seattle.

She thought of the *Gold Runner*'s docking yesterday in the Wrangell harbor. The settlement was scattered around a picturesque harbor, marred by tents, shacks, and abandoned sluice boxes, harnesses, and lumber littering the shoreline. The flotsam of man was at odds with nature's beauty. The Michalesons delivered Aurora to the door of their fellow missionary, the three trying to keep out of the mud by walking on boards placed helter-skelter between buildings. An Indian woman answered their knock, calling back into the house in her language. As she turned, the left side of her face was revealed—the skin drawn in, puckered, tugging down her eyelid. Realizing her exposure, she clapped a heavy black braid to the side of her face.

Astrid Swenson strode to the door, a smile creasing her weathered countenance when she saw her visitors. "Bathsheba, Porter, I knew the Lord would bring you back," she said, her Scandinavian accent giving a cool precision to her words. She grasped both of Bathsheba's hands first, then Porter's. Then she greeted Aurora with a firm handshake.

"Aurora needs a place to stay," said Bathsheba.

"Of course, you are most welcome to use the storeroom. It's tiny but has a comfortable bed," said Astrid, with an abrupt affirmative nod towards Aurora.

"I'm grateful," said Aurora just noticing a rifle resting on pegs behind the door, wondering how many times Astrid had used it. The Indian woman disappeared.

"That was Eleanor. Not her Tlingit name; the name she took when she became a Presbyterian. She is still a bit reticent around whites."

"Oh, Astrid, you have made such a nice little home here," complimented Bathsheba. "How did you manage to get this furniture and rugs from the Outside?"

"The Lord works in mysterious ways. They were shipped here for a new hotel. The owner was shot last week by a woman who worked for him, so they auctioned off all the materials, even the lumber, which had been dumped on the shore. Thank goodness the furnishings were stored in a warehouse."

Aurora thought this a rather gruesome event to attribute to the divine. But if a tragedy offered some benefits, why not be sensible about it? After a simple meal of soup and bread, the Michaelsons returned to the ship. Aurora felt a painful jolt of separation, as if her parents were abandoning her. She kissed Bathsheba's cheek and clasped Porter's hand in both hers. "You've been wonderful to me. I can't thank you enough." She forced down the rising lump in her throat as the couple headed back, carefully negotiating the zigzagging path of boards.

Yet she was happy to be in this house with Astrid and Eleanor as the Indian woman filled a huge pot with water and placed in on a pot-belly stove. Although the day was warm, the interior of the little log house was chilly. Eleanor filled the tub with water, and Astrid placed a hinged screen on the side that faced the door. As Aurora soaked away the grime of the voyage, her dirty clothes were spirited away and replaced by a flannel nightdress which was draped over the screen. Pinned to the material was a piece of paper with child-like printing: *Charge for hot water: 25¢ Charge for laundry: 50¢.*

"I've been telling Eleanor to put a value on her work. You know the Tlingit are ambitious. I think she's taking to this quite well, don't you?" asked Astrid when Aurora emerged from behind the screen.

Aurora was relieved to be charged a fee. It would make it easier to speak frankly about the cost of her room and board. "How long has she lived with you?"

"Over a year now. I expect you've seen her face. A stampeder tried to rape her. When she fought him off, he pushed her into a hot stove. The man has never been brought before the judge, although he's still in town. There's not much justice for protecting whites in Wrangell, and even less for the Natives. I expect one day Eleanor's relatives will deal with the man," she said with some satisfaction. "I hope you'll stay with us for a few days."

"Thank you. I'd like that—to get my bearings for the next part of the journey. It's good to be on land again."

"That is settled. I am grateful to be having company fresh from the Outside. Bathsheba didn't mention where you were from."

"The northern tip of Michigan's lower peninsula, near a little town called Blackbird. My husband inherited a farm from his great-uncle, so that's our home." It was strange talking about the farm, thousands of miles away.

"Why have you come so far?"

"To find my husband." And without any more questions from Astrid, Aurora began telling how last Christmas she knew she needed to find Martin, how without doubt she decided to put her old life aside and step into the unknown.

‍‍‍‍ ‍‍‍‍ ‍‍‍‍ ‍‍‍‍ ‍‍‍‍

On Christmas Eve, while the snow gathered in little triangles in each corner of the window panes, she sat at the kitchen table and rubbed lavender leaves between her palms. The pungent, clean aroma released summer into the kitchen. Marble and the cat lifted their heads to sniff. She was making a gift for Marisa, little sachets, something feminine for her friend who had so little time for treating herself to anything nice. The lavender and other herbs, grown in a patch outside the kitchen door, had been hanging upside down in bunches in the pantry for months.

Aurora delved into a frenzy of gift-making to keep her fears at bay. A knit cap for Pat and a pie for Clyde Kleckner. No word from Martin since the letter she had received in early September. And he had written it June 5! She had sent two letters during the fall, both to Fort Liard. The last letter was slipped inside one of the woolen socks she had knitted. In the other sock she inserted a bag of peppermints, and a sprig of balsam from one of their trees. *"Here's your Christmas gift. I hope you'll be opening it in a warm, safe place,"* she said in her letter. Had Martin reached Fort Liard? Was he past there? No news from her husband for months. And then last week the letter from Martin's parents, whom she had met just once, at her wedding, when they made the trip over from Pelican. Included in their letter was a slip of paper, a note from Martin. This note to her had been folded inside a packet comprised of a letter to his parents and a letter to Mr. and Mrs. King, telling them of Frank's death.

My dear daughter-in-law began the other Mrs. Starr. *I am forward-ing this note from Martin. If its contents are similar to ours, there isn't much news. It is a terrible blow for Frank's parents. We can only pray that Martin comes home safe to us.* Aurora thought it was telling that Mrs. Starr said *to us,* rather than *to you.* But perhaps she was being too sensitive and looking for faults in her mother-in-law, who had been polite, in person and in letters, but never warm towards Auro-ra. She often wondered if there was some young woman in Pelican whom Mrs. Starr would have preferred as a daughter-in-law. Most likely someone with more enthusiasm for church—and one who did not drink alcohol. Aurora remembered Mrs. Starr's rather prickly refusal of the cherry wine Aurora's mother served to the wedding guests.

The folded slip of paper was darkened with what looked like grease stains over the letters of her name. It was a seal declaring deprivation, loss of dignity. She thought of Martin and his tidy ways. The stained piece of paper alarmed her.

Ring out the narrowing lust of gold. Forgive me for being selfish.

He had not signed his name. She was quite sure the first sentence was from one of Tennyson's works. Their second summer of court-ship, they had taken to reading the Tennyson volumes from her mother's glass-fronted bookcase. The next sentence created a sick desperation in her. She grabbed the table top to steady herself. The air hummed and her familiar surroundings swirled before her eyes. Martin sounded defeated, a word she had never associated with her dreamer husband. Frank was the one who had planted the idea in Martin's mind. She didn't think her husband would have initiated such an undertaking, but he couldn't resist going on such an adventure with his friend. How did Frank die? How alone Martin must feel, although, thank goodness, he was with other men whom he seemed to get along with.

Being separated for all these months had given Aurora time to reflect on her marriage. When they said their vows on that lilac-scented June day, she had a twinge of doubt that she was being too hasty, too easily prey to social pressure. At twenty-five, she was nearing the spinster stage. She loved Martin, but would she in ten years, twenty years? Martin was younger and less educated (at least in a formal sense) than she, but she felt a deep connection to him. And of course, the almost animal longing to be near him, her "Pelican boy" with a whimsical, dreamy quality that she had never encountered before. At the same time he was skillful with tools and with horses. He had an innate mechanical sense. And there was his physical beauty, his enthusiasm for starting a fruit business—and Uncle Ethan was leaving him the farm, so the couple would have a ready-made, established homestead. Aurora would not have to leave the place she loved.

Her time in Mount Pleasant had shown her a bit of the larger world, one she still wanted to experience at times. However, the episode with Mr. Malcolm had tainted her enjoyment of being an independent young woman on her own for the first time. Perhaps she was a coward, but she did not want to go through anything like that again. The sense of powerlessness and being at the mercy of another, the underlying wickedness of human nature. A woman alone was more likely to encounter that in the cities, and in places where she had no friends or relatives. She knew most everyone at home, and she saw Blackbird as a refuge when she finished her courses at Mount Pleasant. And there was Libby Gray, alone in the house, depending on neighbors to look after her when she retreated into an illness. She could not leave her mother. Martin had been the answer; he offered her a safe way for her future, though now she saw, it was a false safety.

She wrote a note to her in-laws, thanking them for sending word from Martin. She did not mention how disturbing his short message was. What had he written to his parents? Perhaps they were upset as well, although Mrs. Starr had given no indication of that. *I'm keeping a positive outlook through this time; Martin's return cannot be too soon for me. I'll send condolences to Mr. and Mrs. King*, she ended the note to Pelican.

Christmas Day. She was going to dinner at the Bartek's. She was thinking she should have made some sachets for Jory, to sweeten his clothes, but he would think her odd. For him, she made a tobacco pouch, stitching together two squares of leather and punching holes along the top through which she'd woven a drawstring. For the children, she had made another batch of taffy.

Clyde came over early that morning to clear the wagon path from the road to the barn. He dragged a set of old bedsprings weighed down with stones behind his team, mashing down the snow and creating a wide passage. Since Aurora had been tutoring Pat, Clyde had done favors like this without any spoken agreement between them. He seemed proud of his nephew's ability to read. She knew it was best to not try to formalize an exchange of services. Clyde was a man who operated best with an informal barter system. Aurora considered it more than sufficient compensation for teaching Pat, who was reading everything he could get his hands on. He seemed less sad, less unsure and shy since he'd become a reader.

She was out in the dark stillness of Christmas morn to milk the cow and put down feed for the animals. *I saw three ships come sailing in on Christmas Day in the morning.* She hummed the tune of the carol her mother had loved. As a child, Aurora had looked out at the water hoping to see three ships laden with gifts on the horizon, heading for Blackbird's harbor. She laid extra hay before the cow. *Merry Christmas, kicking beast.* Now in the gray morning light, she hooked the horse to the wagon and placed a soft balsam wreath decorated with a scrap of red ribbon around the horse's neck, then tied a string of bells to his harness. The horse snorted softly and nosed the pocket of her good gray coat with red piping and astrakhan collar for a carrot. She had none, so went back into the barn where she had stored some in a straw box.

She would attend Christmas service at the Methodist church before going to the Bartek's for dinner. Although raised a Methodist, she felt less and less comfortable in the church since the death of her mother. In fact, during the few times she attended Sunday services, she had been irritated by the smugness of the minister and the tired meaningless pieties and stale doctrine. But after all, it was Christmas, and she wanted to be in a crowd of people singing Christmas carols. She liked to think if Martin were here, he would come along.

A dense cloud cover created a gray, pearly bowl whose rim met the top of the bristly tree line. The sun, hidden by the atmosphere, caused the sky to be gray and bright at the same time; a few fat snowflakes floated down lazily. As she headed into town, following the tracks of an earlier wagon, she caught her breath at the magical duet, the merry jingling of the harness bells and the more serious bells of the Catholic church five miles south in Blackbird. In the midst of the whirlpool of worry for Martin was a small, still spot of peace, of acceptance, an awareness of herself. She was an orphan, a gold widow, or maybe spinster would be more accurate, yet she felt tranquil on this cold Christmas morning.

Down the hill, the Sawyersville mill was quiet. There would be no delivery of logs from the surrounding forests today. The men who lived in the lumber camps scattered all over this northern end of the county had a day off. Those who lived within ten miles traveled the icy roads to get home. Others stayed in the camps where a Christmas dinner was served. Aurora imagined it would be the best Christmas dinner in the county. The lumber camps had a reputation for having food in quantity and quality, and hiring the best cooks. A typical breakfast was steak, eggs, pancakes and syrup, oatmeal, potatoes, coffee and a selection of pies.

During the weeks before Christmas, sleighs from the camps dropped off towering loads of logs at designated points along the railroad. The train on the narrow-gauge ran constantly, picking up logs and delivering them to the mill. Aurora learned to differentiate between the stretches of the roadbed that had wood rails and those that had steel rails. She liked the small thunder of the train moving over the wood rails more than the higher pitched steel rails. Last year Aurora and her students walked to the mill for a tour. Many of her students knew more than she did about how trees became lumber. Harold Jankowski's father worked loading the logs into the "soup holes," and Harold told her that this was where loose bark and dirt were removed, before the logs were loaded onto the conveyor. Aurora watched as a sawyer eyed and handled each log, turning it on the carriage for the best cut as it headed toward the band saw. She nearly swooned from the fragrance as the logs were milled into planks. The new lumber was taken by tramway to the docks in Blackbird.

As Aurora drove the wagon south towards Blackbird and crested the final hill, she saw a sailing schooner out in the bay. At least she had seen one sailing ship on Christmas day! It seemed a bit risky for a ship to be heading across Lake Michigan for Chicago, or even just down the coast to Muskegon, at this time of year. But the bay had not frozen over yet, and some boats would run lumber as long as possible. Aurora wondered if she would live to see every tree in the county felled in order to satisfy the insatiable demand for wood. The acres of forests— maple, beech, ironwood, elm, oak, hemlock, which her mother had taught her to identify—were nearly decimated. The land to the west had a vulnerable, unprotected look, scarred by stumps and unwanted limbs.

"And how is your dear husband? Will he be coming home soon with lots of gold?" The new minister's wife was just inside the door, greeting the Christmas worshippers. Aurora had hoped to slip by and into a pew at the back, but the woman grabbed her by the upper arm, leaning in with peppermint breath to get the latest. The dreadful woman had come all the way out to Starrvation Corner last summer to inquire why "they hadn't seen Aurora in the Lord's house" and to press upon her that "she needed to be in the fold of Christians while her husband was away." She had been appalled that Aurora allowed wild animals, referring to the cat and dog, to live in the house.

"I just heard from him. Things are going according to plan," she said, while managing to keep moving. The organist assaulted the keys with all stops out and "Joy to the World" released her from the woman's grip.

She breezed out the door after the service, avoiding eye contact with those who had known her parents and would surely want to talk. Singing carols had warmed her spirit and she sang out, her breath wreathing around her face, as she drove the wagon to Barteks.

The fat, lazy flakes had organized, and now the snow was falling vertically, steadily as Aurora pulled into the Bartek's yard. "Merry Christmas, Mrs. Starr," said one of the older Bartek girls, her round face beneath a huge wool hat a replica of Marisa's. The girl came down from the porch to take her horse to the barn as Aurora gathered her gifts from the wagon.

"If your mother doesn't mind, I'd like you to call me Aurora. I'm sorry. I promise I'll learn all your names today."

"I'm Delia, next to oldest." She deftly unhooked the horse and draped the reins over one hand. "I've never seen a horse decorated so. He's very pretty." She stroked the wet, snowy nose, then stood on tip-toe to plant a kiss just under the animal's eye. Aurora understood this desire to kiss a horse, the deep affection a young girl has for a large, gentle animal. She had kissed her horse, another horse, when she was young. It touched her to see this girl with the same inclination.

With all the Barteks home and in the house, the interior was steamy. The front entryway was dotted with little pools of melting snow from various pairs of boots. Aurora removed her high laced boots and slipped on shoes she rarely wore, red shoes made of soft kid with a little heel and with tiny bows on the outside. She had been saving them for a special event, but as the months went by, she was learning she must declare which events were special. Today was such a day.

As Aurora moved down the hallway toward the kitchen, she glanced in the open doorway of the dining room, which the Barteks had converted into a storage area—bags of flour, grain, tubs of lard, sleds lining the walls and harness and tackle in the middle of the floor. The room had been cleared, and the long table from the kitchen, where they usually ate, had been moved in here and covered with an embroidered tablecloth.

"Merry Christmas, Aurora," shouted Jory. He was securing a five-foot balsam in a bucket in the living room. "The children, they insisted we bring this tree inside." All the children, except Delia, were weaving popcorn through and laying dyed corn husks on the boughs. Jory, a boisterous man, spoke with a strong accent. He left his homeland as a young man, came to northern Michigan, where some of his relatives had settled, looking for work. He met Marisa, who was a second-generation Bohemian, and they married, producing a child every other year.

"It's a lovely tree. I'll go and give Marisa a hand."

The kitchen, compared to the drafty parlor, was hot. Steaming wet socks and scarves hung over the bars at the sides of the wood range. Aurora knew the family had attended mass, earlier than the Methodist service. Planks on sawhorses, set up in the space where the table had been, bowed under the weight of the food. There were two roast ducks, crackly skins glistening—probably from the creek, probably descendants of the ducks Aurora fed as a child. "The children have disappeared. Could you carry this pot of potato soup into the dining room? There's a little burner on the table to keep the pot warm," said Marisa, her face flushed, her ever-present apron on over a rose-colored broadcloth dress. Aurora marveled at her energy. She was only four years older than Aurora, and a mother of six! Yet she did not look worn out and haggard like so many of the women with lots of children.

Aurora set out her corn relish, something that didn't need to be heated. She kept her hands in her lap, her eyes downcast, as the family prayed and crossed themselves. Then the food was passed, the ducks, the soup, ladled out at the head of the table by Jory into cups, bread dumplings and the corn relish. Aurora let the children's banter and their parents' responses wash over her like some healing warm sulphur water. She was lucky, she thought, to have found a family to belong to. Would she and Martin ever have a family?

As if tapping into her thoughts, Marisa asked softly, "Any word from your husband?" The table grew quiet.

"Only a short note. His companion, Frank King, died," said Aurora, and Marisa crossed herself. "I don't really know where he is." She looked down at her plate, as her eyes swam with tears. "I don't know what to do." This last utterance ended in a sob, surprising Aurora. She had done so well to keep a brave face, but now she did not care if the Barteks knew she was afraid.

The children went still and looked down at their plates. Jory sent a look across the table to Marisa that said, *Well, what do you expect when a husband goes off chasing rainbows?* After the dinner, Marisa and Aurora were alone in the kitchen washing up. The children had cleared the table in no time. As the rinse water heated on the stove, Marisa asked, "Is there some authority you can write to? Perhaps he's sick and can't get word to you."

Of course. It sounded so obvious coming from Marisa. She would write to the Canadian government, perhaps in Vancouver. She would feel better doing something. Why wait, working herself deeper into a hole of worry. It was time to take action. She bent down to hug Marisa.

Marisa untied her apron and threw it on a hook on the wall. "Let's open our gifts. It's time to get out of this *kitshen*." Aurora wrapped one arm around Marisa's shoulders and Marisa encircled her tall friend's waist with a plump arm. They hurried down the hallway, drawn by the piney scent of the tree and the excited chatter of the children.

Back home, Aurora wrote a letter to *Whom It May Concern Regarding Americans on the Edmonton Trail*. She would send it to Vancouver, British Columbia. At the post office she might find out how to address the envelope properly. But late on Christmas night, having completed the letter, she knew it was not enough. She had to do more. Who else would look for Martin if not her?

ll ll ll ll

The day after her arrival in Wrangell, she lingered under the quilts, savoring a few moments of privacy before being thrust into a new place with new problems to deal with—how to get passage on a boat going up the Stikine, where to get provisions, and most of all where to go. Her satchel was nowhere in sight. She put on a pair of woolen socks draped over the foot rail and pulled open the heavy log door of the storeroom, which squawked mightily, and tiptoed to the kitchen.

Astrid was in a rocking chair in the corner by a window, a huge, floppy Bible on her lap, reading spectacles perched on the end of her long nose, which was buried inside the *Seattle Post-Intelligencer*. "Good morning, dear," said Astrid, peering around the newspaper. "I hope you don't mind my helping myself to your newspaper. Eleanor found it when she was emptying your bag. Help yourself to bread and porridge."

Eleanor's greeting consisted of lifting her head from her task and looking briefly at Aurora. The Tlingit woman wielded a charcoal iron; the smell of hot cotton, close to scorching, filled the room. Aurora recognized one of her skirts.

"Good morning to both of you. Someone in Seattle suggested that a newspaper would be one of the best gifts I could bring. You must keep it."

Astrid insisted on accompanying Aurora to buy supplies. "The Lord was with you when you chose Wrangell, not "yea," said Astrid, hooking her arm through Aurora's as they left the house. Next door, a plump woman sat outside in a velvet chair wearing a long chemise and drying a cascade of dun-colored in the morning sun. Her little house was decorated with window boxes holding nodding yellow tulips.

"Good morning, Genevieve," said Astrid.

"Bonjour, Mademoiselle *Sweenson*," replied the woman from behind her veil of hair.

"Another of the demimonde," Astrid informed Aurora after they emerged onto the main street. The smells and noise and dust of Wrangell stunned Aurora.

"I know it takes some getting used to. Last year the construction continued all night. They built hotels and saloons by moonlight. It's better now. I assume your husband did not come this way. He took the Edmonton Trail?"

"Yes. He and a friend set off together. Martin, my husband, wants to start a fruit exporting business. We, well actually, he was hoping to find gold so he could forget about being a farmer, you know, hire others to actually take care of the orchards."

"So many men, all ages and occupations, come through," said Astrid. She exhaled slowly, sadly. "Most will never reach the Klondike. I pray that they will just get home safely."

"You mentioned Dyea earlier. Why is it better that I chose Wrangell?"

"I expect someone would have told you before you tried to head there—Dyea has practically disappeared. It was a one-year wonder. Once the railway through the White Pass was completed, the place shut down. In the summer of 1897 there was only a trading post; within a year there were hotels, an opera house and all kinds of businesses. Thousands of stampeders passed through that town. Now I hear it's a ghost town, with weeds growing up in the streets."

Aurora shivered. Could Martin be there? She pictured him walking the deserted streets, looking for gold. She felt Astrid's arm tighten as they passed the "Eldorado Entertainment Palace." Several men sprawled on the porch, drunk and snoring. Laughter and squeals floating down from a half-open second-floor window. Aurora looked up and saw the silhouette of a naked woman move behind the gauzy curtains. A few months ago the sight would have shocked her.

"Why do you stay here?" asked Aurora.

"This is where the Lord has placed me; my mission board supports a church here. I feel needed, helping some of the misguided creatures who come here as prostitutes. Many of them think they can be dance partners and earn a living, but soon most of them have to start 'mining the miners' to stay afloat. Now maybe in Dawson a girl could make a living working in a dancehall, but it's tougher here." She nodded to a prosperous-looking man whose watch chain looped across his satin vest, glinting in the morning sun. "He owns three saloons here, but was a banker back home," whispered Astrid after they had passed.

Aurora was beginning to understand how this wilderness could enchant people, hold them and swallow them. It cast a spell on Outsiders. It wasn't just the lure of gold, it was the chance to become someone else, to throw away the rules and familiarity of daily life. Was this what Martin was after? And, if she were honest, did not the possibility excite her just a bit?

At the first store, at Astrid's insistence, Aurora purchased a net designed to go over a hat, extend down to the chest and tie under the arms, and a bottle of Alaskan Skeeter Preventative. "The mosquitoes and black flies will seek to devour you," said Astrid, as if quoting a passage from the Bible. Another necessary item were high boots, much sturdier than the ones she had with her. *Botte Sauvage* repeated the clerk several times as she tried them on. Astrid approved; they were water-proof and lighter than winter boots.

As they left the store, Aurora jumped as gunshots cracked, cutting through the street noise. They seemed to come from inside a building in the same block. A young man, bearded and without his shirt and shoes, tore out of a doorway, another man appearing seconds later on his tail. The pursuer held his pistol at shoulder level, took aim at the retreating figure. His intention was ruined when a stocky woman in a short nightgown pounced on his arm, sinking her teeth into the wrist. The man howled and dragged her back inside, shaking his arm as if to dislodge an attacking animal.

"I wish the Mounted Police were in Wrangell. They do such a good job at keeping order," sighed Astrid, gunplay being a regular daily annoyance. "The Americans have an odd way of approaching law and order. They wait until things are completely out of control, and then they send in a gunman to set things right. They tried to hire Mr. Wyatt Earp as deputy when he came through town, but even he turned it down."

A wave of homesickness washed over Aurora. She longed for Marisa's kitchen, for Pat's bright hair as he bent over a book, for the buzz of saws and even the stink of the tannery. This was superseded by a spurt of anger at Martin for making her go through this, for having to fear for her life in a wild-west town.

Astrid directed her into a store that sold mining equipment and guns. "Just a small one, dear, that you can fit in your bag."

"I can't. What if I actually killed someone? I could not live with that." While in Seattle, Aurora heard stories about the Winchester widow in California, a wealthy woman by now, who believed she was haunted by ghosts of all those killed by Winchester rifles. She hired carpenters and craftsmen to redesign her house to deal with the spirits of the murdered. The newspaper accounts depicted the Winchester widow as mad, but Aurora felt pity for her.

"Aurora, you most likely won't have to pull the trigger. It will bring an unruly man to his senses to see you with a gun. And you may need it for defense against wild animals."

So Aurora became the owner of a Remington Derringer. The clerk assured her that although second-hand, it was in good condition. Astrid examined it, clicking the trigger several times, holding it before her in a firing position, aiming at shelves holding piles of tack.

Aurora did not tell the missionary that she had no idea how to use it. Astrid most likely assumed that any woman who would venture into the interior looking for a lost husband would know how to use a gun. Martin tried to teach her to shoot when they were first married, but she managed to find one excuse after another to avoid his lessons. She had a natural aversion to firearms: the ripping, final sound; the hard, machine odor of the oil to clean them; the acrid smell that lingered after they were fired; the deadly weight of their metal.

"You can get a ticket to go upriver right here," said Astrid.

"No need for a ticket, Missus. Just show up at the dock. It's not like it was before," said the clerk, shaking his head. Aurora was unsure if this last sentiment was based on sadness or on wistfulness.

One last stop and she loaded up with food for the trip: evaporated onions and potatoes; dried beef; rolled oats; split peas; roast coffee; condensed milk; salt; sugar; evaporated apples, peaches and apricots; matches; candles; tar soap and lye soap. In Seattle, Aurora had gained weight, straining the seams on her dress. Now less than a week in Wrangell, she was pared down. The plain food, unadorned by sauces, and absence of desserts, gave her focus. The noisy, jangling town transmitted a nervous energy that burned off pounds. She was "wound up tight as a top," the way she remembered Martin being, especially when he was ignited by a new project.

Sunday arrived and Aurora went to the little wooden Presbyterian church with Astrid and Eleanor. Like most of the buildings in Wrangell, except for the established dance hall/saloons, the church was constructed of unpainted boards. Its steeple looked naked without a bell. Astrid said the members were trying to raise money to buy a bell, which would have to be shipped from Seattle. Just as back in Michigan, here the hunger for lumber was insatiable. The Wrangell newspaper said that the river steamer Aurora was taking up the Stikine was carrying a load of 30,000 feet of lumber, in addition to 40 tons of freight. Thousands were leaving Dawson in the Yukon, some returning to the Outside, but many heading for gold sites in Alaska, where boomtowns were popping up all over.

Half the congregation was Tlingit. Aurora wondered what there was in Presbyterianism that appealed to the Tlingit. What did Astrid say or do to convince them to leave their native religion? When the congregation stood to sing "Rock of Ages," one verse was sung in English, the next in the native language. Aurora glanced at Eleanor, who sang lustily, not hiding her damaged face, at home in this group. There were two rough-looking characters, filling the Presbyterian air with a miasma of whiskey, tobacco smoke and sweat. Eleanor turned around, fixing them with a disapproving stare.

The traveling minister was up in Glenora, so Astrid delivered the sermon. She stood on the small dais, to the side of the pulpit, her hands clasped in front of her stomach. Her voice was precise, yet warmer than Aurora had heard it, as she spoke of the light and the dark in human nature, how both could be found in each of us, that if we looked for the better side, the light in our fellow humans, we would ourselves reveal what was most God-like. Her brow wrinkled. She tightened her clasp, bringing her hands just under her chin. "God has made us with a capacity for choosing both wise and unwise ways of living on this earth. Now some say that God hates the sinner. But how can that be when He has made us? Would He make something he hates?" Several heads were moving in the negative to her question. "We all experience the sun and the shadows as we walk here on earth. That is part of our being human. Native or those who have come from the Outside, we all must deal with these two necessary parts of our nature."

That's the way Aurora felt. Her life now seemed to alternate between light and dark. She had fears for Martin and for herself, for their future, which was counterbalanced by the helpful people who had been placed in her path. When the offering basket was passed for the church's bell, Aurora put in two dollars.

As Aurora was packing that night for the morning's 8 a.m. steamer, Eleanor came to the storeroom leading a dog on a rope. The dog was gray and white, thick-coated, with suggestions of sled dog and of wolf in its body, but a gentler breed in its face. Even on the end of a rope, the dog maintained its dignity, his clear brown eyes resting on Aurora as if to say, "Well, let's get acquainted. I'm willing to try if you are."

"Better than a gun," said Eleanor, handing the rope to Aurora. "Go with God—and with dog," she said, emitting an unexpected chuckle at her little joke in English.

Totem pole in Ft. Wrangell

Chapter Ten

Mosquitoes—To Prevent Biting

Dilute a little of the oil of thyme with sweet oil, and dip pieces of paper in it. Hang it in your room or rub a little on the hands or face when going to bed. It is said that petroleum is a good mosquito-bar if used in this way. A little coal oil is dropped on some raw cotton, the excess of it squeezed out, and the cotton then rubbed over face and hands. It is said that the little pests will not come near it. To us the remedy seems nearly as bad as the disease; to those who do not mind the smell of kerosene it may be useful.

As she traveled up the Stikine, closer to Martin with each mile, Aurora grew more optimistic now that she could actually picture Martin in this setting. She had boarded the 100-foot steamer *Skeena*, named after the river it usually navigated and owned by the Hudson's Bay Company. In Wrangell, she heard lots of grumbling from returning stampeders about the Canadian enterprise that ran all the trading posts and on which all gold-seekers depended. Astrid escorted her up and down the streets as she asked men who had come down from Glenora if they knew of Martin Starr. No one had, although she was told that a cripple camp existed on the upper Liard and relief had been sent to bring disabled men out to the coast. She was sure this was the same group she had heard of through Mae's sources. And she was sure that Martin was disabled in some way.

The *Skeena* was also carrying relief supplies—food, medicine, clothing—for stranded stampeders. The trip up to Glenora was about 150 miles. "Give me two days," said the captain. The scenery was frightening and beautiful. Countless glaciers and rugged mountains rose on each side. Aurora drank in the pure air, warmed by the sun, cooled by the glaciers. The seasickness that had incapacitated her on The *Gold Runner* was absent. The dog, abandoned on the streets of Wrangell and brought home by Eleanor, made her feel safer than did the gun, which was nestled, unloaded, in the clothes packed in her satchel. He sat close to her, sometimes leaning into her, as if seeking physical contact for assurance. In turn, she felt protected. She began calling him "Wrangell," which seemed to suit the dog, who cocked his head and pointed his ears straight up as she tried out his name. "Wrangell. Wrangell." He took a piece of beef jerky from her hand, gently, then swallowed it in one gulp. "You must chew your food," she admonished.

There were no cabins for passengers, only a lounge and two small closet-size toilets with chamber pots. On board were two officials from the Hudson's Bay Company, who kept to themselves. The other passengers consisted of a small man with a waxed moustache accompanied by three women in trousers. They had a supply of liquor with them. Aurora thought of Sally and her bloomers. Where was Sally now? The gold rush into British Columbia and the Yukon had slowed. Now America had its own gold fields, easier to reach than the Klondike, far less treacherous.

The stop that night on the river was a Tahltan village. Like the Tlingit, the Tahltan saw the arrival of whites as a business opportunity. Since no treaties had been formed with the Canadian government, the Indians considered themselves sovereign. This was their land, their resources, and they charged for anything taken from it. When Wrangell dived into the river and emerged with a flashing salmon in his mouth, a Tahltan man approached Aurora. "Two bits," he said, his open palm thrust under her nose. She paid the man. Two bits seemed to be the cost of everything. Firewood collected along the riverbank was two bits, bread was two bits.

The crew slept on the boat; the passengers had their choice of trying to sleep on the benches in the lounge, out on the deck—or paying for crude shelters in the village. Aurora and Wrangell slept in a wooden shack. She paid "two bits twice," amused that Wrangell was charged, too. The one curtainless window let in the light of the long day, whose sun would not disappear behind the hills until nearly midnight. She secured a piece of gunny sacking, from a pile in the corner, to the little window. After coating her hands and face with the mosquito repellent, she snuggled under the scratchy blanket that smelled of horses. It was disconcerting to sleep while there was still light, but finally she fell asleep, lulled by the rushing river, the dog's snores, the low conversation of men sitting by a fire.

The next day the *Skeena* passed through a little canyon studded with whirlpools. Aurora could nearly reach out and touch the rocks on each side of the ship. She watched a young boy, one of the crew, carry two chamber pots to the railing, and dump each in turn over the side into the olive-green swirling water. She assumed they would have emptied them last night, dug a hole and disposed of the waste on land. It seemed sacrilege to foul this wild, beautiful river.

The steamer was jerked and jostled for half a mile, but when it at last moved into calmer, wider waters, everyone commented on the warmer temperature and began taking off jackets and coats. The dense lush forests disappeared, and Aurora noted tall pines and quaking aspens. There was no undergrowth here on the other side of the canyon. A person could walk freely under the great trees in the open natural park. The imposing mountains had moved into the distance; less intimidating rolling hills lined the river.

The unloading at Glenora took hours. The captain was going to stay overnight, then turn back down the Stikine. He pointed out a battered scow, a tottering affair with a bunkhouse built on top, that could take her on up to Telegraph Creek, ten more miles. Why was it named that? she asked. The captain told her of the Western Union's project back in 1865 to lay a cable across Alaska and into Russia, thus hooking up Europe and America. "Stampeders taking the Spectral Trail said they could see the rusty wires and rotten telegraph poles among the trees." He shook his head. "Another great plan eaten up and spit out by the wilderness."

Aurora and Wrangell found the post office. She explained to the gruff man behind the window that she was trying to locate her husband. Were there any letters or messages for a Martin Starr?

The man ducked down and pawed though something on the floor. Aurora pressed against the grill, peering down to where he thumbed through several long wooden boxes of mail, apparently arranged alphabetically.

"No," he announced.

"Can you double check?"

"If there was a piece of mail for your husband, you can be sure I would hand it over," he said defensively. "I know the importance of mail."

"I wasn't questioning your integrity," Aurora replied.

"I'm not like my predecessor. Of that you can be sure." The man, tight-jawed and red-faced by now, glared at Aurora.

Later, Aurora learned that the previous postmaster, overwhelmed by avalanche of letters and parcels coming into Glenora in the spring of '98, had burned several piles of mail. He escaped downriver as a gang of stampeders chased him through the streets with a noose. Hearing yet another story of the chaos and wildness of the previous year made Aurora grateful that she had not been here then.

The moment when Eleanor had handed over Wrangell to her, placing the rope in her hand, was the last time the dog had worn the rope. Aurora packed it in her bag; a length of rope might come in handy. Wrangell stayed at her side, quiet and watchful, when they walked. As they left the post office, the dog whined, a questioning, puzzled sound. She looked down to see the fur along his spine raised in a standing ridge. There ahead of them, a man walked across the street, eight feet above the ground. A wire had been secured between two buildings on either side, and a slender figure, black tights and scarlet waistcoat balanced on the wire. He held onto a long wooden rod, longer than he was tall, that helped in his walk above the street. People had gathered below. "Don't sneeze," yelled out one loud-mouth.

Aurora and Wrangell joined the audience. When the tight-rope walker made it to the other side, there was applause and whistling. A little boy began a jaunty tune on a miniature accordion, while a girl, his sister most likely, walked in and out of the crowd with a china bowl. The clink of coins against china created a descant to the accordion. As Aurora dropped her money into the bowl, she observed that the girl, probably nine or ten, had an affliction of the eye; her left lid drooped, giving the child a sleepy appearance. Her right eye was bright and defiant. What a thing for a girl to endure, she thought. The girl seemed oblivious to the little dog, a dingy ruffled collar framing its rat-face, that twirled on its hind legs beside her. When Aurora stooped to pet the little dog, Wrangell growled softly. "No need to be jealous," she told Wrangell. The performing dog danced away from them, like a mechanical toy.

That night she stayed in a former saloon. A missionary from the Presbyterian Church of Canada had taken over an abandoned saloon and transformed it into a hotel and mission. Although the woman at the reception desk was a bit dubious of Wrangell, Aurora paid a bit more for him to sleep beside her cot. She liked to think that back home, Marble was sleeping beside Pat's bed, that his uncle had relented on his "no dogs in the house" policy.

Aurora and her dog boarded the scow the next morning. The "captain" reeking of sweat and whiskey stumbled down the ladder from the bunkhouse. Aurora handed over the fare. The only other passengers for the ten-mile ride upriver were two Tahltan men. One of them took a long look at Wrangell, then commented to his companion. Wrangell cocked his head, ears perked up, as if understanding their language. Aurora wondered if Wrangell had lived among the Indians. She had a sinking thought that these men were going to reclaim their dog, but was reassured when they lit up their pipes and stared out at the river.

"Have you heard about stampeders coming down from the Liard to Telegraph Creek?" Aurora asked the captain, keeping some distance between them.

He studied her with bloodshot eyes, then dredged up a gob of phlegm and hawked it over the side. "Lots of cripple camps up there on the Liard. Getting all the sick fellas down here will take a while, but this is the way they'll come. Why do you want to know?"

"I think my husband is up there."

"I hope you weren't planning on taking a train, you know, one with tracks." He barked a nasty laugh. "In January of '98 they had all these big plans to build a railroad from Telegraph to Teslin Lake. They even built twelve miles of grade, but that's as far as it got."

"No, I haven't heard of a railroad. I'm not sure what I'll do after Telegraph."

"There's a pack train leaving Glenora this week. It will pass by here. Maybe you could travel with them. Hell, they might even give you a mule to ride." Another bark.

"How far does this pack train go?" Aurora wasn't sure what a pack train was.

"All the way to Dease Lake, where Hudson's Bay has a warehouse. They store their cargo there, then take it across to Laketon and then to all the downriver posts."

"You know a lot about what goes on." Aurora meant this as a compliment.

"I should. I've been a packer on that trail. Nothing more ornery than a mule with 450 pounds on its back. The damn things have to be blindfolded while you're loading and unloading them." He stopped to hawk another pearl of mucus toward the railing. His aim was short. "Now they're running thirty-eight mules."

"So why did you stop?"

"Me and the head packer didn't hit it off. I'd rather deal with this flat-bottomed rig than four-legged and two-legged jackasses," he said.

"I don't know if I could ride a mule," said Aurora.

"Oh, I expect they'll have some saddle horses along. Course, knowing how greedy the Company is, they might make you buy the horse," he said, an ugly look of discontent taking over his stubbled mouth. Wrangell shifted position on the deck, wrinkled his lip and made a low wolf-like sound. He didn't like this former mule packer.

"You keep your dog under control, or I might have to shoot him," he said.

"This dog is under control. He'll only attack if I command him." Aurora had no idea what Wrangell would do, but talking rough seemed to be called for with this man.

The captain weaved his way toward the tiller. Aurora sat on a pile of cargo covered with a piece of canvas, as the scow moved upriver. The way to Telegraph was strewn with the relics of last year's rush. Shattered toboggans, saddle bags rotting on the riverbank, clothes, a rusty skillet, boxes of candles and matches. She turned her head away from the sight of the carcass of a horse, its upper half decaying on the bank. Birds had been feasting on it, and its bones shone white. She did not want to contemplate the grisly inventory beneath the Stikine's surface.

She pulled the brown notebook from her satchel. She savored each entry, like eating the sections of a sweet orange, slowly. Martin wrote of camping in a meadow on the Fourth of July, last summer, and of Frank's injury, the fall that killed him.

Boat-building, Ft. Nelson

Chapter Eleven

July, August 1898

*O*nly when one of the men mentioned the Fourth did Martin realize the date. Back in Blackbird, Rory would probably be at the town picnic. But the Klondikers had their own celebration, for they had arrived at an oasis in the land of spruce swamps and muskeg: a meadow of thick tall grass and flowers of brilliant orange, yellow and purple. Martin passed around Rory's package of taffy. The taste of maple brought tears to his eyes, and he turned to quickly blink them away. He pictured the sugar maple on the farm, and everything back home seemed so precious that he wondered what had ever possessed him to leave Rory and plunge into this hopeless quest. Her letter with its homey details made him more homesick and wretched than he'd felt so far. Two brothers had picked up the package at the Lesser Slave Lake post and caught up to their party. One advantage for the late-starting Klondikers was that a trail had been broken, so they could travel more quickly than those who had set out in February.

They were reluctant to leave the meadow, but after several false starts of trying to follow the blazes, they were on their way. A northeast flowing river, not on any of the maps, mystified them. It was deep and more than a hundred feet wide. Unable to ford it, they constructed a bridge from huge spruces that grew on the banks. Several parties met there on the banks of that nameless river; the congregation numbered fifty-eight men, one hundred fifty-eight horses and forty-five head of cattle. After watching a dozen cayeuses fall off the makeshift bridge into the water and then hoisted back onto the logs, the little party decided to not put their horses through that. The poor beasts had endured too much hell. Upstream about a mile they found a place to ford animals and provisions across.

The blazes made by the half-breed scout were not easy to follow. After several days of traveling due north, an acrid smell enveloped them as they were looking to make camp for the night. The horses smelled it too and slowed down, twitching their big nostrils and ears. They encountered a huge burnt area, which stretched on and on as far as they could see in the waning light. They made camp at the edge of it. "Indians must have been through," said Frank. Martin thought him too quick to assign blame for any misfortune to the Indians. He had not noticed this trait in his friend before, but the grueling expedition brought out some of the least pleasing parts of men's natures.

"No sign of Indians," said a man from Edmonton, who had been traveling with the cattleman's party. "I'd say that scout let his campfire get away from him."

This meant there was no grass for the horses, so once again the little party of five broke off from the larger group to look for graze. After some time they found a small clearing of grass. Martin was once again shocked at how little attention was paid to the horses. Even though many of the gold-seekers were from small towns and had never taken care of animals, by now they should have learned that their survival was linked to the health of their animals.

For the next three days, the stench of burnt trees was with them, permeating hair, skin and clothes. Some of the timber was still on fire, and they worked their way around smoldering heaps of fallen trees. In some ways the fire had cleared the way, but it had also destroyed the blazes.

On the third day, Frank climbed a tall spruce, one that looked unscathed by the fire, to see if they were nearing the end of scorched earth. He was about fifty feet off the ground, standing on a sturdy-looking limb, when it snapped with a thunderous crack. He fell with a scream, his descent broken by the lower boughs. The others watched in shock, then ran to where he had fallen to the ground. Martin cradled Frank's head in his lap, while one of the men ran to the creek where the horses were drinking. When they bathed his face, he came to, but moaned in agony when they tried to move him. "Just shoot me. Just shoot me," he repeated.

Camp was set up right there, under the spruce from which Frank had come tumbling. His face and hands were badly scratched, but his worst injuries seemed to be internal. Martin stayed by his side that day applying hot flannel compresses to the bruised areas on his torso. He had collected the yellow flowers of the arnica plant at the last meadow, and prepared medicine to spread on Frank's bruises, but still he moaned all night. "You men go ahead; I'll stay here with Frank. We'll catch up with you later," he told the other three. But without hesitation, they all said they would wait until Frank was ready to travel.

When Frank could stand being upright, though unable to walk, he was put on Martin's saddle horse, and that animal's load was re-distributed among the other horses. No sooner had they left the burnt-over country behind than they were swallowed by yet another stretch of swamp and muskeg. In nineteen hours, they traveled six miles, spending half the time in water up to their waists, pulling on the reins, tugging at wild-eyed frightened horses as they sank into the trap of fallen timber and bogs. This was agony for Frank, for he had to dismount, urge the horse while clutching his midsection, then climb back on. Martin feared his friend would expire that day. At 1 a.m., they finally stopped at a spot to camp. Frank slid off the horse and stayed on the ground. Martin got a blanket under him and then bedded down beside him.

When daylight came, evidence of Indians all around their camp-site was visible. The Indians, called the Dog Ribs, a branch of the Slaveys, used signs similar to the Cree at Peace River. Hatchet marks, charcoal messages and the remains of several fires encircled them.

As they moved on, the five passed through several old camps. Empty brush houses, food caches, and tattered clothing were witnesses to the Dog Ribs' winter life.

They stopped the next night at the site of an abandoned winter camp. Soon two Dog Rib men approached the campfire. Frank, unable to move without pain, regarded them suspiciously from his pallet by the fire. The Indians seemed merely curious. Using a burnt stick on a piece of old canvas, they drew a crude map showing the trail as turning to the southwest. They pantomimed a journey of "three sleeps" to *Willeequah*, which the Klondikers guessed must be their name for Fort Nelson.

ll ll ll ll

The last week of July. After the Indians had walked off into the night, having the remaining pieces of Rory's taffy as thanks for the information, the five pledged to stay together. Even Frank, who has been all for turning back several times, knew it would be easier to press on to Fort Nelson than return to Edmonton. Martin did not want to speculate about what would happen after Fort Nelson. They had been warned that as early as August the coming arctic winter would make itself known; provisions were down to about one hundred pounds of flour per man. They agreed to pool their money and use it to buy provisions at Fort Nelson. Frank had $10; Martin $75; the butcher a $20 gold piece; and the other two hardly anything money-wise, but they had larger horses.

The Dog Ribs' information was based on humans who had no horses and carried few provisions. It was possible that they had never seen horses before because they were frightened yet fascinated by the whites' animals. Because the Dog Ribs traveled without exhausted horses and heavy packs, their "three-sleeps journey" turned into a ten-day ordeal for Martin and his group. They got little sleep for they could find no dry ground on which to pitch tents at night. They were again in muskeg and had to place poles on the ground, then spruce boughs on top to keep them out of water. They rolled up in blankets and were attacked by armies of mosquitoes, whose noise blocked out all other night noises in the muskeg. Their smoky fires were no deterrent to the solid black clouds of mosquitoes, as the men burrowed into their blankets to avoid the fiends and tossed about on spruce boughs. The only good thing was that they were not wading through water and that the horses were getting a break.

For those ten days they often had to lay poles on the ground for the horses to walk on. One of the older horses, emaciated and confused, fell on a stump and had to be put out of his misery. They dried much of the meat, but ate fresh steaks that day, giving Frank the thickest piece, "thick" being a relative term regarding the poor old horse. Frank had been coughing up blood and was weak. They tried to keep up his spirits with the hope there would be a doctor at Fort Nelson.

Martin's sole goal was to reach the fort. He no longer thought about finding gold, or about dreams of owning orchards and exporting fruit. He only wanted to stay alive—and keep Frank alive. On August 2 they came to Fort Nelson, situated on the other side of the Nelson River. The Hudson's Bay Company trader was Will O'Grady, a good sort it seemed, who sent a boat across the river to ferry their provisions. The swift river was 800 feet wide, but they managed to swim the horses across. The Dog Ribs' word *Willeequah* made sense now; the place was named for *Willy's store.*

Martin's rough estimation was ninety days since leaving Peace River, 650 miles on "the trail of death." From now on there would be no more trail blazes. As difficult as it had been to follow the markings at times, there had been some comfort that Edmonton's hired scout had been through. The Boosters paid the half-breed to mark a trail to the Pelly River, but now they learned that he had given up at Fort Nelson, going by canoe with the Indians up the Nelson, crossing over to the head of the Peace and down to the Catholic mission, his starting point last April. Word had drifted back to O'Grady that the scout was telling other poor devils just leaving Peace River that lots of gold was being mined on the Nelson and the Liard Rivers with stampeders making thirty dollars a day.

The majority of men congregated at Fort Nelson were planning to go overland to Fort Sylvester, the name for the Mud River or Lower Post on the Hudson's Bay Company maps. The small company of five knew they could face no more muskegs or unmarked trails, and Frank would fare better on a boat than overland.

The doctor left for the coast just two days before they arrived. Frank was able to walk a bit, though he found it difficult to straighten up. At night he slept in a sitting position to get his breath. He drank some tea made from plants that the Sikanni Indians had given him on their visit to the fort following their annual hunt up on the Sikanni River. They were ninety hunters, small and wiry and full of energy. Although they had been converted to Christianity, they maintained their native practices, possessing a facility for sustaining two belief systems without difficulty. The priests taught them to shun profanity, so when Frank let out a good "God damn it!" when pain overtook him, they shook their heads and pointed to the sky. However, that night they brought him the dried leaves with which to make tea. He slept without pain until morning. They blended religions in a tangible way by erecting crosses next to their carved totems which stood on prominent points along the banks of the Nelson River. The Sikanni owned rifles and gave a salutatory volley of shots when they passed the totem/cross sites. O'Grady told them that the medicine man visited these spots for meditation and rituals. The trader was more acquainted with the practices of Indians than with those of whites.

The new travel plan was to sell the horses, build a scow and proceed down the Nelson to the Liard, then ascend the Liard and converge with the "all-water routers." O'Grady said hundreds of them were going up the Liard now and Martin's group would have just enough time to get the boat ready, head down the Nelson and get on the tail end of the procession up the Liard. O'Grady warned them about Hell's Gate and Devil's Portage, canyons on the Liard impossible for boats. They would have to pack their goods and boats and portage over the mountains.

Mac, still in charge of the Philadelphians, low in number and low on food, had yet another idea. He was directing the building of a raft to take the horses with them. Once they reached the portage, they planned on making grubstake packings for other parties. Although Martin was glad to no longer be associated with Mac, he had to admire his tenacity and inventiveness, even though much of it was foolhardy.

O'Grady bought furs, dried moose meat, moose tallow and bear fat from the Indians. In turn, the Klondikers bought moose meat and tallow from O'Grady. They cleaned out his supply of flour—four hundred pounds. He claimed to rarely eat bread, that he had his first piece just a year ago. He had been raised in a family of twelve children at Fort Liard, 160 miles downriver, all of them raised solely on moose meat. Although he looked healthy enough, it sounded a tedious diet to Martin.

From the spruce trees around Fort Nelson, Martin and the other healthy three whipsawed lumber to build a twenty-four foot scow. Their vessel would be accompanied by two others, one captained by a Frenchman and the other by a seasoned adventurer from near Pelican Rapids. In fact, he knew of both Martin and Frank's parents. It was a bright spot, almost like having the support of family as they embarked on the waters of the Nelson on August 18, 1898.

Dog Rib boy kills a bear

Chapter Twelve

July, August 1898

Tanning—Old-Fashioned Way

The first operation is to soak the hide, as no hide can be properly tanned unless it has been soaked and broken on a fleshing beam. If the hide has not been salted add a little salt and soak it in soft water. In order to be thoroughly soaked green hides should remain in this liquor from 9 to 12 days; of course the time varies with the thickness of the hide. The following liquor is used to remove hair or wool, viz.: 10 gallons cold water (soft), 8 quarts slaked lime, and same quantity of wood ashes. Soak until the hair or wool will pull off easily.

Before the heat gained force, Aurora set out early for her monthly shopping trip to Blackbird. Since Sawyersville had only one store, which catered mostly to the sawmill workers, Aurora went into "town" for supplies, not just because there were more businesses, but because she was hungry to be among people and to hear news that may not have reached Sawyersville. Another attraction was the busy station where locals entertained themselves watching the summer resorters arrive, disembarking with trunks and boxes, children and pets. The influx of city-dwellers from Detroit and Toledo increased each summer. Chicagoans who could afford a summer away sailed across Lake Michigan by steamer, then took the Grand Rapids and Indiana Railroad north to breathe the "pure air" and spend time in an atmosphere "free from all kinds of offensive insects," as advertised in brochures. She wondered how the resorts managed to banish the blackflies and mosquitoes, which plagued her out at Starrvation Corner. In May, she suffered hard, red welts around her hairline from blackflies. Martin said that was because they liked "sweet flesh." He never seemed to be bothered by them like she was. The clouds of mosquitoes assembled at dusk in summer, forcing both to wear long sleeves and hats outside and to burn little blocks of pyrethrum in the house.

Aurora avoided the July 4th celebrations in Blackbird, although Pat had come over and set off some fireworks out in the field. She chose to reconstruct from memory that holiday when she was six, when her parents were alive and her world was full of wonder and possibility.

ff ff ff ff

Libby Gray had just tied the bow at the back of her daughter's dotted-swiss dress, whose sleeves were puffy, ending in lace trim at the wrists. At six years old, Aurora was at odds with what was expected of her in dress and manners. "If you go outside, stay on the front porch. We're leaving in fifteen minutes." Her mother lifted the gold watch that hung from a chain around her neck and rested on her neat bosom. "Eleven o'clock," she said, pointing to the number on the clock face. Every direction to her daughter was an opportunity for teaching.

"Yes, mother," said Aurora, already moving towards the door. Her parents were occupied with getting ready for the July 4th picnic at the church, the country's Centennial celebration. Her father carried a hamper packed with food to the trap. He'd been up early grooming the horse, and now let his daughter weave ribbons through the horse's mane. "Now Floy," she murmured from her stool, placed near the horse's head so she could reach, "you'll be the prettiest of all the horses today. And if you get scared when they fire the muskets, I'll cover your ears." She leaned sideways to kiss the horse just beneath its huge glassy eye.

Her parents had noticed early her affinity for animals. Their daughter expressed no fear toward any creature—fox, snake, beaver, even a black bear who had come into the yard. Aurora was less than one and had just been placed on a quilt after her bath in the big copper washtub by the back steps. It was an enticing spring day, a day no one could imagine staying indoors. Libby, hanging clothes on the line, her mouth bristling with wooden clothes pins, jerked around at the rank scent that overpowered the odor of lilacs and new grass. A bear was standing still at the edge of the lavender quilt, on which Aurora was playing with her rag doll. Aurora put down the doll and regarded the bear. Then she seemed to welcome the animal with a beaming smile as she extended her chubby arms. The bear turned slowly and went back down the hill towards the creek where it had been fishing. Before Libby could react, the danger was past. She tasted blood on her lips from biting down on the clothes pins. Relating the incident to Grenville that evening, she told how the whole thing had happened in near silence. The clothes slowly swishing against their neighboring fabrics in the breeze, the solid padding of the retreating bear—those were the only sounds she could remember.

The Grays had moved up to northern Michigan from the central part of the state just the previous year. The town of Blackbird was growing "like Topsy," as Aurora's father said, and he planned to be in on the development. Since the 1600s it had been a trading post, then a Catholic mission and a sleepy Indian village, safe under an 1856 treaty stating that Ojibway and Odawa could claim land in and around the village. In 1875 that came to an end with the influx of white homesteaders like Grenville and Libby Gray. They entered the raw, noisy, burgeoning village on the Little Traverse Bay with their five year-old daughter Aurora.

Today they could have walked to the United Methodist Church, which they did every Sunday except in the worst winter weather; it was only a half mile from their house, but their load was heavy, and Aurora had begged to take Floy along. The church was up on a bluff overlooking the growing town, which was built down to the edge of the harbor, more than a hundred feet deep. This was encompassed by the bay, and beyond the inland sea called Lake Michigan, or just *the big lake.*

The large grassy meadow surrounding the church, redolent from the herd which used it for grazing, was full of people. The town council had hired boys to shovel up the manure; the nation's 100th birthday was to be free of cowpies, but the barnyard smell lingered, mixed with the sharp resin of tan bark from the tannery down on the shore. The odors of baked potatoes and smoked fish were fresher and more compelling.

This was not a church function, but a gathering for all the towns-people of Blackbird. Spread over the green expanse were long tables being loaded with food, a croquet course, a canopy for getting out of the sun, as well as a wooden platform where a cherry pie-eating contest was starting. A straw-lined pit lined with blocks of ice protected several freezer cans of ice-cream. Aurora took all this in while registering the muted clangs from the horseshoe pit, and the resultant groans and cheers. Wagons, buggies, and the horses and ponies that pulled them surrounded the meadow's perimeter.

Aurora's parents were recruited for a three-legged race. Their copper-haired daughter looked on as they stood side by side and put their adjacent legs into a gunny sack. As Libby pulled up her yellow skirt to make room for her leg in the sack, Aurora noticed several of the men looking at her mother's long brown calf. Her mother often bared her legs while working in the garden or washing clothes in the yard.

"Go and play croquet with the Johnson boys," Libby called over her shoulder as she and her husband executed a fast walk/hop across the grass. Her parents were happy, having fun together. The sight of them jerkily making their way in a gunny sack made the young Aurora secure. However, she had no intention of seeking out the John-sons, the family that lived nearest to them. The two boys, seven and eight, were smelly and mean, especially to cats. She avoided them whenever possible.

For a bit she hung on the edge of a circle of older girls making daisy chains. The meadow was dotted with ox-eye daisies and clover. One of the girls smiled and handed her a circlet of daisies. Aurora put it on her head as some of the older girls had done, then walked back to check on Floy, who was standing under a huge maple with a water bucket nearby. The horse lowered its head in greeting and Aurora placed the daisy ring on the horse's head.

Even surrounded by the crowd and activity, Aurora felt alone. Not lonely or afraid, just conscious of herself as a separate being, moving through a world of other separate beings. Patting Floy on the nose, she headed around to the front of the church, which faced the water, and ascended the wood steps, whose boards needed another coat of paint before the next winter when the onslaught of wind and snow off the lake would buffet the building.

The church's interior was a cool relief from the July day. Aurora looked up through a small rectangle in the ceiling through which the rope made its long descent from the belfry. She resisted the impulse to unwind the end of the bellrope from its davit on the wall and give it a good yank. Every Sunday morning old Mr. Carr dragged himself up the steps and pulled the rope, causing the bell to resonate out over the town and bay in solid, metallic tones. That morning, with the help of some grown boys, he had rung out one hundred peals for the country's birthday. Aurora sat in the rocker on the porch, counting, "Ninety-eight, ninety-nine, one hundred!" Her mother standing in the doorway, smiled. She had taught Aurora the alphabet and num-bers at the kitchen table, along with the Johnson boys who had come over for sporadic lessons. Aurora absorbed the lessons quickly, while the two neighbor boys squirmed and grimaced as if being tortured by knowledge.

There was a faintly acrid smell of old ashes. The stove at the back of the sanctuary had not been cleaned out since its last use in April. A voice in Aurora's head (sounding a lot like her mother's) told her she shouldn't be in here, especially alone. The stillness, the ashy-smelling coolness embraced her as she climbed the twisting stairway to the choir loft, situated above and behind the worshippers in their wooden pews. Aurora stood on the "children's stool" so she could see out the little round window, five feet off the floor. The town was spread out below the bluff, only one wagon kicking up dust as it moved down the sandy main street. Even the tannery was quiet today; two schooners loaded with hemlock bark waited patiently in the still harbor. Aurora could see her father's dry goods store, nestled between the drugstore and post office. The unending waters of the big lake shimmered with tiny hexagons of sunlight. A ring-bill gull, its band of yellow split in half as the bird opened its beak and screamed, soared past the window. The gulls would be circling the meadow, ready for scavenging opportunities. Aurora wondered what was on the other side of the lake, for surely the lake had to end somewhere. Was someone gazing out a window on the other side, trying to imagine the place that was her home, her universe?

II II II II

Now in summer of 1898 she was an adult with more urgent matters to attend than gazing out at the lake. On her last trip into town, she read a notice on the bulletin board outside the post office: *Highest market price paid for hemlock bark. 1,000 cords needed immediately.* Hemlock bark produced a rich tannin, which when brought in contact with animal skins made the glutinous hides insoluble. The leather company was increasing production, and she could smell its sharp, rancid scent from the post office. The owners called it *the leather company*; everyone else called it *the tannery*. Situated where the river emptied into the bay, it stained the banks and water a deep orange. The Indians were angry about this desecration of their fishing spot. Aurora didn't blame them, but here she was contributing to the company's fouling of the waters. And she was involving the Indians, too. They needed the work. It seemed such a sad progression: the fishing spot no longer provided the native people with food, so they had to work for the company that had destroyed their fishing spot. That morning she contracted with Sam Agawisso to clear a stand of hemlock. Sam and his crew would cut the trees, peel the bark and deliver it to the leather company. Aurora would split the profit with them. She received no teacher's pay in the summer, but would not touch the money from the sale of her parent's home and business. No matter how stretched her finances, she felt secure knowing that money was squirreled away. "Someday we'll have need of it," she told Martin after her parents had died, "but let's live as though it's not there."

She thought back to Martin's suggestion of passenger pigeons as a source of income. The birds still arrived in early spring, but not in the huge numbers of her girlhood. She recalled the churning of her stomach, the ache in her throat when the pigeons swept down from the Arctic, the distant thunder of their approach bringing the people of Blackbird outside. The birds approached the town like a dark advancing army: the continuous coos and the beating of wings frightened her. The huge swarming formation blotted out the spring sun. The roar of the flying pigeons was punctuated by the cracking of tender limbs as the pigeons landed, coating every surface of the branches.

When the advancing pigeons were being pursued by hawks, the formation became magical. Aurora remembered seeing the black cloud divide into columns, the columns turning into ascending spirals, like twirling black snakes or tornadoes.

But what she dreaded most was the fate of the birds, which had come south to breed, nest and raise their young. The whites learned pigeon hunting from the Indians, who used crude means of capturing the birds. Aurora had seen the Odawa men cut down small trees that housed many nests. The squabs, not yet fliers, were thrown from their nests and fluttered about helplessly on the ground. The women and children then grabbed them, decapitating the young in one quick jerk. The trembling bodies were tossed on an every-growing pile, one belonging to each Indian family. For the larger trees, the men used long poles or bow and arrow to dislodge nests on lower branches.

Aurora first witnessed pigeon slaughter after coming out of her father's store on a brisk April afternoon when she was about ten. The village, just opened to whites after the expiration of the 1856 treaty with the Indians, was a fascinating potpourri of smells: fish, tan bark, horse manure, sawdust and woodsmoke. She stood on the boardwalk in front of the building as her father locked up for the day, then grasped his hand for the walk home. She often spent the afternoon with him at the store, after the morning lessons with her mother. At the edge of town, there was a group of about forty Indians in a grove of maple trees.

"What are they doing, Father?" Just then a nest tumbled to the ground as it was poked by a long pole. The naked little birds flopped on the sandy ground as a woman and two girls rushed forward to snap off their heads. Aurora screamed. The woman turned and laughed.

Her father nodded to the woman and sighed as his daughter, her red braids swinging behind her, tore off to the house. She refused to come down to supper that night, crying herself to sleep. Her mother explained that the birds provided food for the winter months. The birds hardly felt anything. But Aurora did not believe this. She had held the airy pulsing body of a young robin, fallen from its nest. The exquisite terror of the bird entered her own body. Her mother told her to leave it there, under the cedar tree, where it remained, frozen, for an hour. When she checked its progress, it had disappeared. She wanted to think it regained its stamina and returned, somehow, to its parents, so she did not closely study the paw prints in the dirt surrounding the spot the robin had occupied.

As she grew older, Aurora became acquainted with the steps of squab preservation: rubbing the scale-like feathers off the tender bodies, cutting up the flesh and packing it in crockery for the trip back to the Indian camps where the meat was smoked. She knew what was done, but she never did it herself. She would not now.

On the way back to the farm, she drove past the house where she had grown up. It was now owned by a boisterous Bohemian family. Six children ran through rooms she had inhabited as a child; six children, rather than a solitary child, explored the woods and fields that sloped away from the house to the river. She felt the salty sting of tears as a woman came down the back steps with a basket of wet clothes. Aurora reined the horse to a stop and watched as the woman untangled sheets from the basket and fastened them to the line, holding spare pins in her mouth. They would dry in no time on a warm, breezy day like this with the wind coming straight off the lake. Two children, about five years-old, raced around their mother, ducking under the flapping sheets. The woman looked towards the road and beckoned. She took the pins out of her mouth and called, "Come in for a bit." She knew who Aurora was.

"Thank you. I will another day." She waved and clicked the horse into motion. The contrast between her living situation, a childless married woman whose husband was thousands of miles away, and the Bohemian woman's bursting household was too much for her. Also was the fact that she missed her parents and did not wish to encounter their ghosts inside her old home. Her father had died from blood poisoning after cutting himself on the quarter hoop of a barrel of molasses in the store. Her mother sold the store and took to her bedroom, visited by one infirmity after another. Libby Gray lived to see her only child married, but succumbed to a tumor of the breast. She had told no one about the growth, disguising her misshapen bosom with loose garments. Aurora could not believe her strong mother, who had taught her to be brave and independent, had given up so easily, had not put up a fight. "I don't know what else to do with my life," she confessed to Aurora. She could have been a widow who took over her husband's affairs. Women had done it before. Look at the widow Rudolph who now managed the chair company just on the other side of Sawyersville. Her husband had gone down on a lumber schooner heading across Lake Michigan to Chicago. She stepped in, still wearing her widow's weeds, and now the company was thriving. Aurora missed her mother, and at the same time was angry with her for deserting her. Aurora let the tears splash onto her breasts, covered today in a white summer-weight cotton dotted with tiny blue cornflowers. She indulged in crying freely and unashamedly. She looked back over her shoulder at the bedroom window over the porch roof. It had been her mother's room, where the bed had been moved in front of the window so her mother could watch the sky. Her mother had died in that room. Neither of her parents reached the age of fifty. Both sets of grandparents had died before she moved up to Blackbird with her parents.

Martin's family was quite the opposite. His grandparents from both his mother's and father's sides were in their seventies and in good health in Pelican Rapids. His great-grandmother lived with his mother's parents and a great-grandfather with his father's. Such an abundance of generations staggered Aurora's imagination. Having an array of family elders was something that Aurora envied.

Uncle Ethan had been Martin's great-uncle, who died at 73 after wearing out three wives. On Decoration Day, Aurora put a bouquet of yellow hawkweed and cowslips on Uncle's grave, and the wives' graves too. The three were buried beside him in the family graveyard, or "stone orchard" as Martin called it, situated in a little enclosure off to the north of the house, near to the intersection of Sawyersville Road and Starr Lane. The women's stones were spaced in a semi-circle around Ethan's, all equidistant from their husband. Aurora wondered what the last wife, Lenora, thought when she saw two stones of predecessors out in the family plot. Off at an angle from Lenora's resting place was the tiny stone of *Infant S.*, where Aurora lay a circlet of ox-eye daisies. She assumed the baby had been Lenora's. Ethan had no living children from these three marriages. His second wife had been a widow with two children, but they were grown now, and Ethan did not name them in his will. Aurora often thought of the dead infant, wondering if it had been stillborn—or had lived briefly here at Starrvation Corner. Very briefly, she thought, for the baby had not been named. Martin knew no more than she did about the dead child.

Aurora remembered Ethan coming into her father's store: tall, white- streaked, black hair with a hawk-like gaze which could pin down and hold the object of his interest. Aurora thought Ethan must have Indian ancestry, but again, Martin didn't know. The elder Starr strode in purposeful way, as if there was much more to accomplish. The one time she had seen Lenora, before she met Martin, was when the petite, neat woman accompanied her husband to the store. She bought a yard of flannel cotton, and several skeins of yarn. Aurora admired her pretty, pert features and matching dress and bonnet. Lenora's hands told the story of her daily life—the palms with their yellowed calluses; reddened, raw knuckles; and broken nails.

Ethan Starr had been a Civil War veteran, so was allowed to claim 160 acres; most settlers were allowed only 80. A bronze GAR marker guarded his stone, and under his name was etched the square and compass symbols of the Freemasons. Aurora's father had been op-posed to the Masons, saying the country did not need any secret societies. So the symbol made her uneasy as she placed the yellow bouquet at the base of the stone.

Aurora and Martin lived five miles north of Blackbird. In bad weather, it seemed a hardship, but today Aurora was enjoying the ride home. The soft thud of the horse's hooves on the sandy trail, the insistent, penetrating heat of the sun, and the chittering squeaks of hummingbirds squabbling in the pines diluted her sadness and brought a peace she could only find in nature. "bout a mile before Starrvation Corner was a huge bed of huckleberries. The horse sensed that she wanted to stop here and slowed to a halt in a spongy needle-covered clearing under a grove of tall pines. One end of the patch was stripped of fruit; the birds and, from the snapped off twigs and tracks in the sand, a bear had been eating here. The other end was still laden with clumps of dense blue. The fruit fell into her palm when she touched the stems.

She grabbed a small bucket from the wagon, and squatted in the sand, smiling as the soft pings hit the tin bottom, then diminished as a deep blue filled the bucket. Martin loved huckleberry pie; he had shown her this patch, feeding her berries from his hand. They both laughed at the blue mouth and teeth of the other. They first kissed here—a deep blue kiss of summer. And they returned to this spot the next summer to lie down together back behind a shelter of pines. *Martin, where are you? Are you safe?* To keep her spirits from spiraling downward, she concentrated on picking enough berries for two pies: one for Pat and his uncle; one for her—and Martin.

The summer progressed with intense sweetness, making her miss her husband even more than in winter when longing and discontent seemed to fit the season. Wherever Martin was now, she hoped he found a patch of berries.

Chapter Thirteen

July 1899

Canvas—To Make Water Proof

White lead 4 pounds, spirits of turpentine 1 fourth part, white vitriol half ounce, sugar of lead half ounce, and boiled oil to make it thin; apply with a paint brush . . .

Aurora had been with the pack train for three days; it would be another three before it reached the head of Dease Lake where the Hudson's Bay Company warehouse was located. The head packer and small crew were more congenial than the owner of the scow had been. They charged her a modest sum for food, and made her feel welcome when she joined them for meals. Wrangell had neither lifted his lip nor growled at any of them, so she took this as a stamp of approval. He trotted along beside her horse, only leaving her when the mules moved out of line or balked. The dog's herding instinct went into play as he crouched, then charged, nipping at the heels of the temperamental beasts. As the day advanced, and the temperature rose, large flies congregated on top of the rich mounds of mule and horse dung.

Whenever they stopped, they lit a fire to keep the clouds of mosquitoes at bay. Aurora had nearly used up her bottle of insect repellent; she wore the net constantly as she rode on the horse "leased" to her for the trip. In spite of these measures, the back of her neck was peppered with itchy welts, as well as the backs of her hands.

To distract herself from physical discomfort, she let her mind drift, entering into past experiences. The years of teacher training had not prepared her for travel by pack train in the wilds of Canada to search for a missing husband. What would her students think to see her now? What would her mother make of this situation?

ʺ ʺ ʺ ʺ

When Grenville Gray died in 1892, Aurora's mother insisted on sending Aurora away to school. A portion of the money from the sale of the store paid her tuition for the next year. Her mother, experiencing a brief reprieve from her ailments, accompanied her to Mount Pleasant and stayed overnight before heading back north to Blackbird.

Libby Gray was ready to shed her role of mourning wife and assume the next phase: Mrs. Gray, widow. She left her bombazine mourning dress at home and wore a new green plaid cotton one with matching sunbonnet. She considered staying a while longer to see that Aurora got settled in her new surroundings, but, she reminded herself, this was Aurora's adventure; her daughter needed to have a chance to explore the world without her mother hovering.

The streets, houses and businesses of Mount Pleasant were more polished, less raw than in Blackbird. Some of the homes were huge brick structures, larger than any Aurora had seen. They had no trouble finding her student lodgings. It was on an elm-lined street, set back from a broad sidewalk with a brick path curving in an "S" to the front door. Aurora inhaled the sharp scent of marigolds, growing in abundance as a border for the bricks. The leaves of oaks and maples here had barely started to turn color, only a suggestion that summer's green was on the wane, no splashes of red and orange that already marked the trees up north. And something else was missing: the stench of the tannery and the perfume of freshly sawn lumber, as well as the noises that accompanied those industries.

The house was approved by the administration as a residence for female students at the Central Michigan Normal School. The landlady installed a cot in Aurora's room for Libby, at no charge. "I'm glad to meet the parents of my residents," said the woman, whose high collar did not do an adequate job of concealing a goiter on the side of her neck.

Libby and Aurora walked to a restaurant the landlady recommended. They laughed afterwards, calling it their "meal in white": boiled chicken, boiled potatoes, steamed cauliflower and white Parker House rolls. Even vanilla ice cream for dessert!

Aurora slept well that night, her mother sleeping only a foot away. She insisted that Libby take the bed. In the cot, she felt like a child again, secure that an adult was there and the world was safe. Her mother's hair was a duller shade of Aurora's, some silver strands threaded through the long mass that spread out on the pillow. There was a gas lamp on the wall—"all the modern conveniences for my young ladies," the landlady said with pride. There was a soft pop when Aurora turned the key on the fixture and the light went out.

"Good night, mother."

"Sleep well, Aurora. I enjoyed today. The first day I've enjoyed in a while."

During the night Aurora awoke and saw that the bedclothes were thrown back, her mother gone. Aurora opened the door to the hallway and heard coughing from the bath, two doors down. She knocked softly, "Mother?" Another cough, ragged as if torn from the lungs, then the door opened to reveal a white-faced Libby, trembling slightly.

"Just a little spell. I think I'll take some of my medicine." Libby leaned against her daughter as they walked back to the room. Libby removed a brown bottle from the tapestry bag that was always at her side and poured some reddish liquid into a teacup. Fumes of alcohol filled the room. Aurora realized her mother often exuded this "medicinal" smell. She had for years, Aurora admitted to herself.

Their landlady informed them that Isabella County was dry, so that they should not expect any wine for dinner when they headed out to the restaurant. Pushing back the worry about Libby's "spell," Aurora smiled as she crawled back into the cot. Her mother had found a way to circumvent the dry laws.

ıı ıı ıı ıı

The packers were all Canadians, and although Aurora could not say exactly why, she felt at ease in their company. Perhaps because she was on Canadian soil, and because they were taking her closer to Martin.

"We got word to bring more saddle horses for the real sick fellows," said one. "A mule isn't the easiest thing to ride."

"Are there lots of sick men?"

"Yes, and they're the lucky ones. They made it through the winter on the Liard. So your husband didn't come through this way last year?"

"No, he took the Edmonton Trail. He met his friend in Minnesota, so it was closer for them to travel that way. And they were told it was faster, 1500 miles from Edmonton to Dawson."

"I'd say your husband's a fool to have left you at home just to hunt for a few nuggets in the largest God-forsaken wilderness there is." The head packer cleared his throat harshly, as if to cover up for his forwardness. "The men who travelled up the Stikine still had a thousand miles before they hit Dawson."

Aurora could hardly comprehend the vastness of this part of North America. Her part of Michigan was wild, but the lakes, except for the Big Lake, rivers and hills were manageable. Not a threatening landscape. Here a human struggling up rivers, through the forests, across the mountains was an insignificant creature, smaller than much of the wildlife, moving toward a promise of something grander than the life left behind. "He wanted to find gold to start up a business." She caught herself using the past tense, as if she knew Martin's dream was dead.

"Few ever find enough gold to even pay for the trip," said the one who had helped her set up her tent the first night. She had purchased a small canvas tent in Wrangell, and slept under a giant pine apart from the men. At first the dog Wrangell slept just outside the flap, but when she heard him snapping at mosquitoes, she took pity and brought him into the shelter of the tent.

Now at dawn on the last day of the trip, Wrangell whined and Aurora unfastened the flap and let him out. She smelled coffee and heard the clang of iron on rock as the skillet was set on the three-stone fire. The breakfasts so far on the trip consisted of fried potatoes and trout, caught in the river. She tried not to think of the human excrement dumped from the ship, the carcasses of horses, perhaps of men, too, beneath the green waters. The men took turns cooking; since Aurora was a paying passenger, she was not asked to prepare meals. She was grateful to let someone else attend to the routine matters. With few women in the wilderness, men had to take on jobs considered to be in the domestic realm back home. Here everything was for survival. Cooking was as important as shoeing a horse.

"None of you has caught the gold fever?" Aurora asked, balancing a tin plate on her lap.

"I was up in the Cassiar last year. My uncle works a mine up on Snow Creek," said Clyde, the man who had helped her with the tent. "He went up there during the first rush into that area, and he's been there for twenty-four years. He pulls out about $10 a day. It's decent, but too remote for me. It's like being on the moon. The lakes up in the mountains sit above the clouds. The water is the coldest, purest you'll ever find."

"He must be lonely."

"Well, I think he's so used to that way of life, he's unfit for civilization. But I know he liked having me there, shoveling gravel into sluice boxes. Boring work." He shook his head and reached for the coffee pot. "I'd rather tangle with mules. More interesting."

Aurora smiled, then sprang to her feet, her plate hitting the dirt. Off in the trees came a series of high, frenzied yelps. Wrangell. She hadn't seen him since she let him out of the tent at daybreak. She started to run toward the sound, but Earl, the head packer, stopped her. He grabbed his rifle and motioned to Clyde to come along.

They returned carrying the dog between them. The dog's muzzle was wrapped in Earl's bandana. "He snapped, so I had to tie up his mouth. I think he tangled with a bear, from the look of his leg."

Wrangell moaned, his eyes locking with Aurora's. "Oh," she gasped, mesmerized by the glistening muscle laid bare where fur and skin had been peeled back on the dog's flank. The men put the dog on a horse blanket under a pine. She removed the bandana and offered him some water from a battered tin bowl, which he lapped at out of politeness. He struggled to stand, but yelped and collapsed onto the blanket.

"We need to stitch that flap, then cover it with a poultice to keep it from getting infected," said Earl. He went to his saddle bag and returned with a large needle and thread. "I even do a bit of sewing on the trail," he joked. "This is used mostly on canvas and heavy wool blankets. Don't worry. I dipped it in the boiling water we used to make the coffee." Pulling out a flask from his pocket, he soaked a folded handkerchief with the contents. "I don't know if this will help, but it's worth a try." He pressed the cloth against the dog's nostrils. Wrangell twisted his head, then sneezed.

"Here, you try. The fumes might take his mind off my stitching him up."

Wrangell put up less struggle as Aurora put the handkerchief under his nose.

"Now tie up his muzzle again and hold his head. Firmly."

Aurora put Wrangell's head in her lap, placing a hand on either side of his head. She crooned nonsense to him as Earl first washed the wound, then pulled the thread in and out, securing the flap of skin. Only once did the dog try to wrench his head from Aurora's hands. But she held on.

Earl went back to the fire and brought Aurora a heaping serving of oatmeal. "Save some of that for a poultice." Since Aurora's breakfast was in the dirt, where it landed when she heard Wrangell yelping, she gobbled down most of the oatmeal.

In her tent, she retrieved the sanitary cloths she had brought along. One she tore into strips, and borrowing Earl's needle and thread, she constructed a poultice holder that was secured by the strips that went under the dog's belly and around his leg. She tied this clumsy device to his flank. Wrangell sniffed the oatmeal through the fabric. "You rest and don't eat that," she instructed as the dog struggled to stand. "Lie down." She knew it would be difficult to keep him down for long.

One of the more compliant mules pulled a small wagon. The crew redistributed the load on to the pack mules, and Wrangell and Aurora rode in the wagon for the last leg of the trail to Dease Lake. They were cushioned somewhat by the bags of flour and oats spread on the bed of the wagon. Wrangell winced when the wheels hit a hole. By tonight she would see Dease Lake, a huge body of water, thirty miles long and two miles wide, the men told her. They bet her husband would be there among others waiting for the pack train to take them back to the Outside. She stroked Wrangell's head, filled with a mixture of anticipation and apprehension at seeing her husband again, after almost a year and a half. They had both been changed during their separation. How great the change remained to be seen. Would she still love him? She had the same doubts during her two years of study in Mount Pleasant, but once she was back home in Blackbird, she felt on stable ground, sure of her feelings for Martin Starr.

ƒ ƒ ƒ ƒ

In May of 1894, the year before she would marry Martin Starr, Aurora was twenty-four, large-boned, yet slim. She honored her height of nearly six feet by piling her auburn hair in a sumptuous mound and securing it with various combs, which she chose with care to complement her dress.

In two weeks she would receive her certificate after two years of study at the Central Michigan Normal School. During her first few months away from Blackbird, she had been desperately homesick, ill with longing for the familiar. When her mother left, she nearly backed out of the idea of getting an education, justifying her fright with reasons why she should be back home: her mother's poor health and the expense of her tuition being high on the list. But after a week, she was growing fond of her landlady, even of the woman's goiter, which at first she found repulsive. She knew the names of her housemates, all young women in their twenties. As the only northerner among them, the rest from central and southern counties, she had a special status. She was given the nickname "Eskimo." It pleased her because she had never had a pet name before, other than Martin Starr calling her Rory. Her parents called her Aurora, always. These girls delighted in assigning names to everyone, including the landlady, whom they had deigned "Mrs. Big Neck," or just "B.N." Although Aurora got along well with them, she had not formed a special friendship with any one girl, the type of friendship she hoped might develop, a bosom friend.

While at Mount Pleasant she corresponded with Martin, who was working in the family flour mill business. He confessed to Aurora that he hated it, but was trained for nothing else. Through letters, she was coming to regard him as friend who shared confidences, though she knew they were in territory beyond just friendship. When he came to his great uncle's farm each summer, they spent all free time together. Martin was anxious to be out on his own and encouraged Aurora to see more of the world "south of Blackbird." *I wish it were possible for the two of us to go adventuring. Both of us should experience things beyond the net of our families,* he had written.

In spite of her feelings toward Martin, she was seized by an uncontrollable crush on her botany instructor. It was as if once she left home, a band of emotions was unleashed to overwhelm and confuse her. She knew Ira Hedges was married, with a young son, but she could not keep fantasies from filling her head. During a field trip in the woods near campus— called Normal Woods by the faculty, and Abnormal Woods by the girls in her house—Aurora walked at the front of the group as Mr. Hedges led them in looking for trout lilies, spring beauties, Dutchman's breeches. His sandy hair and sandy brows gave him a tousled, puppy look, at odds with his size. He was a big man, making Aurora, larger than the other women students, feel dainty. The golden hair on the backs of his large hands glinted in the spring sun. The students crowded close, those nearest, like Aurora, squatting under their long skirts, as Mr. Hedges pointed a pencil at an emerging jack-in-the-pulpit. Aurora imagined that hand on her waist, a gentle, firm pressure. It intrigued her that such an imposing figure of a man was so careful in dealing with the small, delicate flora of the Michigan woods. It was like God bending down to tend to a sparrow.

She spent hours drawing the plants and flowers she observed, filling a notebook with them. "You have an eye for detail, Miss Gray," said Mr. Hedges, as he turned the pages of her notebook, while she looked at the cross section of a wild leek sprout under the microscope. "This is a work of art," he complimented her, running his fingers over the fabric cover, a piece of silk with a fleur-de-lis design she had fashioned herself.

She could do no more than mumble, "Thank you," keeping her face pressed against the eyepieces, pretending to concentrate on the minute striations of the plant, while the sharp, oniony scent arose from the stage of the microscope.

Toward the end of the course, she began to dread and anticipate class in equal portions. The presence of Mr. Hedges confused her, made her inarticulate. Yet when she was out of his presence, she thought of him and began to plan for how she could impress him at the next class: some penetrating botanical question, perhaps a rare plant she would find and bring to him; combs for her hair to emphasize its lushness; a new waist she had purchased at a shop downtown, the bodice interwoven with lavender and pink ribbons. Would it be too dressy for class? Would her attempts to impress be considered girlish and transparent?

On her own she had begun pressing flowers, making a portfolio that she intended to show her instructor later. She followed the directions in her text for preserving and drying botanical specimens:

> *The plants to be preserved should be gathered when the weather is dry. Place the ends in water, and let them remain in a cool place till the next day. When about to be submitted to the process of drying, place each plant between several sheets of blotting paper, and iron it with a large smooth heater, pretty strongly warmed, till all the moisture is dissipated. Colors may thus be fixed, which otherwise become pale, or nearly white.*

Aurora borrowed her landlady's iron to press violets, lady slippers, and forget-me-nots along with all the other blossoms from the walks in Normal Woods.

"What do you think of Mr. Hedges?" she asked Nell, a housemate and her partner during botany lab. Nell had been raised on a farm in Oceana County.

"Don't you think it a bit strange for a man to be interested in flowers?" Nell's brow was furrowed as she unraveled a piece of knitting she had just begun as the two sat on kitchen chairs in the side yard. The spring evening was full of warm, moving air and the sharp robin sounds punctuated their conversation. Nell had fair hair, but black eyebrows, which caused one's eyes to stay with her face longer than usual to study the contrast.

"Well, goodness, Nell, he's a scientist. He doesn't pick them to put in a vase; he studies them." Nell could be a bit thick at times. "Have you ever seen his wife?"

"My, aren't we a nosy Parker," said Nell, looking up from the tangled mess of yarn in her lap. "No, why?"

"I just wondered. Natural curiosity." Aurora knew that if she decided to confide in someone about her feelings for Mr. Hedges, it would not be Nell. "I wonder if his wife is named after a flower?" she laughed, turning the conversation in a lighthearted direction.

"You mean like Violet, or Rose, or Iris?"

"Maybe Pansy, or Hollyhock."

"How about Trillium? Marigold? Actually that sounds kind of nice. Marigold," said Nell. "But certainly not Geranium or Hepatica." Aurora pictured a broad, red-faced wife, matching her husband in physical stature.

"You didn't mention Skunk Cabbage," laughed Nell.

"I think that may be it, Nell. Skunk Cabbage Hedges." As she said this, it defused her longing for Ira Hedges, at least for that evening.

One final incident contributed to Aurora's emotional maelstrom during the final weeks of her time in Mount Pleasant. She was still teetering; should she return home or apply for one of the many teaching jobs in towns like Grand Rapids, Muskegon, Lansing? She had not seriously considered teaching away from home when she came to Mount Pleasant, but lately she had wondered what it would be like to live in a new town, to be unknown.

She was assigned a critic teacher known for his fussiness. Mr. Malcolm was mimicked for his habit of evaluating his student teachers with pursed lips and narrowed eyes, diving down periodically towards his ledger, like a heron after a fish, to scribble madly, often perforating the paper with his pen. Aurora had been disconcerted to find the man staring at her during his observations of her teaching, rarely writing down a thing.

Aurora was late for her appointment with Mr. Malcolm, who had completed his last observation of her the previous day in a class of fourth, fifth and sixth graders at a nearby school. The day had turned chilly, with a few snow flurries, a cruel May joke, but one which Michiganders did not take seriously. Winter could not return now. Aurora rushed into the faculty office, shared by all critic teachers. It was a bleak room—high tin ceiling; drab olive walls; desks, tables, chairs scattered throughout its space like driftwood cast upon the beach. The sound of her heels against the bare floorboards echoed. She was out of breath, almost choking from the tightness of her coat, which was buttoned all the way up; one comb was coming loose, causing her abundant hair to shift on one side. She sat down in the chair placed beside Mr. Malcolm's at a long table, on which sat the infamous ledger.

"I'm sorry for being late." She left on her coat, for the room felt as chilly as the outside. Because it was May, there would be no more indoor heat, no matter what the weather.

Mr. Malcolm was alone in the room, polishing his rimless spectacles with a square of flannel. He looked exposed, almost frightened with the flat planes of his face fully exposed. He hooked the earpieces securely on his ears, adjusted the lens at the temple and blinked slowly at Aurora's approach.

He patted the seat of the chair beside him. With the other hand he pulled a tin of peppermints from his jacket pocket. "Miss Gray?"

She took a piece of the candy, feeling that she'd entered the wrong room or was here for a reason she had no knowledge of. "Thank you."

He replaced the tin and leaned towards Aurora, unbuttoning the bottom two buttons of her coat. She froze, the candy turning bitter in her mouth.

"Never sit down with a coat buttoned across your lap. You'll stretch the fabric," he said, turning to open the ledger.

Mr. Malcolm's voice was a background buzz. She watched his full, molded lips— his only attractive feature yet so out of sorts with his gooseberry eyes, plastered down thinning hair and jug-handle ears— that they were an aberration. He was discussing her lesson yesterday, but she could not process the words. She could still feel the pressure of his hand against the coat which pressed against her lap.

He handed her a slip that had her name and Pass for the practice teaching portion of her course. She wanted to be out of this room, away from the smell of peppermint and the camphor scent of Mr. Malcolm's jacket. "I'd be glad to recommend you for any position you desire, Miss Gray." He placed a hand on her sleeve as she stood. "Is there a particular school, perhaps nearby, where you would like to teach?"

The chair screeched as she pushed it back. She moved to put distance between her and Mr. Malcolm. She felt dizzy and breathless, yet managed to say in a voice, her voice, surprising her with its firmness. "I have not made a decision yet." She headed for the door, her hand on the knob. But suddenly Mr. Malcolm was behind her, his broad hand splayed on the door, at the level of her eyes. Hearing voices in the hallway gave her courage.

"Is there something you want or am I to be kept a prisoner?"

"I'd like to take you to dinner. You are no longer my student. It would be quite proper." She turned and saw the sensuous lips wet and moving towards hers. Aurora turned the knob and jerked open the door, hitting Mr. Malcolm on the forehead as she passed through, clutching her slip of paper. "The devil," he swore. Later she wondered how Mr. Malcolm would explain the bump on his head to his colleagues.

Now she could laugh, remembering the awful Mr. Malcolm. She could even be amused at the crush on Mr. Hedges. She had given the portfolio of pressed flowers to Martin as a birthday gift. He declared it his best gift ever. She had smiled, too, reading Martin's notebook last night about the just desserts dished out to Mac, leader of the Philadelphians.

I restrained myself, but wanted to yell out a cheer when we passed the Phil-adelphia party with all their rafts, loaded with horses, stuck on a sandbar. Mac was on a raft directing the men who were in the water, leaning into their handspikes to pry the rafts free.

But Martin's account of the three-day float down the Nelson River was the only bright spot in his record of what transpired in August, September and October of the previous year.

Chapter Fourteen

August, September, October 1898

For three days Martin and his companions had a reprieve as they traveled the one hundred miles of the Nelson to where it joined the Liard. No calamities befell them, but Martin had grown superstitious of voicing aloud any good fortune or piece of luck for fear a hardship would hit them. Therefore, he kept from cheering when they came upon Mac's party lodged on a sandbar.

When they reached the confluence, he was not encouraged by the appearance of a half mile-wide churning, rushing water pushing its way around sand bars and snags. At that point they were forty miles below the lower entrance to the Liard's Grand Canyon, known as Hell's Gate, the next destination on the ascent of the Liard.

Frank, still unable to do any lifting and pulling, was in the stern at the steering oar. Even this task was too much for him; the pain was in his face, but he kept at his post. Harry, Ulrich, Jim and Martin were in and out of the water hauling the scow upriver by the 300-foot track line. They could not have done the job without this piece of equipment, which Martin had made from thirteen cinch ropes, saved when he sold their horses. They were sometimes obliged to climb the bank to work their way around obstacles in the water, and then back into the river in a waist-high swift current. On a tough day they made three miles; on a good day seven. The only reward was that at night when they secured the boat, they camped in a dry place; they were free of the muskeg for good. They managed to stay with the other two boats that had left Fort Nelson with them. At night the three groups camped together and shared the stories they'd heard from all-water routers along the way.

Several parties who had come from Edmonton by the all-water route passed them. It was too late for regrets, but hearing their tales confirmed what they already knew: they had chosen the worst way by going overland. The all-water Klondikers had traveled two thousand miles downstream with few of the hardships the overlanders had battled. But now they, too, were having trouble. They were inexperienced at tracking, and because their boats were loaded down with provisions, they were having a time moving their crafts upriver.

On September 1 they reached Hell's Gate, all of them working from the boat. The narrow passage did not allow for tracking. They used boat hooks, pike poles and sore, bloody fingers to grab hold of the canyon walls. Afterwards, Frank, looking at their raw, scraped fingers, declared they were all "up to scratch."

Martin did not know which name was more fearsome—Hell's Gate, through which they had been delivered, or the Rapids of the Drowned. At Fort Nelson they heard a story of two ill-fated boats belonging to the Hudson's Bay Company years before. The entire cargo and crew had been lost. The bodies of a few turned up now and then on snags downriver, but most had disappeared, claimed by the Liard. As if responding to a curse, the boats began to leak. They camped for a few days on the high banks, recaulking the seams with spruce gum. While repairing boats above, they watched other parties battle their way upriver, knowing they would soon be doing the same. It was at this point that the Frenchman's party turned back, even though they discovered some gold near the campsite, just above the rapids. Fear overcame their desire for gold. Martin proposed staying and mining, though it was late in the season. The other four in his party said it was impossible to mine enough to make it worthwhile. They voted for moving on. Martin went along with the group, though still convinced they could have at least gotten a grubstake out of that spot if they'd stayed a bit longer.

Back on the river, Frank and Martin took turns at the sweep, though Frank's shift was half of Martin's. They were the designated steerers, perhaps because they were more familiar with water, having grown up on the Pelican River and Pelican Lake. The other three men worked the line, being leery of navigating a boat in these waters. The banks were high and steep, with no place to stand in the water. So four men pulled from the top of the cliff, while the fifth steered the boat one hundred feet below. Because they could not find purchase at the cliff's edge and had to walk back a ways, they often ran out of track line. When this happened, they tied a pole to the end of the line and dropped it down to where the man in the boat would grab the pole, release it and tie the rope to the bow. Then hand-over-hand the crew pulled the boat up the river.

"A fool's paradise," said Ulrich in his jocular way. Indeed they saw the darker striations announcing gold's presence in varying degrees in the bars, banks and benches of the Liard. So far there had not been enough at any one site to make it pay. And they all still had the goal, in theory at least, of a big payoff when they reached the Klondike. But each man wondered on his own if the Frenchman and his crew had not been wiser.

At Devil's Portage sixty men unloaded boats and packed their goods over the mountain. The river ran through an eight-mile long elbow-shaped canyon that gradually narrowed from half a mile to sixty-seven feet. And then the falls, a deafening roar of water that rivaled Niagara. They had to shout to one another as they set out in the early morning on the portage trail, a total of four miles: a thousand feet of steep ascent for two and a half miles, then a drop for the last mile and a half. By afternoon they were making another trip with more weight on their backs. But one more trip was necessary. The next day, all except Frank, whose skin had a grayish cast, made another trip on the portage trail, each carrying one hundred pounds across. Martin could not have made another trip; he exhausted all energy. He marveled that Indian packers often carried two hundred and fifty pounds, and many of them were smaller in stature than the whites.

At night the men congregated around one party or another's campfire and entertained themselves with an evening "jollification." Each man took his turn at presenting music, in song or on an instrument, a story, a joke or recitation. Many of the stories featured legendary Klondikers. One such larger-than-life figure was a Scotchman named Jack Russell from a party who had already gone through. The massive Russell, so went the legend, had carried six hundred pounds on his back for a mile just for fun; another time he had slung his horse around his shoulders to ford a river.

Martin was constantly impressed by the diverse bunch of men lured by the promise of gold. There were older family men, some with established businesses back in their hometowns. Some were well-educated; others were illiterate and could barely follow the maps. A West Virginian from the all-water routers had brought his violin (he called it a *fiddle*) with him. How he managed to keep it dry for thousands of miles was a mystery. He played a sweet, haunting tune, an English ballad, he called it. The music stirred something in Martin; it seemed to be coming from centuries before, perhaps around a fire like this with people in layers of wool and leather listening, being strengthened by the music as they journeyed through unknown territory. Martin felt a bond with all adventurers and travelers. The fiddle tune brought the immensity of history and the tragedy of human endeavor to weigh on him.

There was one suspicious character, known only by his last name Jensen, who was with the all-water routers. He joined in on these jollifications, but there was something false about him that set many of the men's teeth on edge. Jensen claimed to have been on the Liard far back in 1882 and 1884. He was back again for gold that was further upriver. At night he spread out on his blanket reports from government geologists that proved there was gold to be had on the Liard. Later, the men present that night would discover he was a liar, one of many sent out by the Edmonton boosters to keep hope, mostly of the false nature, alive among the discouraged Klondikers. Almost all convened here at Devil's Portage expected to find paying gold on the Liard, if not at this spot then on farther up. And if not on the Liard, then over the divide in the Yukon basin. There was always one more place further on where a man could strike it rich.

The next Herculean task was taking the boats through the canyon. Martin recorded in his notebook that it took five days to get their boat and the boat of the party headed up by the Minnesotan, who had embarked from Fort Nelson with them, to pass through. All the while, they wondered where the group headed up by the Frenchman was now. Although discouraged, Martin was driven by stubbornness and a sliver of hope that he and Frank would find enough gold to be able to return home without shame.

The Minnesotan's boat was first. Most of his party were stationed at the end of their track line. The old adventurer himself was at the sweep and one of his men knelt in the bow with a pike pole for avoiding the rocks and an ax to cut the line if there was imminent danger of capsizing. At the initial yank on the rope, the boat darted into the current and then veered back towards the shore. Before anyone could react, the fully loaded vessel was spun around in a vortex and capsized. The man in the bow was quick and cut the rope as the boat twirled in the eddies of the river. The two men managed to stay with the boat, and as the vessel came spinning towards them, the others grabbed the sides of the boat and held on for dear life. They lost three boxes of ammunition and some guns, having decided to not portage those things over to the other side. Now they were sorry, but it was too late for regrets. Martin thought that the bottom of the Liard must have enough items to outfit several trading posts.

They patched up the damaged boat and tried again the next day, this time with success. Everyone was for taking a day off before moving the second scow through the canyon. So they rested, although with each day the water was growing colder. They couldn't spend hours wading in the water as they had done in August. In the mornings, the Liard wore a light skin of ice in the places where there was no current. Back at the portage, some men talked about Rivere des Ventes, or Windy River, a tributary of the Liard, as a good spot to quarter for the winter. So twenty miles above Devil's Portage, they stopped to build a temporary home. The two parties which had been together since Fort Nelson became neighbors, each building a cabin of sixteen by twenty feet beside the Windy River. The bear and moose tracks along the banks were promising for food. With the beginning of October, winter was already upon them.

// // // //

The leader of the other party, the fellow Minnesotan, was named Chauncey, the oldest of all of them. They respected him for his know-how for surviving in the Yukon—and for his tireless activity in carrying out projects. While the cabins were under construction, Chauncey had been working below the mouth of the Windy. He and his right-hand man constructed a grizzly—a contraption that worked as a sluice box for washing fine gold. It took a day to thaw the gravel over a fire. Next they shoveled the gravel into the grizzly and washed it. When they brought the gold into the cabin to weigh it on Chauncey's well-used gold scales, everyone gathered around in excitement. The big pay-off: forty-three cents! They all let forth a volley of curses on Jensen, the lying imposter in the employ of the Edmonton boosters. As well as promoting the Liard, he declared there was gold up on the Windy. Even Chauncey had believed him.

They worked long hours to tighten up the cabins for winter. Martin's party finished a stone fireplace on one side, with bunks around the room. With timbers from a wrecked boat in an inlet, they fashioned the door, table and shelves. But the windows were the most inventive feature. Jim, who was the group's photographer, scraped the film off four-by-five camera plates and used them as window panes. They were proud of their humble winter home.

Frank was growing progressively weaker, and with the completion of the cabin, he took to his bunk more and more. One gusty October evening while Martin made a gill net out of some cord, a skill he learned as a boy fishing on the Pelican River, Frank hunched over pen and paper at the table. "Put these in a safe place and deliver them when you return. Promise me," he said, handing Martin a note to his parents and one to a young woman he had been courting back in Pelican.

Martin tried for a jolly tone, but tears started up in his eyes. "Once you have some extended rest, you'll feel like a new man." Frank had already turned away to burrow under a pile of clothes and blankets on his bed. No matter how much wood Martin added to the fire, his friend could not get warm.

Around 3 a.m. Martin awakened, alert, up in the top bunk, above Frank. The varying timbres of the snoring men filled the cabin. The fire had gone out and an icy fuzz covered his beard and hair, the result of the men's exhalations condensing and taking solid form. Then he heard a soft rasp, "Martin," from below.

He jumped down to the cold, slippery planks and lit a lantern on the table. Frank's head was tilted over the side of the bed with a pink froth, now quickly freezing, around his mouth and in his beard. "Frank, Frank," he yelled, lifting up his friend's head and placing it on the bed. There was only silence and the gaze of his vacant eyes. He could not reconcile this corpse on the bunk with his lifelong friend.

The presence of death disturbed the sleep of the others, who soon gathered, wrapping their arms around their torsos in the cold, at the bunk. Martin drew the blanket up over Frank's face, and each man murmured his own farewell. "Be with God." "Rest in peace now Frank." "You're in a better place. You'll surely find some gold up there." Ulrich, the only Catholic, crossed himself. There was nothing they could do until daybreak, so they all crawled back into their bunks. Martin did too, but stayed awake, unable to sleep, with Frank's corpse beneath him.

In the morning they wrapped Frank in a blanket. Martin stored his effects, along with the notes he'd written the night before, in a pack bag for the day he'd return them to Mr. and Mrs. King. The ground was already hardening under a foot of snow, but using picks and shovels, they dug a shallow grave behind the cabins. Once Frank was in the ground, they overlaid his grave with timbers cut from the surrounding woods. At the head of this wooden platform they lashed a birch trunk, which Harry peeled and then carved:

> *Frank King*
> *b. Oct. 10, 1872*
> *d. Oct 10, 1898*
> *A son of Minnesota,*
> *a faithful friend,*
> *a brave Klondiker*

Martin hoped Frank was pleased with the symmetry of his life, short though it has been. Martin and he were born the same year. A black guilt settled over him. Frank had been ready to turn around at several points, and Martin persuaded him to continue. Martin had helped him to an early grave.

Chapter Fifteen

July 1899

The pack train arrived at the warehouse late in the evening, the sky still full of light. Dease Lake was a mirror, the perimeter broken by a series of wooden docks extending out into the water. Blindfolds were put on the mules to calm them while the packs were unloaded by the warehouse crew. Earl offered his hand to Aurora as she climbed, stiff and aching, out of the wagon. The two of them lifted the dog and steadied him as he wobbled on four legs, sniffing the drooping poultice still tied to his flank.

Beyond the far side of the warehouse, Aurora observed smoke from wood fires sending gauzy fingers upward. A cluster of tents circled the fires. Men moved disjointedly, slowly in the quiet evening. The sound of a harmonica drifted over, its peaceful, melancholy sound competing with the grumpy protestations of the mules. 'bove these sounds, rose a ragged cheer from the encampment. A small group, a few on crude crutches, moved towards the pack train.

"Is Martin Starr here?" she asked the first man she saw.

"Who might you be?"

"His wife."

The man said nothing, but pointed towards the tents. She and her limping dog headed over. Her stomach rumbled from eating nothing more than some jerky and bread, which she shared with Wrangell, since the morning's oatmeal. The smell of stew wafted toward her. First she went down to the shore of the lake and rinsed her face, staring at the wavy image. Her hair, sticky from sweat and dust, was loose from its combs. She rearranged it as best she could. A bath would have to wait. She had grown used to the smell of her own sweat, and it no longer disgusted her, the way it would have back home.

A man was bent over the nearest fire, stirring a pot. Something in his shoulders, his crouching stance stopped time. Aurora stood still. Wrangell whined softly. The harmonica player had stopped in the middle of his sad tune. Past, present and future condensed into this moment. She could not breathe. The man raised his head as if sensing her presence behind him. He wore moccasins, trousers too large and flapping as if they'd been made by a sailmaker, and a winter underwear shirt, stained under the arms. His black hair, choppily cut near chin-level, was threaded with gray. Still holding onto the long-handled spoon, he straightened up and turned. He wore no beard, but a dark shadow of new growth covered his face like a mask.

"Martin, it's you," she said. Only the eyes, robin's egg-blue, identified him, and they were disconnected from the rest of his features. They were expressionless, an ornamentation.

"You must be hungry. There's plenty tonight. I have another pot over there." He pointed to another fire with his spoon.

"Martin, it's Aurora. Don't you know me, Martin?" Even as the words were leaving her mouth, she knew the reunion she had imagined—her rushing into his arms, Martin overwhelmed with joy and surprise to see her—was not to be.

Martin stared past her, dropping his gaze to the dog. "It's injured."

"Yes, I think a bear ripped open his leg."

An old man sitting near walked over to Aurora. "Good evening. A woman is a welcome sight, almost as good as the pack train. Woolsworth," he said, extending a gnarled, brown hand.

Martin turned back to his stirring. "He doesn't know me," she said to the old man.

"He does. He's just locked up right now. Once he gets to the Outside, I expect he'll improve. He wants to get every last man who ever spent the winter on the Liard back to safety. He's worn himself out. But I can't stop him. Maybe you'll have better luck."

Martin dished out a bowl of stew, rabbit it seemed, and handed it to Aurora.

"Thank you, Martin. Do you have something I could use to feed the dog?"

He spooned more stew into a dented tin bowl and placed it on the ground. Wrangell lapped tentatively, unused to being served hot food.

"His name is Wrangell," Aurora told him.

"The men are going to Wrangell," he said.

"So are you. *We* are; I've come to take you home."

"I can't leave; there may be more coming down. They'll need someone to care for them." He turned and walked toward a man propped up on what looked like a chair made from a cut-up sled. The man's face was mottled blue, black and red. He opened a toothless mouth like a baby bird waiting accepting food from its mother as Martin spooned in broth from the stew. Other men staggered about on bandaged limbs, some with only one leg, one arm. The scene resembled the aftermath of a battle. But in this case the enemy was not human, and these men never had a chance to win.

Oddly enough, Woolsworth, who Aurora judged to be the oldest in the camp, seemed the most physically able, along with Martin, who although thin and fragile-looking, burned with energy as he executed the endless tasks—cooking, washing, nursing.

"It's a shame you can't talk to the other men who were with Martin," said Woolsworth. Harry was rescued right after the break-up; Jim and Ulrich were more able-bodied and should be back home by now."

"I wanted to thank Ulrich. He sent me Martin's notebook." She glanced over her shoulder. "How long has he been like this?"

"He's been more and more wound up since Cranberry Rapids. Some days I think he'll just spin off into the sunset. I thought now we've nearly reached the Outside, he would calm down. Be patient. He's a good man."

Aurora felt numb. Woolsworth showed her where she could pitch her tent, beside the one he shared with three other men. "I expect you know his friend died. Then that Harry had his toes amputated. Martin feels responsible. Lately Wiggins weighs on his mind." The old man pounded in a stake. "I told him I heard Wiggins had made it to the coast, but he can't be persuaded."

Martin was making his rounds, moving from tent to tent. Aurora assembled her toiletries and headed for the shore of the lake, where some bushes provided a low screen for privacy. Seeing no men close by, she left her dirty clothes in a heap and waded into the still water to her waist. Submerging quickly in the cold water, she shampooed her hair, ready to brave any creatures in the water for the feel of a clean scalp. She stood up and soaped her body, rinsed and hurried back to a clean nightdress and a blanket she had brought to the shore. The temperature was dropping, and mosquitoes swarmed around her head, whining like miniature saw blades. Wrangell gave one sharp bark. Aurora looked up to see Martin walking towards her. He stood there, an apparition of her husband. She waited, hoped, for him to speak. He bent to pick up a large piece of driftwood, then walked back to tend his fires.

You need rest, Aurora told herself. *This is your only concern now. You need to be strong and rested for the trip tomorrow. What if Martin refuses to go with the pack train back to Glenora? What will you do then?*

During the night a man screamed. This was followed by the sound of feet running between tents, then a frantic voice, interspersed with low, soothing murmurings. Somehow Aurora returned to sleep immediately, waking to the sensation of warmth in her pelvic area. The feeling was pleasant, sensuous and somehow related to a dream of Earl, producing stirrings of desire. As she reluctantly struggled out of the dream, she recognized the warmth as wetness. When she threw off the blanket, drew up her nightgown, her thighs were coated and the back of her nightdress soaked with blood. What a joke, she thought, allowing herself a bitter smile. Seeing her husband again had brought on her monthly. She was fertile, she was married, at least in the legal sense. Martin was alive, yes, she was thankful for that, but in his present state he could not act as either husband or father. She positioned a sanitary cloth into her underclothes.

In the twilight of midnight, Aurora made another trip to the lake to soak the blood from her nightdress. Venus was a ghostly presence in the sky. The blood on the bedroll would have to stay. If she washed it now, the heavy thing would have to be spread out (over the back of a mule?) to dry during the trip back. If it didn't dry during the day, she'd sleep in a damp bed. Not something to look forward to after a day on the trail. And she had no desire to cause the men to speculate about her wet bedroll.

In the morning when she emerged from the tent after a fitful sleep, Earl was squatting on the shore, a shaving mug and brush balanced on a rock beside him. She blushed to think of his appearance in her dreams, but boldly announced herself as she drew near.

"Good morning."

"So you found your husband," he turned, straight razor in hand. He wore no beard nor moustache, but light bristles dotted his deeply tanned skin.

"I've found Martin Starr. He no longer seems my husband," she said, scrubbing the cloth with a piece of lye soap. "You've seen him? You know which man is Martin?"

"Yes. He seems in need of care, if ever he can stop caring for others." Earl flattened the skin under his jaw line, and pulled the blade down his neck. Aurora observed the head packer's profile, his strong, slightly curved nose, the cords in his neck.

"He's a stranger. I don't know what to do." She looked down the shoreline in the other direction as tears smarted in her eyes.

"Do you have family to help? Mail a letter when we get to Glenora. Mail service is much better this year." Earl moved over to her, dabbing her wet cheeks with a bandana that smelled of pine and tobacco.

Martin's parents. She could not avoid telling them. Martin's mother would probably want to have her son in Pelican Rapids where she could administer her own therapies. Aurora thought if Martin could be back at Starrvation Corner, their home, perhaps his trauma along the Edmonton Trail would diminish. She prayed her money would stretch far enough to get them home. Otherwise, she'd have to get work, perhaps in Seattle. She wondered if Mae would give them a room. "Thank you," she said to Earl, the smell of his shaving soap bringing a fresh surge of tears.

"Don't worry, Aurora," he said, using her Christian name for the first time, "we'll make sure your husband is on the pack train."

Martin had been up early preparing a meal of pancakes and bacon, made possible because of the supplies brought in on the pack train. The men ate with purpose, but quickly. They were anxious to be on their way. The harmonica player, sitting on top of his gear, pressed the instrument against his mouth with his right hand; he had no left, his damaged arm ending in a knobby stump just below the elbow. A few men joined in with the song as they dragged or carried their packs toward the waiting horses and mules. "We've Camped a Little While in the Wilderness," sang these worn-out stampeders. Their voices brought tears to Aurora's eyes. She noticed that Martin was not singing. She had tried to help him with breakfast, but again he treated her as if she were a guest, someone he may have met once or twice before.

Now she surveyed the former campsite. The tents had disappeared, but men had left behind what had once been necessary: several abandoned canoes, one caulked with faded-red winter underwear; rusty prospector picks; gold scales and pans strewn on the ground. She stepped on a broken compass, no longer needed. Its owner knew where he was going: out of here, back home. Martin was cleaning up the dishes and utensils down at the lake.

Wrangell, wet from his swim, limped towards her. His gait was off-center, as if his compass point was askew, making him approach the world slightly off true. He stopped inches from her and shook himself. She had disposed of the poultice. The stitched-up wound, which Earl had inspected earlier, showed no evidence of pus or inflammation.

"You'd make a good doctor," she praised Earl.

"Maybe for dogs and horses, but I wouldn't trust myself on a person." He scratched the dog behind his ears, causing Wrangell to emit soft grunts of pleasure. "We'll put this fellow in the wagon part of the way. He shouldn't be on his feet all day."

Aurora watched as Woolsworth walked to the shore and talked to Martin. The old man squatted beside Martin, who today had a long leather apron over his clothes. Together they walked back, each carrying pots and pans.

Aurora waited for them near the smoldering fire. "Martin, it's time to go. Do you have what you want to take with you?"

Martin turned his head as if it were being adjusted slowly by pulleys. He fixed a dazed look on her, as if he had no idea what to do, as if all purpose was gone from his life. He turned towards the warehouse, where the men who could walk were loading their packs onto mules. Earl and his crew carried some of the invalids over. The worst scurvy cases had been given lime juice last night, but months of deprivation and horrendous diets had thinned their blood, making their bodies appear severely bruised, their skin a palette of ghastly colors. Yet with the frightening hues, the faces were puffy, as if the skin were bread dough which could be kneaded and formed. Most had lost their teeth and were suffering with soft, bleeding gums. Their dry, chapped lips were crusty with dried blood. Aurora thought it was only their tattered clothes, if they could be called *clothes*, not skin, that held their bones together. Their outfits were strange to behold:

ripped Mackinaw suits, torn overshirts and all manner of inventive footwear. One fellow had attached rubber soles and heels, most likely from wading boots, to knee-high wool socks. Another had used the tops of rubber boots and sewn strips of gunny sacking to fashion an odd-looking sandal.

Of the forty men in Martin's cripple camp, ten had to be tied onto saddle horses. There they sagged, eyes sunk in their heads, but murmuring, "Giddy up. Let's go home."

Aurora was relieved as a docile Martin mounted a mule. "Where are the cooking things? The food?" He twisted to look behind.

"All your things are in a load on one of the mules. Woolsworth marked it," she reassured him. She placed a hand on his bony thigh. Thank God, at least he didn't show any of the ravages of scurvy, though how he'd managed was a miracle. Martin looked down at her hand on his thigh, studying it. She joined him in his observation, taking in the broken nails, the scratches and scabs and insect bites on the backs of her hands and wrists. He made no move to touch her.

"Wiggins," he said. "We must look for Wiggins." He dug his heels into the mule's sides, causing the beast to sit on its haunches. Martin clung to the animal. Earl saw what had happened and came back from the head of the train to coax the mule into an upright position.

"These are temperamental animals, so go easy with them. They'll get you to Glenora," said Earl to an unresponsive Martin.

Aurora rode behind him, watching her husband's body sway on the mule, pitying him. Inwardly she cursed the deprivations and horrors of the Edmonton Trail that had unhinged his mind, loosed it from its moorings, and from her. But now she was here. She was his wife. When they stopped to rest, Aurora made her way into the woods to change her bloody cloths. She had no choice but to bury them in shallow graves, where they would no doubt attract animals.

She longed for darkness. The constant daylight, the sun absent from the sky for only four hours, confused and disoriented her. Only Earl's pocket watch told them when it was time to stop. The birds sang at all hours, probably worn out and longing for the respite offered by a dark world. When they stopped to make camp, Martin slid off his mule and stood, his arms dangling listlessly at his sides. Aurora approached him, her husband, a pitiable figure, so lost, so alone. "Martin, would you like to sleep in my tent?" She kept her voice low, as if talking to a frightened child.

"No thank you. I need to see to the men." Suddenly he sped off, possessed with his mission. The men still needed him, at least until they reached Glenora. Aurora was aware of change in the demeanor of the disabled. Several good meals had given rise to a jauntiness, a cheerfulness in realizing they had survived and were going home. The group reminded Aurora of a bunch of hopeful scarecrows.

The packers and the former Klondikers all ate together, Martin and Clyde doing the cooking. Aurora was impressed with Martin's cooking skills, one positive by-product of his mental state. That night she slept with Wrangell; Martin shared a tent with Woolsworth.

The second night on the trail, she was awakened by Wrangell's growling and the rough whisper of canvas as the tent flap was thrown back. Wrangell stood up, the fur raised in a ridge along his back. The man crouching in the opening, stood up and let the the flap fall back. She heard shuffling footsteps retreating.

"It's all right, Wrangell." The dog grunted and stretched out at the entry. It had been Martin. Did he know she had his notebook? She would be sure to keep it out of his sight. It was her only source, other than the men, of the events that had changed her husband.

The man who had written in his notebook was not the man who appeared in the tent opening. She admired the man who wrote of surviving a winter on the Windy; she was afraid of the man who crouched, bathed in the light of a long summer night.

THIS WAS LEFT BY CREE
INDIANS AT JUNCTION OF
WHITE MUD LAKE TRAIL AND
WAS TO DIRECT OTHER INDIANS
TO A CACHE TWO MILES
UP THE WHITE MUD LAKE TRAIL

Chapter Sixteen

October, November 1898

*F*rank was scarcely in his grave before they made plans to leave the camp to hunt for fish and meat. The long winter loomed like a white specter. Chauncey and two of his crew took Martin's gill net and headed for the nearest of the Fish Lakes, up at the head of the Windy, about eighteen miles. The party of four set out for moose in a valley about twenty miles from camp. For a week they waded through knee-deep snow by day, slept together in a tent at night, eating only bannock and tea. Bannock, a staple of the Cree, had been adopted by the Klondikers. It was a simple bread to prepare: mix flour and lard by hand, then throw in baking powder and salt. If they were lucky enough to have currants or raisins, they added those for flavor, like the Cree did. Then water was added to make a dough, which was divided into lumps and wrapped around sticks. Usually there was not the luxury of an oven, so the bannock was propped over the campfire, watched and turned until golden brown.

Martin and the other three returned to the camp without a moose. They had seen no tracks. The fishermen returned and were smoking their catch. Chauncey laughed when he heard where they had been. "You don't want to be tramping around in the valley. Them old moose go up to the mountains at the first sign of snow. They'll be up around the timber line until February or March."

Martin and Harry talked about heading up into the mountains, but changed their minds when two all-water men stopped. They stayed the night, first paying their respects at Frank's grave, then sleeping end-to-end in Frank's bunk. When the pipes were lit up that night before bedtime and the story of the fruitless hunt was recounted, one of them said, "We killed two moose last week down below the Devil's Portage, at those sulphur springs where the moose have a yard." When Harry asked, they explained that a yard was an area where a herd congregated and tramped down the snow to create a safety zone against wolves.

Another piece of news was that Mac had drowned in the Nelson River, not long after they had passed the Philadelphians' rafts. They all grew quiet. None of them had liked Mac, but the death of any man in this wilderness, so far from home, was an event worthy of respect. The hand of nature was indiscriminate—snatching the strong and the weak, the braggart and the meek. Martin gave the all-water men a letter for Frank's parents, telling them to pass it on to anyone who could get it to a trading post. He had no assurance that it would reach them, but he had to try. Martin wanted to deliver in person the notes Frank wrote before he died. It was the least he could do. It seemed a callous act to send them out now. Maybe the notes would comfort his parents and lady friend after the news of his death had been absorbed.

In the sad letter to Mr. and Mrs. King, Martin slipped a note for his parents and for Rory. What could he say to Rory, other than to ask her forgiveness? He had not been a good husband, and had shown poor judgment.

So though gold seemed more remote, less important now, still they had to stay alive. Martin and Harry recaulked the boat and packed meager provisions: flour, tea, compressed vegetables, along with a teepee tent, blankets, rifles and ammunition. It seemed they were going backwards, revisiting that dangerous canyon from which they had escaped, tempting fate. Jim and Ulrich would go up into the mountains. They had to find meat at one of these locations or they would not survive the winter.

Martin took the helm and Harry the oar, and they made it to the portage unscathed. Three all-water parties were building cabins there for the winter. They invited the two men to join them, and that night around the fire, they feasted on moose steaks, sugar in their tea, even syrup on the bread. Then the all-water fellows proposed a swap. They had left their boat on the lower side of the portage. Would Martin and Harry take that boat and leave their own for the all-water men? Martin and Harry looked at each other and nodded, so the deal was struck.

The next morning the two sledded their gear over the portage to the boat they had traded for. They launched it into open water but before long saw that the bay was frozen. The whole day was spent breaking ice to get the scow downstream to the edge of the rapids. The night was a bitter, blood-freezing ordeal in the tent, made worse by the knowledge they would be tackling the river the next day. At daybreak, when Martin pushed aside the hide over the tent door, he cursed in dismay to see the floe ice moving quickly past, with lots of slush ice.

Harry heard his curse and joined him at the tent door, his eyebrows and moustache bedecked with tiny icicles. "What else can we do? We have to keep moving."

They were at the mercy of the river. After a mile, they joined the main current. It was futile to try to work the sweep. A pack of floe and slush ice carried the boat along, and the two men became part of the whirling frozen mass. Before long they were stuck in a jam at a bend in the river. Harry shrugged in helplessness at the water rising around them. The roar of the water muffled his yelp as the jam broke and the water level plummeted. The vessel plunged eight feet. There was no time to consider their fate; they were moving again as another burst of pent-up water and ice shot them downstream, locking the boat in a fifty-foot ice pack. Powerless, they did not even try to communicate with each other as they were carried sideways. A fresh roar filled their ears—the voice of the Rapids of the Drowned. They had planned to land above the deadly rapids and snub the boat down, but that was no longer in the cards. It was impossible to get to shore; they could not even steer the boat. A spark of resistance flared in Martin; he refused to join those who had perished here. Then suddenly the churning water broke up the ice, and they were free!

"Pike pole!" screamed Martin as he worked to swing the bow toward downstream. Harry scrambled to join him at the bow and poled against the ice. They barely missed a rock as they were propelled into the final cascade of the rapids. His throat raw, Martin screamed again: "Down!" and his companion dropped to the bottom of the boat as the boat lurched downward, filled with water from the curl of the back current. The poor boat creaked and shook but remained upright. They were soaked, as were their packs. The boat, carrying more than a foot of water, was pushed towards the shore, as if the river had had enough of them.

Martin spotted a fairly sturdy looking white birch leaning out over the water. "Try to hold her steady," he yelled with no guarantee that Harry could hear him. He lept from the boat, stern line in hand, into knee-deep water. Chunks of ice bumped into his legs. He took a turn around the birch's trunk and stabilized the battered boat. Their clothes were frozen stiff, making it difficult to move on land. Martin had tucked some extra matches in an inner pocket—that saved their lives. He started a driftwood fire in the overhang of a cliff. Harry was making slow headway chopping their packs out of the ice that had formed in the boat.

They kept the fire going all night, drinking tea, and adding sugar, a gift from the men back at the portage. They removed the outer layers of clothing, draping them over a stick frame as near the fire as possible without scorching them. Underwear and shirts steamed dry on their bodies. As morning neared they pitched the tent and climbed in, covering themselves with Harry's lynx-skin robe, a seven-foot square, worth more than gold, for they were warm immediately. Harry had made this invaluable purchase back at Fort Nelson from a discouraged Klondiker financing his trip home by selling all his goods. The story of the robe was that the former owner had traded with the Indians for the skins. For an additional $75 he had the skins sewn into a robe and lined with woolen blankets. Martin reckoned the temperature to be 20 below zero, for a wind had come up and the river was frozen solid. After sleeping for two hours and reluctantly leaving the comfort of the robe, they determined to leave the tent and head down to Sulphur Creek. They were almost out of wood and needed to scare up some more, and they wanted to see if they could spot moose tracks.

When Martin and Harry reached the creek, there were no moose tracks on the bank, no yard now. Had the men who had stopped with them up at Windy River been lying, or had the moose moved on? At least they found some wood and returned to their dismal campsite. They prayed the others had found moose up near the timberline. They chopped up the boat that had carried them through the icy rapids and spent a day making sleds for returning to the Windy River camp. The first day back was discouraging; the ice so rough that the sleds were useless. They abandoned them and loaded the packs on their backs to begin a slow, laborious routine. The bumpy ice heaved up, and pan ice edged the river, making it treacherous for walking. The two men inched along, taking turns going ahead with an ax to test the ice. At dusk on October 30, they came upon a flat area, where in warmer weather there would have been a creek with flat, sandy banks joining the river. A mix of alders, poplar, birch and spruce made it a good spot to camp.

Martin could not have wished for a better traveling companion. Although he wasn't as talkative and entertaining as Frank had been, the butcher was tireless, uncomplaining and possessed the skills for staying alive. While Harry scraped away the snow, Martin cut down boughs for a bed as well as poles for the tent. He started a fire; then together they put up the tent. They were back to rations of bannock and tea, with a little tobacco for their pipes. "Pretend it's moose meat," said Harry, biting into a piece of bannock, softened a bit by dunking it in tea. Martin laughed, and for a moment things were less grim.

The comforting ritual of puffing away on their pipes while hunkered next to the campfire at the end of the day—little fire and big fire—kept their fears at bay. Martin had never smoked until becoming a Klondiker. He hoped if he made it back to Michigan, Rory would not mind his new habit.

In the morning, new snow covered the tent. Martin went further back from the campsite to get more wood, and seeing a fallen spruce limb sticking at an angle out of the snow, gave a mighty pull, dislodging a snowy mound. A piece of frozen canvas poked out—a tent, caved in on one side by the weight of snow. With a dreadful intuition, he called to Harry. They cleared off the snow and managed to open the stiff flaps. Curled up inside a pile of blankets was a shrunken man, his long sandy beard and hair flowing out from the top. "God bless him," said Harry, his voice shaking. They both realized the dead fellow could be either of them.

And then the rage and futility of the whole expedition threatened to undo Martin. "Put this man's picture in your pamphlets, Edmonton boosters," he screamed at the frozen river. "Let everyone see the face of a real Klondiker!"

Harry put a hand on his shoulder and guided Martin back to the revived campfire and placed a cup of tea in his hands. After a few bites of bannock, they fortified themselves to go back and look for any traces of the man's identity. Unwrapping the corpse from its cocoon of blankets was grisly business. The poor chap wore an overcoat, and in the pocket was a small diary identifying him as Samuel Haines from Oxenbridge, England. To have come so far and end up like this! He had chronicled his journey from Edmonton in August of 1897, and leafing ahead they read January 7, 1898 as his last entry, ten months ago. It was a marvel that animals had not found him. It took all day to give Samuel Haines a burial.

Without picks or shovels, they had to devise another way to bury him. The morning was spent cutting down small trees, the afternoon sawing the wood into equal lengths and piling them around the body, which was wrapped in his tent, his shroud. They placed spruce boughs over this construction. Harry carved the man's name, his town and the date of his last day on the trunk of a living tree near the site. Here were two men unknown to Samuel Haines mourning his death.

Around the fire that night Martin read Haines's diary out loud as a final tribute to the Englishman. He had been a barrister at home and had come to North America with his law partner, Edward Fealey. Haines's feet became frozen in November of 1897, and his partner had "deserted him, taking most of the provisions." Haines had walked "eight miles one day on painful feet." His last entry said only: "I am here alone on the banks of the Liard, far from home. The agony of my feet and legs makes me wish for death."

Martin added this diary to his other burdens and vowed to mail it to Haines's hometown at his first opportunity. A heartless man like Fealy should be exposed. It occurred to him that they might yet encounter the heartless bastard.

It took them another week to return to the cabin on the Windy River. As they approached "home" on November 7, smoke curled from the chimneys of both cabins and light shined through the "camera plate windows," indicating Jim and Ulrich were back from the mountains. Though they had no moose, Martin was thankful they had not ended up like the unfortunate Haines. They at least had this to return to—shelter, companionship and loyalty.

Jim and Ulrich found no moose either, but Jim had shot a bear, literally running into it as they rounded an outcropping. He reacted more quickly than the bear, raising his rifle in the nick of time. They dragged it on a sled to the cabin and salted and roasted the meat.

The bear meat tasted like ambrosia on Thanksgiving as they gathered around the plank table. They set a place for Frank, and bowed their heads as Martin offered, "We thank the bear for giving us sustenance." A group "Amen" followed. They ate bannock, of course, baked in frying pans in the fireplace, a pint of beans Martin had been saving since July, and tea with the remaining sugar.

The day after Thanksgiving, Martin and Harry announced they were heading up to the mountains. "I think you *guyss* are going on a vild goose chase," said Ulrich. He was peeved that Martin doubted the lack of moose in the area he and Jim had just hunted. Martin assured the other two that he felt guilty for not finding one with Harry and that maybe their luck would change this time. Martin would come to regret this trip. They still had some strength and a chance at making it out to the coast by way of Glenora. Why hadn't he tried to convince the others to get out while they could?

As soon as Martin and Harry left the river, they were struggling in snow up to their waists while pulling a toboggan. They had a bit of bear meat from Jim's kill and looked forward to the greasy treat when they made camp that night, about halfway up to the timberline. Like the trip down to the Devil's Portage, they followed the same routine when they stopped: make a fire, pitch the tent, smoke their pipes. Finally they reached the timberline, but still no trace of moose, though they were sure they heard a bull snorting. After two nights up in the heights, they had to go down to the river, defeated.

The accident occurred about eight miles from the cabin. Once they reached the Windy, Harry stayed out front dragging the nearly empty toboggan over its frozen surface. Martin was behind the toboggan, downcast and discouraged. His lapse in attention would haunt him forever after. If he had been out front checking the ice, his friend would not have suffered the way he did.

One moment Harry was on his feet, the next only his torso and head were sticking up through the ice. The toboggan had not yet broken through. Martin extracted one of the tent poles from the load, and scooted on his belly, extending the pole. "I think I'm done for," Harry said as he made a feeble grab. (Later they would agree that the temperature must have been about forty-two degrees below zero that morning. When they had crawled out from under the lynx robe, they could hear their breath collide with the frigid air. They took care to breathe slowly and not too deeply.) Now Martin gripped Harry's forearms yelling "kick, kick!" After several tries, he was out of the hole, horizontal on the ice. He struggled to get up.

"I'll make a fire. We can burn the toboggan. You wrap up in the robe," Martin told his friend. "Once you're warmed up, we'll head for the cabin. I'll come back later for the packs."

But Harry shook his head vigorously. Through chattering teeth, he said he'd freeze on the spot if he waited for a fire to get going. It would be better to walk with frozen feet than to try to rewarm them here. Later Martin learned that he was right about this. He watched as his friend took off in a strange, jerky half-trot at a speed his frozen clothes would allow. All he could do was take up the toboggan rope and follow Harry home, praying the ice would not take him as well.

He found Harry in the cabin sitting with his feet buried in a bucket of snow. Jim and Ulrich had decided to stay in Chauncey's cabin to save on fuel. Without a fire in their cabin, the interior was below freezing. Martin quickly started a fire going. Seeing the smoke, Ulrich and Jim came back to the cabin. Over Harry's protestations, they took his feet out of the bucket and took turns rubbing them with snow. His feet thawed after nearly two hours; then the pain set in. They stuck a bit of moose jerky in his mouth to bite down on when the moans turned into screams. It was dreadful to hear.

That night they took shifts to keep the fire going. The next morning Harry's feet resembled sausages bursting in their skins, misshapen, purple, with darker splotches on the soles. There was no choice now but to close up the cabin and get him to a doctor. They had heard a doctor was camped with an all-water group at Brule Portage, twenty-six miles upriver. Harry needed medical attention, and the group needed meat.

Chauncey and his party would try to stick it out at the Windy River camp for as long as possible. They still had some smoked fish. Martin told them his group would come back for their things if they were able, but the wisest course would probably be to join the winter encampment up at Brule Portage.

Martin assumed the heavy weight of responsibility for this situation; his guilt spurred him to action. He quickly whipsawed some birch and fashioned a new toboggan with a chair back and a support for Harry's feet. They took as much as they could pack on the toboggan, along with a large heated stone to keep Harry warm. He didn't seem in as much pain right now, though tears filled his eyes as his companions installed him, wrapped in the lynx robe, in the toboggan. "I'm fortunate to have met up with you fellows." No doubt he was thinking of poor Haines. He wanted his knives next to him, which were stored in a folded piece of hide, with a separate pouch for each.

Martin took a moment to walk back to Frank's grave to say good-bye. He hated to leave him here; he belonged in Pelican Rapids. It was time to leave. Chauncey and his men came out and shook hands all around. "We'll look for you up in the Klondike," Chauncey yelled as they set out. Martin had no doubt that Chauncey would make it, but Martin knew he would never see the Yukon. Out on the frozen river, Jim and Ulrich pulled the heavy toboggan; Martin walked out front to check the ice.

Chapter Seventeen

August 1899

Nervousness

The cure of nervousness is best effected by restoring the healthy action of the stomach and bowels, and by the use of proper exercise, especially in the open air. The stomach should not be overloaded with indigestible food, and the bowels should be occasionally relieved by the use of some mild aperient.

The Strathoon was waiting when the pack train reached Glenora. The ship's whistle sounded, a startling reminder of civilization that brought cheers from the men. They hobbled, limped or were carried to the deck. As the ship headed down the Stikine, several raised their crutches in the air, whether in joy or in defiance at having escaped, Aurora wasn't sure. By the time they reached Wrangell, Martin seemed less concerned with the men around him. Woolsworth made sure Aurora had Martin's pack; it was light, as if he'd shed all material things.

Off the ship, the men gathered to thank their caretaker. While he shook their hands, some missing fingers, some having to use a left hand in the absence of a right, Martin remained expressionless. "God be with you," several said to Aurora. "He'll snap back," another assured her.

Martin stood woodenly by the gangplank as Woolsworth embraced him, then patted him on the back. The old man was returning to his home state of Iowa, though he hadn't lived there for decades. He declared he was done with gold-seeking this time, for sure.

Aurora led Martin to Astrid's house, the dog trotting with a slight limp ahead of them. He seemed to know where they were going. As on Aurora's first visit, Eleanor came to the door. She nodded at the two humans and bent to stroke Wrangell's head, then ran her fingers over the stitches, shaking her head.

"This is my husband." Eleanor reached and grasped Martin's forearm to pull him into the house. She seemed to recognize him at once as another injured creature, in need of attention like Wrangell. Astrid was at the church, she said. Eleanor buzzed around the main room, tidying up and retrieving two letters propped up against a crockery honey pot on the table. These she handed to Aurora. Then she ordered Wrangell to lie down. She retrieved a pair of sewing scissors from a basket on the shelf and snipped the stitches on the dog's flank. He kept his eyes glued to Eleanor's hands but made not a whimper.

Two letters from Pat. She was disappointed that there was no word from Marisa. She had written both friends and given them the Wrangell address before she headed up the Stikine.

end of June, 1899

Dear Aurora,
I hope by the time this reaches you, Mr. Starr has been located. I found your description of the scenery out west exhilarating. I would like to see it myself. Marble and the cat are doing well, although Marble spends most of his time over at your farm. He's waiting for you to return, I think.

The tenants have left. So now your house is empty, but I'm taking care of things. I'm reading poems by Longfellow and Edgar Allan Poe. Quite a difference!

Your friend and student,
Patrick

"Martin, do you remember Clyde Kleckner's nephew? He's taking care of the animals for us, and keeping an eye on the house."

Martin had moved a chair close to the window and stared out at the house next door, where Astrid's neighbor was hanging several lacy bits of underwear on a clothesline. He made no response.

Aurora opened the second letter. "Oh, no." Her hand flew to her breast. Eleanor turned from the stove, lines of concern on the un-damaged side of her face. Martin maintained his motionless posture at the window. This letter was written less than a week after the first one. Clyde Kleckner had died working out in the fields, felled, like a tall pine, by apoplexy. He had left the farm to Pat, never expecting his heir would take on the property at the age of fifteen. Pat, on advice from neighbors, would be renting the Kleckner place to a family in town who were going to try farming. The place was established, so this family would not find it as difficult as starting from scratch as homesteaders. He wanted to move into Aurora's house until she and Martin returned, but a group of concerned church people had told him he was too young to be living alone. So for now, he was living with the Methodist minister's family in Blackbird. *They weren't too happy about me bringing along Marble and the cat, but I told them we were a family,* Pat added at the end.

Aurora took a deep breath. Her world was crumbling. All the familiar people and routines were disappearing. She started to relay this news to Martin, but seeing his slack, still body, as if the spirit had been sucked out, she knew it would make little impression on him.

As before, Eleanor filled the tub with water. Aurora realized how used she'd grown to the smells of the trail. Martin smelled of sweat, old and new, and woodsmoke and mules. Eleanor opened the lid of a trunk in the corner and dug out shirts, trousers, socks, underwear. "The churches on the Outside send these clothes," she said, holding them out for Martin to inspect. With great effort, he turned his head to look at the denim clothes held by the Tlingit woman. He reached out, rubbing the fabric between his fingers. "You take bath. I'm going out," she said, draping the clothes over a chair back. Her nod to Aurora as she passed acknowledged Aurora's burden, yet conveyed no pity. And this nod comforted Aurora, more than a sympathetic look would have.

She had to take charge. Gone was her husband, her lover, her friend. "Martin, you need to take a bath." How quickly she adopted the manner of treating him like a child.

He stood and walked to the galvanized tub. "Let's get off these awful clothes," she said, growing gentle with him. He started to unbutton the stained flannel overshirt, then dropped his arms, as if the task were too much for him. She got him undressed, holding her breath against the released stench. She took the clothes and threw them in a pile outside. As she came back to the tub, Martin was getting in, and she saw the white bony shanks, the sunburned skin of his neck and forearms, his vulnerable back which seemed stooped like an old man's, each vertebra pushing up through the skin. She rolled up her sleeves and grabbed the tar soap. Eleanor had placed a dipper beside the soap, and Aurora started with Martin's head, wetting his matted hair. She should have combed and cut it first, she realized. She averted her gaze from his genitals, still and pale as fish at the bottom of a pond.

Could this be the same man who had undressed her at Indian Beach? They had gone to their favorite spot the summer before he left. They were alone on the stretch of white sand with a semicircle of cedar and pines behind and the still expanse of Lake Michigan in front. After Martin unbuttoned her dress, she stepped out of it and draped it over a large log, polished white by the water and wind. "This too must come off," he announced solemnly as he lifted the cotton camisole over her head. He kept his eyes on her breasts as he unbuttoned his denim shirt. His torso was as starkly white as the piece of driftwood; a determined line of black hair started at his sternum and continued to that wonderful destination below his waistband. "It's a black arrow pointing the way," she said the first time she had seen him naked. His forearms, neck and face were a reddish brown, giving him a disconnected appearance. When both were naked, he grabbed her hand and they sprinted across the sand into the water. It was shallow for yards until at last the bottom slanted downwards and they floated in the water. Now and then, Aurora, a bit nervous at being naked out in the lake, kept an eye on the beach. But no one came then, nor later as they laid together in the dunes, a wind-sculpted cedar tree offering shade.

When he was dressed, Eleanor offered to cut his hair and shave him. He was passive, looking now and then at the floor where his hair lay in tufted piles. Aurora handed him a mirror, but he turned his head away from his new image.

They slept in the same bed that night in the storeroom. It was the first time they had shared a bed in a year and a half. When she leaned over to kiss his cheek, he did not exactly flinch, but he moved closer to the edge of the bed.

"It will not always be like this," she said, as much to herself as to the man next to her. "You're going to get well, Martin. I'm taking you home."

She awoke in the middle of the night, alone in the bed. She tiptoed out into the main room to find Martin again at the window. The prostitute's delicates still hung on the line, little white ghosts suspended in the pale light of the Alaskan night. She left him there and returned to bed, but sleep would not come.

ƒƒ ƒƒ ƒƒ ƒƒ

When Martin had first left for the Klondike, she had fallen into bed every night exhausted. During the first few months of his absence, the daily routine of chores was her sleeping tonic. The week after he left a blizzard blew over the lake and hit Sawyersville and all the northern towns with four feet of snow. The school was closed, and Aurora could not even make it to the nearest neighbor. She went into a frenzy of housecleaning, telling herself she would keep it neat as a pin for Martin's return.

She shooed the dog and cat into the front room. They moved reluctantly, not wanting to be away from the enveloping comfort of the wood range. After sprinkling sand and potash mixture over the floor boards, she soaped up the brush, and on her hands and knees applied the bristles to the wood. The water in the cleaning pail was scalding; her hands turned red as she scrubbed the kitchen's pine floorboards.

The work was not rigorous enough to keep her thoughts from her situation. Each time the tears burned, she called up her mother's voice. "Self-pity will not make you feel better, Aurora. Just make a list of all you have to be thankful for. *That* will make you feel better." Well, she had a loving husband, a good house, a job teaching at the school just down the hill. She was healthy and had food for the winter. The horse and cow out in the small barn were dependable—and the cat and dog were faithful companions. She had fields and woods around her. Lake Michigan was five miles west, offering wild, undiscovered beaches. So in the absence of her husband, she would have to embrace these things.

When the floor was dry, she let the cat and dog back into the kitchen from the cold front room, leaving open the door to let the heat spread. She had made a list for the day, so the hours would be taken up with useful, productive things:

Clean kitchen floor
Bake apple pie
Write letter to Martin
Prepare lessons

Aurora like the way her list contained two physical and two mental chores. It gave a sense of balance and harmony to the day. She did not include the normal early morning chores, which were vital to staying alive. When she had opened the kitchen door, snow fell inward across the sill. Before wading through the deep snow in Martin's barn boots, she secured a long rope to the post by the kitchen door, tying the other end around her waist. Two winters ago a farmer west of Sawyersville had been found by his wife, frozen, halfway between house and barn. Aurora had to orient herself to the predawn landscape, changed completely by the snow. The barn seemed out of place, unfamiliar in the grainy gray and white light.

Inside the horse and cow had moved close together. She retrieved an apple from the pocket of her wool coat and gave it to the horse, who chomped it quickly then nosed her side for another. "Yes, one more for you." She thrilled to the huge lips, the giant teeth lifting the apple from her palm. She put hay and oats before him, and some carrots. Half the carrots she grew in her garden were for the horse. The water trough was frozen, so she broke the ice with the handle of the pitchfork.

She put down hay for the cow, still a bit wary around the animal because she was a kicker. Assuming the beast had a sensitive udder, last summer Aurora had sheared all the long hairs around the bag, bathed the teats in warm water, then greased them with lard. Still the cow flung its hoof just when she settled into position to milk. Aurora made sure her fingernails were blunt and smooth, that she soothed the cow in a soft voice before touching the udder. The kicking behavior continued. Aurora sought the advice of their neighbor, Clyde Kleckner, whose farm was kitty-corner from theirs. "To cure that old girl, you got to strap the foreleg." He came over and walked up to the cow in its stall. "Well, now, Bessie, I got something for you." He stood beside the animal, reached down and bent the cow's foreleg, bringing the foot up to the body. He put the strap around his arm and the cow's "ankle," near the hoof, and crossed it between him and the cow. The cow jerked its leg, but the strap held firm. One or two more twitches and the cow was subdued. "You might have to do it a few more times, but then just letting Bessie see this strap will quiet her down." Aurora thanked her neighbor, thinking what she could do to repay his help. Mr. Kleckner was a widower, whose nephew was living with him and helping with the farm. A woman who lived near the sawmill came up the hill to cook and clean a couple times a week.

She had become more comfortable with the cow; still she left the strap hanging on a nail where the cow could see it. Her hands squeezed the teats. The milk hit the cold pail with the sound of metal slivers. In the next stall the horse stamped. Aurora leaned against the cow, drawing warmth from its brown and white expanse. She turned her head and pressed her nose into the cow's hide, breathing in the old, grassy smell of summer pastures. The cow seemed to welcome the contact. She depended on these animals, living and breathing presences, for affection, for physical contact.

She had to clear a space outside the door to dump the manure, which steamed in the snow. The cow got extra hay in case Aurora didn't get out again to the barn until evening. She grasped the rope that connected her to the house in one hand, the milk pail in the other. There was a skin of ice on the milk by the time she reached the kitchen. The cat extended on hind legs to lap from the rim. "You little bandit," Aurora said, but did nothing to shoo it away.

Next she made the pie. Thank goodness she had collected some apples before the blizzard hit. Now, she'd never get to Martin's apple hole. She pared the northern spys, letting the spiral of skins pile up. Martin loved to watch her pare an apple, without once breaking the skin. Standing in the kitchen, the warmth of the wood range heating her from behind, the lap-lap of the cat's tongue in its saucer of milk, she was happy—and then she was ashamed of feeling happy. No matter how relentless her chores, her struggles here on the farm, they were nothing compared to the daily dangers and deprivations that Martin was going through for their future.

Aurora doubted if the school would be open for the next few days, but that evening she made notes on what to cover next time she met with her students. There were ten, four of them from the same family.

Her youngest pupil was six, the oldest sixteen. Teaching was not at all what she had been led to expect at the Normal Teachers College. Her instructors had not emphasized how the lives of the students took precedence over the curriculum. Weather, sickness, the crops, family crises—they were more important than the lessons. She had been rewriting the standard curriculum in order to address the problems of Sawyersville: math questions about board feet and log loads; short essays about the animals and plants, combining science and rhetoric lessons.

She banked the fire in the kitchen range and moved into the front room, where she had prepared a fire in the little parlor stove. At her desk, she started a letter to Martin.

February 15, 1898

My dear husband,

I am posting this letter to Edmonton, trusting it will be waiting for you and will cheer you as you set out into the wilderness. As I sit here in our parlor, I imagine you back in your boyhood room in Pelican. I hope your parents are well; I'll write to them soon.

Because it is but a week since you left, I don't have much news from home—except that last night a blizzard blew in and the school is closed—as well as many other things I should imagine. I tended to the milking first thing this morning. I checked on our beasts a few hours ago and they seem snug enough. I had to force the cat and dog outside to do their business. Since the snow is high all around the yard, I cleared a space for them. I think they'd like to get in bed with me tonight, but their spot by the kitchen range will most likely be warmer than the bedroom. I've had the register open all day so the bedroom should be bearable. At least there should be no frost on the inside of the panes. I'll pile on extra quilts and wish you were beside me for warmth.

I feel like a sissy for complaining about the cold when I know what you must endure. Take care of yourself. I hope the socks are keeping your feet warm.

Lovingly,
Rory

" " " "

That time alone on the farm seemed unreal; compared to her life now, it had been secure and constant. She thought about lighting the lamp and retrieving the notebook, but she did not want Martin to see her reading it. Aurora finally fell into a troubled sleep, disturbed by dreams of armies of men with missing limbs and toothless grins. Martin walked among them, moving past her as she tried to get his attention. He came to bed just as it was getting light.

Chapter Eighteen

December 1898 to March 1899

*M*artin's party made ten miles the first day, arriving at the site of old Fort Halkett, where a few all-water men were camping. When Harry's feet were unwrapped that night, they were covered with huge blisters. He begged Martin to lance them. "Boil some water and use my small boning knife," he pleaded. He thought releasing fluid from the blisters would make the swelling in his feet go down.

But Martin resisted the request. What little he knew about frostbite was that any infection could lead to gangrene. "You'll be seeing the doctor soon; he'll know what to do," he said, trying to reassure Harry. They all had heard stories of men who left the Klondike with boxes of gold dust, but with one less limb or fewer digits than when they'd left home. Harry did not even have the cold comfort of gold.

Around midnight, the wind rose and a blizzard hit. It extended to a three-day blow, during which the men only ventured out the door to relieve themselves. Even then they went with a "buddy" because of the white-out conditions. A man could turn the wrong direction and never get back to the cabin. Harry used a slop pail in the corner. He could hobble around a bit in his "booties," he called them, which he had fashioned from an old torn horse blanket; his swollen feet no longer fit in his boots.

When they were finally able to continue on to Brule, they secured Harry on the sled, and the other three wore snowshoes, for the snow was so deep they sank to their waists without them. The day was brilliant, the piercing blue sky mocking their pain and disappointment with its beauty. The landscape was softened by the sculpted snow and the green-black pines pointed heavenward. It was difficult to tell where the river ended and land began.

Brule Portage was a winter village, a hodgepodge of cabins, shacks made from boat timbers, and tents on platforms with oil-drum stoves—all on a plateau 150 feet above the river. The way to the top of the cliff was a nearly vertical switch-back trail. Calling on all his reserves of physical stamina, Martin climbed the cliff and secured the help of four residents, in hauling up the toboggan with the track line. Down below, Harry was roped in for his ride. Then the toboggan was secured with the track line, and hand-over-hand those at the top pulled up the sled. Ulrich and Jim made the steep climb by foot. "Free haircuts for everyone, if you get me up," Harry yelled. They admired him that he could joke while being hauled up a cliff as an invalid.

Dr. Ritchie was attending another frostbite victim at the Mud River camp, but was to return the next day. They set up housekeeping in a vacant cabin, dirty and forlorn, and once a fire was going, melted snow on the stove and mopped the place out. In one corner was a pile of frozen feces, animal or human they didn't know, but Martin disposed of it in the leaning outhouse behind the cabin. They were especially grateful for an outhouse in winter.

True to his word, Harry opened his barbershop the next day. The four men who helped haul him up the cliff were given haircuts and beard trims. In addition to his butcher's knives, he had scissors, which he filed with his sharpening steel. Others heard of his skill, and he made a tidy sum during the following week. He collected the hair, saying he was going to make "stampeder pillows." He gave Martin a trim, too. Martin thought how he would frighten Rory if she saw him now; even with a trim, his hair was longer than at home. His beard gave him an outlaw's countenance. But being hairy was another way to stay warm. No man had given up his beard; it would be foolhardy.

Dr. Ritchie, a tall, rangy Scotchman with a bushy red beard, showed up the next day, wearing a fur parka, looking like a friendly bear as he entered the cabin. He had done many amputations, and the cripple camps were filled with his handiwork.

He slipped the parka, whose design has been borrowed from the Indians, off over his head, hung it up on a peg, where it dripped as the layer of frost thawed. Those who could afford them acquired parkas, which resembled huge ponchos with hoods, no opening in front or back. The doctor removed Harry's booties to examine the feet, handling them tenderly. He said nothing for a long time, during which the others held their breath, waiting for the medical pronouncement. Finally, "Let us wait a wee bit longer to see if I need to amputate." Harry did not blink at that last word. He had always known it was a possibility. "It takes six to eight weeks before ye can tell if the tissue will heal. I won't do surgery unless it's entirely necessary, lad," said the doctor, clamping his hand on Harry's shoulder. "But for now let's attend to this scurvy."

Most of the men at Brule Portage suffered from some degree of scurvy. Dr. Ritchie pressed his fingers against Harry's gums. "My teeth have been feeling a bit loose," said Harry, as though they were a small concern, compared to his feet.

"Well, lad, ye'll need some vitamin C, though the good Lord knows where you'd get it in this God-forsaken wilderness." He went to his parka, reached underneath to a leather pouch sewn into the inside under the armhole and retrieved a small bottle. "Lime juice. Drink this. Dilute it to make it last longer, and see if it doesn't give your poor teeth some relief." He shook his head when Harry tried to pay him. "I'll not take your money. Ye will have need of it." Dr. Ritchie struck gold back in 1896, returned home, and now was back for more. He offered his services for free, and was considered a saint.

Martin remembered Harry at 200 pounds when he first met him back in May, so long ago. Now the man was now down to 110 with spongy gums, loose teeth, and frozen feet with dead toes. What a hell this place was! Gold fever had brought nothing but hardship and disappointment.

While everyone was in bed, Martin opened the side loading door of the stove, but he didn't add more wood. He threw in the brown notebook. But before he could close the door, Ulrich reached in with the poker and pulled it out.

"Vat are you doing? That book is valuable." Ulrich had seen Martin hunched over its pages, writing of the days, weeks and months of the journey.

"It's bad luck, I'm sure. I don't want to read or be reminded of all the horrors."

"Vell, you don't need to read it, but let me haf it."

Martin shrugged and crawled into the bunk. The smell of singed paper filled the cabin.

" " " "

As Christmas approached, the span of daylight stretched about five hours, from 10 a.m. to 3 p.m. In those few hours, they ventured out to hunt, managing to shoot a few squirrels. At night they played Sheepshead, a card game Ulrich taught them, or sang and recited.

Christmas Day was hardly the festive time it was back home, but their neighbors invited them over for a dinner. These all-water treated could afford some luxuries; their boats allowed them to carry more provisions than the overlanders could carry on horses, or sleds. Among the all-water party was a Negro from Winnipeg. He told them his grandparents had been American slaves and had escaped by the underground railroad to get all the way from North Carolina to Canada. He had never been to the States, and swore he never would. Yet, he was friendly to the Americans, perhaps because none of them was from a southern state.

While the guests contributed roasted squirrel, the hosts provided mountain grouse pot pie, plum pudding with brandy sauce and dried peach pie. The visitors moaned as they ate. Martin had not eaten this well since Michigan. One of the men had designed a tin oven, a little box placed atop the oil drum stove. He used a slip of paper to determine the temperature. When the paper turned a medium even brown, the time was right to put in the dough. The smell of the fresh-baked bread brought tears to their eyes—a loaf of real bread, not bannock, which Harry sliced with one of his knives. For a few hours they forgot the desperate circumstances and were thankful for companionship and good food.

Christmas night, with a full belly, Martin dreamed of Frank and him as boys on the Pelican River. They were floating in the old rowboat, fishing poles over the side. "Let's go down the river as far as we can," Frank said, grabbing the oars. "We have to see where it ends." His fair hair blew across his forehead, and as he brushed it back, his green eyes had been replaced by hollow sockets, his flesh disappearing from his face and hands. Soon his shirt and overalls hung in tatters over a frame of bones there on the Pelican River. Martin woke up his cabinmates with screaming. Jim and Ulrich rushed across the freezing floor to his bunk, then went back to their beds when he quieted down. After that, sleep eluded him. It was true that Frank had wanted to be a Klondiker. He had a raging case of gold fever and persuaded Martin that the trip was worth the risk. But he changed his mind, had come to his senses, although a bit late. Several times he suggested they return home, but Martin could not see going back after all they'd been through. If they'd returned earlier, Frank would be alive in Minnesota, and Martin would be on the farm with Rory. And now, another man was paying the price for Martin's bad judgment.

Harry said he was glad it was his toes, not his fingers, that were frozen. He could still continue his occupation as a butcher, although he might have to spend more time sitting down. On January 15 Dr. Ritchie amputated all the toes on Harry's left foot, and the two smaller ones of the right. Harry showed the least trepidation of all of them. "Let's get on with it, doc," he said. Ulrich, Jim and Martin hovered, shuffling feet, until Dr. Ritchie told them to boil water and move the table close to the window. He boomed the good news that he had some chloroform with him as he brought it out from that inside pouch in his parka. He told Harry, even without the drug, he would not feel much pain during the surgery. They placed Harry on the table. Martin lit the one oil lamp, for although it was 11 o'clock in the morning, the daylight was meager. The three retreated to a bunk and tried to play cards, avoiding glances at the table by the window.

"This will be an easy job, doc," joked Harry. "I've had a lot more challenges carving up a cow." Then as the sweetish odor of the drug filled the room, Harry became silent. The men had watched the progression of the effects of frostbite on his feet, and the toes now resembled little black mummies. Dead tissue, Dr. Ritchie pronounced. It was necessary to get rid of the necrotic so the healthy could thrive.

As they stared at their cards, the dull ping of dead toes landing in a tin can echoed in the cabin. Harry made not a noise, while Dr. Ritchie whistled softly as he worked. "Ye done well lad," he murmured, patting Harry's shoulder. Turning to Martin, he said, "You'll need to keep his feet clean and dressed," then handed him a bunch of cotton rags with remnants of lacy trim. It seemed Harry's bandages had once been a lady's petticoat. Taking one of the rags, he demonstrated how to dress the feet while they healed. For the next few days, Martin dressed his friend's feet, boiling and drying the soiled bandages for reuse. After a week, Harry was changing them himself every few days.

Toward the end of January, two brothers driving a dog team came through. They brought news that Spain had declared war against the United States. It made Martin realize how cut off from civilization they were. His goal for 1899 was no longer to reach the Yukon and Dawson. He vowed to keep Harry alive during the winter, then get him out to the coast for a boat, so he could return to his family in Brooklyn. By now they knew the number of men who had reached the Yukon basin by way of the Edmonton Trail could be counted on two hands, and those hands might not have all their fingers.

For about a month they lived on moose meat, having spotted two who were living on an island below the camp. They hung the meat from a pole over their door, and could not refuse to share it with hungry-eyed, scurvy-ridden men. The whole camp needed provisions to stay alive for the winter. Willie O'Grady back at Fort Nelson might have subsisted on nothing but moose meat, but not Martin. So during the first week in March the four companions headed upriver to the Mud River Post, manned by a heartless Hudson's Bay trader named Trumble. All around his "post," just a ramshackle cabin, were starving, sick men, many of them with the black spots of scurvy on their hands and feet. They heard an extraordinary story of another party who had finally made it after a harrowing journey from Fort Nelson. During their first attempt at making the trip, all their horses died. They returned to Fort Nelson to regroup and obtain more toboggans. They engaged an Indian guide, whose family accompanied him. During a night of intense cold and blizzard conditions, the guide's wife gave birth. The next morning she continued the journey on snowshoes with the newborn in her arms, a one-year old on her back and a three year-old behind on his own little snowshoes! With their adaptation to these rough conditions, the Indians would certainly be more likely to reach the Yukon. But Martin had yet to meet one who was infected with gold fever.

Martin traded his rifle and some extra clothing for food, which was being sold at the highest prices yet encountered: flour, $30 for a hundred pounds; bacon, $60 a hundred pounds; and sugar, 50¢ a pound! Some of the men in tents and shacks around Trumble's building were near death. Martin confronted Trumble, a well-fed man with pouchy eyes, who stared at the newcomer over a pile of fresh pelts on the counter.

"These men and the ones at Brule Portage are out of money and food. We're not asking for free goods. You'll be reimbursed." Dr.

Ritchie had told them that an old agreement between the Canadian government and the Hudson's Bay Company assured that the traders would be paid back for good-will donations.

"I'm not operating a poorhouse here. These men are foolish. Most of them hooked up with no-accounts who left them stranded at the first opportunity." He leaned forward to aim an orangish-brown stream of tobacco juice at its target—a spittoon on Martin's side of the counter.

The stories of Trumble were legion. A month before Martin's party arrived, a starving group of seven, some of them survivors of the Philadelphia party, stumbled in, seeking food and aid for five more members, whom they had left fifty miles back, along with most of their rifles. Trumble stipulated that they could trade provisions for the rifles, forcing two of these emaciated, scurvy-ridden men to return to a dangerous trail. One died of exposure on the way back. Two of the group on the trail died waiting for help. Martin regarded Trumble as a murderer, and considered gathering together the sorry band of men and storming the store.

Nature, harsh and unpredictable most of the time, still comforted and amazed him on occasion. It was right after his encounter with Trumble that Martin felt a visceral connection with Rory. He stepped out of the cabin in his snowshoes to a sky filled with pulsing sheets of red, purple, green light and heard an unearthly crackle in the cold air. Aurora Borealis. Rory. When they watched the northern lights from their farm, he told her she was his northern light, his life's light. Now standing under light which seemed to cascade down from a central axis, quivering with colors, he asked his wife to forgive him for abandoning her. At the same time, he felt charged with power to do something for these unfortunate men.

The next day he wrote up a petition to the Canadian government asking for immediate aid for the "disabled and destitute." After every man at Mud River who was physically able signed Martin's petition, he headed off on snowshoes to Cranberry Rapids. There was a community of twenty tents there, all waiting for the ice to break up towards the end of May. Those at Mud River would have to get above these rapids before the break-up, then begin the long trip towards the coast as soon as the river was navigable. Martin was consumed night and day with his undertaking. He did not have to persuade the men at Cranberry Rapids to sign; they were more than willing, even offering to fit the invalids at Mud River into their vessels. Even in the cold conditions, they were building boats to add to their fleet of five Peterboro canoes. The readiness of the men to take whatever action they could to see justice done was motivation for Martin. He began to live for the day that the greedy, lying promoters of the Edmonton Trail would be punished, and inhumane dealers like Trumble would be made to answer for their crimes.

Funeral of prospector, who was accidentally shot

Chapter Nineteen

August, September 1899

Wrangell stayed in the town for which he was named. His wound was hardly visible except for a patch of sparser fur. "You were a wonderful companion," she crooned to him, stroking his head. Eleanor was happy to have the dog, although Astrid was less enthusiastic to have him part of the household. "We'll be praying for you both," promised Astrid, gripping Aurora's hands while blinking back tears.

On the voyage from Wrangell to Seattle, not on the *Gold Runner* this time, Aurora asked herself the hard questions. Was Martin permanently damaged? Would he ever get better, ever be the Martin she'd known at Starrvation Corner? His manic caretaking when she found him at Dease Lake had changed and settled into a withdrawn, unresponsive condition. He needed help, more than the doctor in Blackbird could give. She was resigned that she was powerless to help him. There were so many things she wanted to ask him, about Frank, about Wiggins, the name he'd muttered in bed at Astrid's, but she was afraid to, for fear she would set something off, which might be worse than his passive state.

"We're going to spend some time in Seattle." She put her arm around his waist where they stood on the bucking deck. Martin's knuckles turned white as he gripped the railing, but thank God, neither of them was seasick. "We'll stay with someone I met on my trip out." She looked at his profile; his nose was sharper, and white streaked in the glossy black of his hair.

When Mae opened the door and saw the couple on the steps—Aurora, her eyes brimming, chin quivering, and a wooden Martin—she asked no questions. "Follow me."

She installed them in Franny's old room, which had a double bed. "Franny lives above her shop now. She's doing very well. You might stop in if you have time," said Mae. "I'll give you the address."

Martin gravitated to the window. Aurora stepped out into the hallway with Mae. "He's not well. His mind has been damaged. I think he knows who I am, but I'm no more to him than a piece of furniture," she whispered.

"Shshsh," said Mae, rubbing Aurora's back. "Take one thing at a time. Look how far you've come. What a journey, and on your own. You need to be proud of *yourself* for what you've accomplished. My God, girl, you found your husband!"

Aurora rested her forehead against Mae's solid shoulder, breathed in the scent of lilac talc, a smell she associated with her mother, and sobbed.

"If you want some advice," she paused, "I do not think it wise to take him back to your house. Not in his condition. I've seen men up in Dawson with mental troubles. He did not find gold, I take it?" When Aurora shook her head, she continued, "Well, he's dealing with other horrors on top of that disappointment. My dear, he's probably dreadfully ashamed before you."

Shame? Could that reduce Martin to this motionless husk?

"I don't know where to take him. His parents? Maybe being in Pelican Rapids would heal him."

That night Martin found the gun, which she had forgotten about, at the bottom of her satchel. A metallic click woke her instantly. The shade was up and the light of a gibbous moon revealed her husband's silhouette, standing on his side of the bed, facing her with the raised Derringer. "Martin," she screamed, throwing herself across the bed in a tangle of bedclothes. The gun thumped to the carpet.

"Aurora, Aurora, I'm coming in," yelled Mae. And there she was, lantern in hand, a kimono patterned in shimmering green leaves fluttering, her hair wild about her face. Mae set the lantern on a round table by the door, marched up to Martin and took him by shoulders, steering him to a wing chair. She bent to retrieve the gun. "I'll take this." She was flushed and shaken. "I'll bring up some tea and cake for both of you."

Aurora kept vigil for the rest of the night, although Martin dozed, exhausted by the episode. She knew she could not handle him, could not feel safe with Martin. She had not loaded the Derringer. Had he put bullets in the gun? Was he raising the weapon with her in mind, or himself? Mae had taken the gun. She wanted to know, and didn't want to know, if the gun had been loaded.

While he slept in the wing chair, she lit the gas lamp on the wall and propped herself up with Mae's sumptuous pillows in the bed. She reached for the notebook. Why did they, why did he, keep going? There was so little mention of gold. What happened to gold fever? What of the burning desire that had compelled these men to leave home, jobs, family? Perhaps Martin and Frank, poor Frank, would have done better to take a train to Seattle and reach the Yukon by that route. Well, it was too late to wonder about the best route to the Klondike now. Martin was finished with looking for gold, or for anything else. What would become of him? What would become of their marriage? She looked up from the page and over at his face, mostly in shadows. She could almost see her husband as he was just before he left to hook up with Frank—a handsome dreamer, worshipful of her, full of energy and ambitions. She could not proceed without believing that her husband could be restored. She must believe that or else . . . she could not imagine a future with him lost to her. Tears streamed down her cheeks, plopping softly on the singed page of the notebook.

At daybreak, Mae entered the room quietly in satin slippers and the green kimono. Martin was sprawled on the floor, sleeping. She beckoned to a nodding Aurora and led her down the hall to Mae's own bed. "I'll keep an eye on him, and you get some sleep. You'll need it."

There was a midday meal prepared by two new girls who were cooking for Mae's household. Aurora and Martin were taking a late afternoon train out of Seattle. "What of Sally? Have you heard from her?" asked Aurora, noting that Martin was eating his food with a mechanical dedication, fork to plate to mouth, with no pause until the food was gone. This seemed a good sign.

"Sally heard that thousands have left Dawson; the town is emptying out. I bet those Mounties are rejoicing to see the backs of all those stampeders! So she turned around and went to Nome. Gold is being found all over Alaska, so now the American government can deal with the chaos."

"What is she doing?"

"Oh, you know," said Mae with a tight-lipped grin. "She says she's making it in a dance hall, getting paid for dancing with the men and getting them to drink a lot, but I'll bet my gold tooth, there's more to the job than that."

As far as a job for herself, in the early hours while Martin slept, Aurora considered staying in Seattle. It was a large city. Perhaps she could find proper help for Martin here. She could live with Mae, find work. It was appealing, but she could not cast off her real life so easily. There was Starrvation Corner, Blackbird, Pat, Marisa. Even now, she needed those places and people to sustain her through a time of uncertainty. She missed Michigan. She knew that was where she belonged, and where Martin belonged. Mae agreed that being in a familiar geographical location might be best for Martin, although she'd miss Aurora and their "talks."

Before the train departed, Aurora sent a telegram to the Great Lakes Asylum in Grand Bay City, telling them she would be arriving with her husband in a few days, seeking admittance for him as a patient. She had no idea what procedures were required, but she felt

Martin needed the safety, the physical presence of an institution. Another telegram went to Mr. and Mrs. Starr in Pelican Rapids, Minnesota, telling them of her plans.

When she attended Normal School in Mount Pleasant in 1892, the asylum had already been open for seven years. As she and her mother traveled through Grand Bay City, the institution loomed up in the distance, an imposing brick fortress, spires and chimneys punctuating the sky. She had heard that the buildings were magnificent inside with carved woodwork, and outside with gardens and even a lake. However, her first glimpse of the sprawl of connected buildings— the force of their architecture softened by the backdrop of trees and rolling landscape— made her think *how awful to be behind those walls, cut off from the world.* In Alaska, everyone referred to the civilized world, the States, as the Outside. Well, she had brought Martin to the Outside. And now what was she doing? She was putting him inside, removing him from contact with his familiar world.

As the train carried them east across the continent, Martin was compliant and detached. She was his custodian. He sat in the day coach next to the window, facing the vistas of mountains, valleys, prairies. They ate silently, like an old couple, in the dining car. She tried making conversation, but Martin would shake his head as if words were too much for him to deal with. He was longing to get back to the window.

How she longed for her mother's sensible comfort. She worked to conjure up Libby Gray's voice: *Marriage is not an easy partnership. Sometimes one of you must carry the weight for a while.* Aurora thought of her father's constancy during Libby's years of illness. She must do no less. Martin was ill. If only his illness were an ailment of the body, one she could observe and monitor.

And Marisa. She felt deserted by her friend. No letter, no word since she'd left Michigan. What would Marisa advise? The decision to deliver Martin to the asylum was hers alone.

Near the end of the trip, Martin showed an awareness of his surroundings. He thanked the waiter who served them breakfast. He shaved himself before the tiny mirror in their compartment. And he met her eyes more often, but not in an affectionate, husbandly way that she longed for. It was if he was studying her, trying to unravel a mystery. "We're going home" was all she said. Not "We're going to the Great Lakes Asylum, where I'll leave you."

ıı ıı ıı ıı

At the train depot in Grand Bay City, Aurora hired a driver. Now at the end of September, the red maples were aflame, the oaks an embankment of orange as they passed through the streets. The houses were mostly wood with small, neat yards, and Aurora imagined their inhabitants untouched by madness or lost minds. But then anyone observing Aurora and Martin riding in a buggy would see a handsome couple sitting side by side, though the man was devoid of animation. Grand Bay was calm, content to separate itself from Lake Michigan, yet at the same time always reaching, stretching towards the great inland sea. In November the gales that roiled the Great Lakes would extend turbulence to the bay.

As the buggy proceeded up 11th Street, another city, a separate city, was revealed—the huge asylum complex spread to the north and south. Martin turned his head toward Aurora. He stared at her, his fixed gaze forcing her to face him.

"This is Grand Bay City," he accused her, a muscle jumping in his cheek.

In Blackbird, as in other northern Michigan communities, people knew of the Great Lakes Asylum, but no one called it that. Anyone who was acting strange or exhibiting eccentric behavior was said to be *ready for Grand Bay City*. Aurora had overheard her students teasing one another with taunts of "Grand Bay City, Grand Bay City," accompanied by the gesture of a twirling finger at the temple. The town's name had become synonymous with the institution.

"Yes, Martin. I don't know what else to do. I'll stay here until I'm sure you'll get some help." She covered his hand with hers. She was grateful he did not pull his away as they passed between two stone pillars and were carried up a long, poplar-lined drive.

The driver announced, "Center Hall. This is where you'll want to go." The man had obviously brought many people from the outside world to this doorstep.

They walked up steps, through the portico and entered a huge lobby, whose floor was tiled with thousands of tiny ceramic squares. A grand stairway rose through the center of the room like an ancient, polished tree, then divided when it reached the landing above. Aurora and Martin stood there transfixed; a radiator hissed somewhere behind the stairway. There was the scent of hot dust and beeswax and lemon oil. A door to the right clicked open, its mechanism conveying solidity and well maintained parts. A man and woman emerged from the shadow of the stairway, the woman hugging the wall until they were in the large, exposed open area of the lobby. The woman, gray-haired, red-eyed, clutched a doll dressed in a white christening gown. The man, her husband Aurora assumed, grabbed her by the elbow and steered her toward the front door. "I need to let Dolly see the flowers," the woman quavered.

Martin had not moved from the center of the lobby where he looked up at the top of the stairs. "Come, let's find a doctor," Aurora whispered. Now you'll get better, she thought; now we'll get some real help. He followed her, glancing over his shoulder at the stairway, as if some revelation awaited him at the top Later, in reading over the pamphlet given to relatives, she was amazed Martin had not bolted. She had approached his confinement in the wrong way, had not prepared him properly. The literature advised that *utmost care should be made to not deceive the patient into thinking he is just visiting, or even staying a few days.* She had done even worse; she had not even told

Martin where they were headed. Of course, his admittance to the institution was not assured. He had to be evaluated first. But would he ever trust her again? The truth was she had been afraid to reveal her plans. What if he turned violent or ran away? How could she stop him, on her own, traveling across the country?

They entered a room whose door said *Patient Reception*. The green-carpeted room was empty of patients. A woman sat behind a desk, hitting the keys of a huge typewriter with frowning determination.

"Yes?"

"This is Martin Starr. I sent a telegram from Seattle." A horrible thought leapt up—what if they had not received her message, her plea?

"Yes. You must be Mrs. Starr." She nodded at Aurora, but did not acknowledge Martin. "I'll go get Dr. Shelby. He'll be doing your husband's evaluation." She kept her eyes on Aurora. "The doctor is on ward six; I'll go get him." With some difficulty the woman wiggled her way out from behind the desk and waddled out the door, her broad backside nearly as wide as her height. Her upper body was deceptively narrow and slender.

"I don't want to stay here," he shouted. His blue eyes glittered.

Aurora jumped, frightened, yet relieved, to hear some emotion from him.

"Martin, you are going to talk to this Dr. Shelby. I've brought you here to get some help. You need help. Can you understand that?" she pleaded.

He started to look at her, then let his gaze slide away

"Do you imagine I wanted to bring you here? Don't you know I wish we were back on the farm, making cider and picking the Maiden's Blush and Transparents?" She stopped as the receptionist with the doctor in her wake entered. Dr. Shelby was a wispy man with a rosy, speckled rash across his cheeks and the backs of his hands. He seemed to be trying to catch his breath. Aurora wondered what he had been doing on ward six, but was nonetheless impressed because he offered his hand first to Martin, who responded with a reluctant, limp handshake. Then the doctor bowed slightly to Aurora before leading them down a short hallway behind the desk with the typewriter, which was again being attacked in an irregular rhythm by the receptionist's surprisingly long fingers. Dr. Shelby ushered them into his office, a space of dark furniture and glass-doored bookcases. Vases of chrysanthemums suffused the stern interior with a magical golden light. The tall curtainless windows were shaded by the swaying tendrils of a huge willow tree. They took two large chairs which faced the huge walnut desk.

"Mr. Starr, do you know why your wife has brought you here?" Dr. Shelby placed his palms together and rested his chin on the peak of his fingers. The gesture struck Aurora as condescending. She wondered if Martin would answer. Suddenly the sharp, insistent scent of chrysanthemums seemed annoying, aggressive. Aurora couldn't get enough air.

"She is afraid of me. My wife fears me," Martin spoke to the face above steepled fingers.

Aurora had been unable to hide this new distrust from him.

"Does she have reason to fear you, Mr. Starr?"

"No. I want nothing bad to happen to her. It's true I've brought harm to others. Maybe she thinks she'll be next."

Aurora opened her mouth to explain about the gun, but Dr. Shelby moved his head slowly from side to side, silencing her.

"How old are you, Mr. Starr?"

"I was born in 1872."

"So you are twenty-seven."

Martin shifted his gaze to a huge arrangement of bronze and yellow mums in a pottery vase on the desk.

Dr. Shelby glanced down at the telegram on his desk. "Your wife said you were returning from a trip in Canada and Alaska. Were you a Klondiker?" he asked, putting emphasis on this last word, as if he were showing off, as if he were proud to know the word.

"Klondiker? It sounds like killer or murderer. If that's what you mean, yes, I am a Klondiker." He gave a hollow laugh, one that chilled Aurora. "I even know where some of the bodies are buried."

"Mr. Starr, I'm going to ask you to step out into the reception area while I talk to your wife. Then I'll have a private chat with you." He pushed a button mounted in a brass casing on the corner of his desk, creating a muted buzz. The wide-bottomed receptionist was at the door. "Flora, see that Mr. Starr is comfortable." Aurora watched her husband leave the room, his gait jerky and unsettled.

Dr. Shelby hands were out of their steeple pose and were busy filling a pen from the inkwell on his desk. "Now Mrs. Starr, just from this short conversation with your husband, I have concluded that he would benefit from a stay with us. However, the decision is yours. It must be you who commits him to our care. And before you sign the papers, a judge must declare him incompetent. Tell me, what was there in his actions or speech that seemed unusual?"

How to explain the unpleasant transformation? "It's as if someone has sucked my husband out of his body and left the shell. He barely acknowledged me after I had traveled thousands of miles to find him, showed no desire to be with me. All his faculties were focused on taking care of the sick men he was with," she said, her voice rising, her face flushed. She stared at the small bald spot on Dr. Shelby's head, pink through his wispy hair.

His pen scratched rapidly in the notebook. "And these changes all occurred after he left home?"

"Oh, yes. His best friend died while they were heading for the Yukon, somewhere in British Columbia. Another man fell through the ice while Martin was with him. This man had his toes amputated due to frostbite. I think Martin feels responsible for what happened to these men, as if it's his fault. He has nothing left for me."

"If he feels acute mental anguish over these misfortunes, it could bring on this depression, which manifests itself in lack of normal affection towards you, his wife. I imagine conditions were brutal, and this may have affected his mind. When meeting the basic requirements for daily survival becomes mentally stressful, insanity often develops." He capped the pen, stood up and walked to one of the bookcases. "Our institution is based on 'moral treatment.' When the patient's own world becomes too agitated, too stressful, or the patient experiences a trauma, a shock to the mind, it is often beneficial to remove the patient from that world and immerse him, or her, in a more ordered environment, an environment created by graceful buildings and planned landscapes, which ensure beauty and regularity." He stopped to take a breath after his compelling explanation. "The Great Lakes Asylum's patients will not be subjected to surprises or changes. Here they can heal." He turned abruptly from the bookcase. Aurora suspected he had been studying her by the reflection in the glass. "Have you ever heard of Thomas Story Kirkbride?"

"No, I don't believe so." Aurora settled back in her chair. The atmosphere had become more relaxed, less charged since Martin left. Even the scent of the chrysanthemums was less pungent.

"He was superintendent for the Pennsylvania Hospital for the Insane, and revolutionized the way asylums are designed. This institution's design is based on the Kirkbride model: the solid, magnificent structures, the park-like grounds with ornamental plantings. Your husband, if you decide to commit him, will benefit directly from Kirkbride's ideas."

The rash on Dr. Shelby's cheeks had deepened in color. His pale eyes glittered behind his spectacles, his thin moustache quivered. "Here are the rules and regulations of the hospital, as well as the consent form. Included is a list of clothing items your husband will need." He extended a batch of papers to Aurora, as well as a piece of paper with the judge's name and office address.

"You can look them over while I speak to Mr. Starr. One more thing. Has he been violent? Why does he say you fear him?"

"He's right. I am afraid of him, although he's not struck me or harmed me physically. Perhaps I'm afraid of the stranger that he's become. God forgive me if I'm being unfair to him. There was that time in Seattle. He found a gun in my satchel." She had been relieved when Mae told her the chambers were empty of bullets. "It wasn't loaded, but he was raising it. He knows guns, so he must have known it wasn't loaded." This reassured her. He had to have known the gun was empty. "But the act of raising it terrified me. I was sleeping and awoke to see him on the other side of the bed with the gun."

"Naturally, that would be frightening to anyone," he said.

She rose from the security of the chair, reluctant to leave the golden calm of this room. "It's strange, what you say about Nature being a curative. Martin was damaged by Nature, his mind unhinged by the destructive and impersonal cruelty of natural forces. And now I've brought him to a place where Nature is supposed to restore his mind." She smoothed her skirt. "Don't you find that strange?"

"I can understand you seeing irony in the situation. However, your husband's experience was with uncontrolled nature. Here man's hand has controlled the surroundings. I believe it is man's responsibility to tame nature for his own benefit." The rash on his cheeks was aflame again, lit up by his convictions.

"Really?" She shuffled the papers in her hand. "Well, you've given me something to think about. I'll read through these now," she said, regarding the papers as an unpleasant chore that must be tackled. At the door she turned. "If Martin is admitted, where will he stay?"

"The men's wards comprise the southern wing of the institution. They all have even numbers. The receiving ward would probably be the best spot for Mr. Starr initially, as long as he shows no tendencies toward violence."

The reception room was empty, the door to the hallway wide open. Aurora heard panting and a breathless Flora came puffing through. "Your husband just walked out. While I was typing. He's disappeared." Her tone implied she held Aurora responsible.

Dr. Shelby came out of his office and took in the absence of Martin. "Did he seem agitated, Flora?"

"Not at all! He was just sitting and staring out the window. He must have escaped while I was filing some records."

"He could hardly have *escaped*," corrected Aurora. "He is not a patient here, or a prisoner."

Flora stared stonily at Aurora. "Mrs. Starr, you come with me. He can't be too far away," said Dr. Shelby, taking her elbow.

Just outside the front door of the administration building, the doctor glanced across the grounds towards Willow Lake, a reflecting pond. The area was empty of people. As a buggy approached the asylum from 11th Street, Dr. Shelby asked the driver if he'd seen a man walking back towards town. No, no pedestrians. The doctor and Aurora walked around the huge complex, to the south where the men's wards were located. A man, wearing denim overalls and a huge straw hat was pruning the hedge under a row of windows.

"Hello, Stan."

Stan glanced up, pruning shears dangling from a meaty hand, while with the other he executed a quick lift of his hat. "Dr. Shelby," he nodded. Then "Missus." He returned to his pruning.

"Stan, did you see a man wearing . . .," he paused and turned to Aurora.

"A brown worsted jacket," Aurora supplied. She was embarrassed that she couldn't recall the rest of his outfit. He was wearing clothes from the missionary box given to him by Eleanor, strangers' clothes. Well, it's appropriate she thought. He's a stranger to me now. "He has black hair and remarkable blue eyes," she added.

Stan pointed beyond the main complex, towards several separate buildings. They quickened their pace. When they were out of earshot, Aurora asked, "Is he a patient?"

"Oh, yes. Stan has been a patient here almost since the asylum first opened for occupancy. He arrived here in 1885, long before I came," Dr. Shelby answered as he gestured toward a two-storey house with a covered porch. It looked like the home for a family with lots of children. "Cottage 32, housing for our patients with tuberculosis."

Ahead the glass panes of the greenhouse glinted in the autumn light. As they came closer, Aurora could see there were actually four separate houses, each about eighty feet long. They opened the door of the first and stepped onto the dirt floor, and were immediately enveloped in moist, peaty air. Two long shelves held pots of chrysanthemums. Now Aurora knew where those in the doctor's office had come from. There were baskets of blue lobelia, and moss containers of exotic lily-like blooms atop elegant thin stems. Martin was not here. They checked the next flower house, then the two vegetable houses, empty of crops, now that summer was over and cucumbers and tomatoes were finished.

Aurora spotted him first and began moving slowly, silently towards him, as if towards a skittish horse in hopes of throwing a halter over its neck. Martin was standing in the orchard behind the greenhouses. He acknowledged her presence by pointing to the row of apple trees to his right. "Wolf River. They should be picked this week." He moved down the aisle of well-pruned trees. "Over here," he gestured to Aurora, and Dr. Shelby who had joined them, giving them a tour as if this were his own private orchard, "are, I believe, the new variety of Winesap, the Stayman. They weren't available to the public until a few years ago." His eyes glittered as he walked on, cutting across rows, ducking under limbs to point out Jonathans and Maiden Blush, most of which had already been picked, being an early fall apple.

"When can I begin?" Martin demanded of Dr. Shelby.

"Begin?" Dr. Shelby plucked leaves and gnarly twigs from his hair and clothes.

"Begin helping you here. I know a lot about apples," Martin offered this as if it should have already occurred to the thick-headed doctor.

With a glance at Aurora, Dr. Shelby said, "Why don't we come back to my office and talk about that? Bring a few apples with you."

The three walked back to the central building, taking a path that led past a carriage barn, where a sleek chestnut horse and buggy were being attended to by three men. Patients, Aurora assumed. "That outfit belongs to the superintendent," Dr. Shelby informed them, resentment tingeing his tone. Aurora walked between the two men: Dr. Shelby keeping an eye on Martin, Martin studying the Staymans he carried in his jacket, like chicks in an apron.

In the reception room, as Flora banged away on the typewriter and Martin and Dr. Shelby talked, Aurora thumbed through the notebook. It remained in her satchel at all times. It was precious, as if holding a key that could unlock Martin's mind. She scanned the pages for the name *Wiggins*.

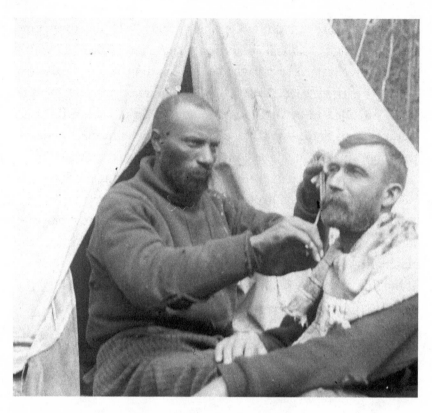

Barber work in Cripple Camp

Chapter Twenty

May 1899

hey had been at Cranberry Rapids since early April, having moved all the sick up from the Mud River Post by toboggans. Harry named this spot "Hospital de la Liard," for it was now one of the largest "cripple camps." Martin was its self-appointed director and was convinced that this was his true calling. The desire for gold and adventure may have been the original motivation, but he believed a higher purpose had led him here, to care for the less fortunate. Starrvation Corner seemed remote and less immediate. And Rory—he still felt a bond with his wife, but he was useless to her. Better that he be in a place where he was needed and able to help others. He was finding it more and more difficult to call up the sound of her voice. The color of her hair was still vivid in his memory, but her features swam in and out of focus.

The population had grown to sixty men, a small village. Since that horrid day back at Mud River Post, he could no longer turn any man away, no matter how short their supplies. He had vowed to keep everyone alive so they could climb aboard the boats and start the long voyage toward the coast.

The look in Wiggins' eyes, like a dog that has been kicked but keeps pleading with its tormentor, was an image that stayed in front of him all the time. Wiggins was yet another straggler from the former Philadelphia party, which finally disintegrated after Mac's death and further disorganization under his brother's leadership. When Wiggins arrived at Mud River Post, he was a walking skeleton, a vacant, yet desperate, expression in his eyes. The man was starving, so they took him into their shack of four when he arrived at their door. How he found them they never learned, but he obviously remembered them from that former association with the Philadelphia party. He hardly resembled the man they had seen months ago, strong and sane. Jim and Ulrich were not enthused about an extra body in the small space, but Harry did not seem to mind. There was an abundance of moose meat then, and the starving Wiggins ate three pans of fried meat as Martin cooked it up. When he toppled over on a bunk in exhaustion, Martin removed his soggy moccasins, the socks inside barely more than rags, his bare toes sticking through.

When Wiggins awoke he wandered around the camp, going from tent to tent begging for food like a dog. Martin watched as he took a loaf of bread down to the river, where he sat on a piece of driftwood and ripped off hunks, stuffing them in his mouth. By supper time, he was back at their place, ravenously devouring stewed moose, bannock, and boiled rice. He could not get enough food. Martin feared he would become ill from gorging himself.

After a week, with supplies getting low, Martin was elected to tell Wiggins he had to move on. "There are camps upstream about every six or seven miles. You can get food at each one," he assured him.

Wiggins begged, "Let me stay just a few days more. Please." This entreaty ended in heart-rending sobs, water streaming from his eyes and nose.

This exchange repeated for several more days. "The ice will not be safe for walking if you wait. You must leave now," Martin told him, giving him new socks and a pair of Frank's moccasins. Wiggins began to cry as Martin put his coat on him, as if dressing a child. Martin accompanied him for the first three miles. Near a bend in the river, he shook Wiggins' hand. "God bless you. Perhaps we will meet again in the States."

Martin turned to go back, while Wiggins stood there on the ice, making no move. When Martin looked back one last time, he was shuffling along, wiping his eyes with his sleeve. Martin, too, wept as he made his way back to Mud River Post, detesting himself for turning the poor fellow out into the wilderness. Harry had assured him that Wiggins would make it out. He was stronger after his stay at the Hospital de la Liard. But Martin wondered. Anything could happen to a man alone.

On May 15 the ice began to move. At first it sounded like thunder, the roar increasing as it came whirling, grinding downriver. Huge masses, some twenty feet across and six feet thick, piled up, some wedged on their ends. The crash as the blocks toppled was an awesome sound, as if the earth were coming to its end. Trees were torn loose by the grinding of the ice along the banks. Added to these were piles of driftwood carried along by this supernatural force. The cripples who were invalids were brought outside to see this show down on the river. The more mobile men carried them to the bluff and put them down on blankets. The noise was deafening, though none seem frightened, except one or two who had lost their wits. This was the sound of hope, the roar as water broke free and ice blocks collided, the sound of promise that soon they could make their way to home and loved ones.

After three days, it was considered safe enough to launch some boats, although towering slabs of ice crowded the shore. Most of the boats were ready and the most disabled, including Harry, were loaded in first. Martin and Harry embraced, and Harry stuffed a piece of paper with his address into Martin's pocket. "Have a safe trip, friend," said Martin. "One day I'll make it up to you."

"Martin, get yourself out. You've done more than enough."

"I need to be here for a while."

That morning Martin learned that his petition to Ottawa had been delivered to a judge in Telegraph. This judge had heard of the desperate conditions of the Klondikers on the lower Liard and had been waiting for official sanction from the government to send in relief boats. But time was short, and government action was slow. The river would soon rise making navigation dangerous. So he took matters into his own hands and authorized the manager of the Canco Transportation Company at Laketon to organize a relief party. The manager, Gardner, fitted out a forty-foot scow and hired eight Indians with their team of dogs to drag the boat across Dease Lake to the head of Dease River. This was dangerous business because by now the ice was unsafe. In addition, they sent 3500 pounds of provisions by dogsled.

Later, Martin learned that while all this was transpiring, the judge received word that Parliament had appropriated $25,000 for relief of the suffering men on the Dease and Liard Rivers, and that the Hudson's Bay Company would carry out this mission. This was typical bureaucracy, he thought. Many men would starve or die of their illnesses if they had to wait for the Hudson's Bay Company to organize a rescue party. It could take a month, or more. Still because of the big name, this company, and not Gardner's outfit, would get all the credit for the rescue. It made Martin's blood boil to think a heartless beast like Trumble would ever be associated with a compassionate gesture.

Provisions from Gardner's company arrived within the next few days; the remaining men ate better than they had for months. Martin assured the relief team that he would write another letter to Ottawa to document that Gardner's company had reached them first and should be fully compensated for their costs. He was also going to add that some of the traders, and yes, he would name Trumble, brought shame to the Canadian government and to the Hudson's Bay Company.

By May 25 only a few men remained. Martin's goal was to get them strong enough to make the trip upriver. The river level was rising every day; when it reached its highest point, navigation would be impossible.

But he knew there would be stragglers, those who wintered further downriver and were making their way to the now well-known Hospital de la Liard. Martin's days were spent cooking, washing clothes. He rigged up a clothesline between two pines, and the smelly rags the men wore were still rags, but clean and dried by the spring winds. Arrivals at the hospital wore strange costumes, clothes they had sewn together from an assortment of materials: horse blankets, tent canvas, animal skins.

He listened to the stories of old Woolsworth, a 78 year-old veteran of the goldfields. "When I was about your age, I was a 'forty-niner' in California. That started it all." He had mined gold in South Africa, New Zealand, Mexico and Australia. "This is the hardest, and I saved it for my old age. I thought the Edmonton trail looked like the best bet," he said, shaking his head. The old man had suffered from scurvy, but had regained the use of his limbs; though he was the oldest, he was in the best shape of all the remaining invalids.

Just yesterday morning, the start of a mild and breezy day, Martin was at the cookstove when Woolsworth summoned him. "There's one poor sucker out of his misery," he said, pointing down to the river bank, where a body had washed up on the shore.

Using an improvised windlass they were able to haul up the body. Neither recognized the water-logged features. How did he drown? If he'd fallen from a boat, surely someone would have retrieved the body. Maybe not. He looked to be about forty, with nothing in his pockets to identify him. Martin dug the grave himself, no one else being fit to help, and Woolsworth exhausted from assisting him with the windlass. Woolsworth put together a crude cross of wood from twigs, and they bowed their heads once the man from the river was in his final resting place.

Martin supported the older man as they walked back to camp. They stopped so Woolsworth could rest, each sitting on a stump. "Martin," he said, wheezing, "you bring to mind a saying my sainted mother had on a painted plate on our kitchen wall. Since I looked at it every day as a boy I committed it to memory: *To pity distress is but human; to relieve it is God-like.*" But Martin could not meet the old man's eyes nor acknowledge his praise, for he was thinking, Wiggins, Wiggins.

Leaving Cripple Camp, packing goods to boat

Chapter Twenty-one

October 1899

Cider—General Rules for Making

Always choose perfectly ripe and sound fruit. Pick the apples by hand. (An active boy with the bag slung over his shoulder will soon clear a tree. Apples that have lain any time on the ground contract an earthy taste, which will always be found in the cider.) After sweating, and before being ground, wipe them dry, and if any are found bruised or rotten, put them in a heap by themselves, for an inferior cider to make vinegar.

*I*n the months she had been gone, Pat had grown a foot. He seemed nearly a man, much more self-assured. It's because he can read and write, she thought. "I'm sorry about your uncle, Pat." She was able to say this to him, eye to eye, for they were now the same height, with more growth ahead for Pat.

"I miss him, in spite of his ways. He's really the only kin I have. Had," he corrected himself. "That is unless you count my pa. And I don't count him," he said emphatically, wiping the back of his hand across his eyes. "Do you want to go out to your farm right now?" Pat was waiting for her with the minister's buggy when the Grand Rapids and Indiana pulled into the Blackbird Station. There were few passengers in October, unlike the summer when the train and station were packed with resorters, and the platform was heaped with bushels of produce sold by the farmers. She liked the town in the weeks after the summer people left, when a calm hovered over the bay and infused the streets and public buildings. She wrote Pat from Grand Bay City, grateful to be in a place where one could count on a letter reaching its destination. She was working her way home, she told him. Pat relayed the minister's wife's invitation to stay at the parsonage. Aurora would rather have slept on the railroad tracks, though she didn't say this. She could not bear being bombarded with questions from the nosy woman, and she was not ready to have Martin's condition revealed to the whole community.

"I need to go out to Starrvation Corner today, but could we first stop at the Bartek's?"

Their yard was littered with yellow oak leaves, at which some stray chickens pecked, rustling and stirring up the ground cover. A cider press ringed with lumpy gunny sacks of apples stood beside the porch. Because it was a weekday, the children would be in school, Jory at the tannery. When Marisa opened the door, she raised her hands to her mouth, dumbfounded at the sight of Aurora on the porch. Marisa's belly was high and round with a pregnancy. Her apron rode up on her dress, its ties strained with the circumference of her. A spear of jealousy stabbed Aurora, a physical pain under her breast. She swallowed.

"You're back! Thanks to God." Marisa threw her arms around Aurora, taking in the empty wagon parked under an oak. She looked at Pat, then back to Aurora. "Is Martin back at the farm then?"

Marisa placed fresh prune bread and tea on the scrubbed kitchen table, slicing an extra piece for Pat. During Aurora's absence they had become acquainted. Pat had been invited several times to eat with the Barteks. Now they both listened as Aurora retraced her odyssey. These were her closest friends, so she was honest in relating Martin's condition, even the incident in Seattle with the gun. When she paused, she found them looking at her in amazement.

"I can't believe you did all that by yourself. Alone. And your poor Martin." Marisa's eyes sparkled with tears. "I did write a letter. Well, I spoke the letter, and my Delia wrote it. She's very good at penmanship. Did you get it? I sent it to that place in Alaska."

Aurora shook her head. Then quickly to counter the dismay on her friend's face said, "But I knew you were thinking of me." She ran her finger around the rim of her cup. "And you. It looks like soon there will be another Bartek."

Marisa breathed in, then looked down at her stomach as she exhaled. "That is for sure what it is looking like," she said. The flat tone indicated she was not overjoyed by the impending event. "Stay here tonight. Don't go out to the farm to stay all alone." Marisa's biggest fear was being alone. From birth to her present life, she had been surrounded by other people, her life circumscribed by duties and chores. It was the only life she could imagine. Aurora wondered what thoughts went through her mind when she was alone for brief periods, like today, when the children were in school, her husband at work.

"I'll be alright. I've been there alone. I need to check things over. I'll probably rent it out again while I'm in Grand Bay City. I have to be near Martin—until I know if there's hope for his recovery." She continued, voice quivering, "Until I know if he'll ever consider me his wife again."

Marisa poured more tea into Aurora's cup while Pat stared nervously at his hands, uncomfortable with the women's frank talk. "Did Mr. Starr find *any* gold?"

"Not that I know of. At least he didn't have any when I brought him back." Aurora circled her wedding ring, loose around her finger. Maybe she should take it off, before she lost it.

On their way to the farm, Pat asked, "What about Marble and the cat? Do you want me to bring them out?"

"No, it would be too hard seeing them only to be separated again. How is the situation with Reverend and Mrs. Hartless?"

Pat did not answer right away. Aurora waited, taking deep breaths of October air. October, her favorite month, a joyful month of lavish celebration of the harvest. October eased one toward preparing for the long winter. The high metal whine from down at the sawmill reached them.

"I guess they mean well, but I feel like I'm being smothered." He clicked his tongue, urging the horse up the sandy incline towards Sawyersville Road. He aimed towards the more solid edge of the road, for the horse was slipping in the soft sand. They were both silent as the nervous beast pulled them up the slope. Aurora marveled at how accomplished this sixteen year-old was at handling the reins.

"Aurora." He stopped, embarrassed to use her first name to her face. Using it in a letter was one thing, this was different. He started again. "When you come back from Grand Bay City, can I live with you, you and Mr. Starr? I'd be a lot of help."

"I know you would, Pat. Believe me, I'd like to have you at Starrvation Corner, but my plans are so unsettled right now. I'll stay in touch with you, so you will be the first to know, right after me, that is." She laughed. How long had it been since she'd laughed? She and Martin used to joke around, play tricks on each other. During the first year of marriage they had been like puppies romping around, in a giddy state of love. Now her laughter sounded hard-edged to her own ears.

The farm looked forlorn, tall brown grasses, now dying, crowded the porch. The dark green trim around the doors and windows was flaking. The tenants had left in May, and Pat had been living in town, so the place had been neglected. What would Ethan Starr think if he saw his place now? No longer a working farm, the animals all gone, his great nephew in an insane asylum. A few strands of blue yarn dangled forlornly from the branch of the tree where she had tied them a lifetime ago. The birds or squirrels had used most of her offering.

"The new owners of uncle's farm have your horse, cow and wagon. They know of your situation. I'll have to take this outfit back into town. Will you be all right here?" asked Pat.

"Yes, I'll be fine. I want to check things over, get the place ready for another renter. You might ask Reverend Hartless to put out the word, or perhaps you know of someone." Her voice drifted off. She was suddenly exhausted. The tasks and arrangements ahead of her seemed too much to think about. How would she make her way through her complicated life? How would she earn money? Her funds were nearly depleted.

The front door was unlocked and gave a lonely, complaining creak as she pushed it open. She stood in the hall, the stairway beckoning to the upstairs. Each step had a shallow dip in the center where the feet of Ethan and his wives had worn away the pine. The air was musty, unused and still. A fine silt of dust coated the banisters and furniture. The house was familiar and strange at once. Pat carried in her luggage, setting it at the bottom of the stairway. He took the box of groceries she had purchased in Blackbird, as well as a gallon of new cider from the Bartek press, back to the kitchen, moving easily through the house, as if he already lived here.

After Pat left, Aurora climbed the stairs to the bedroom, now shadowy because the afternoon sun was lighting up the west side of the house. The bed had been stripped, the sheets folded on the ladder-back chair, the quilt hung submissively over the blanket stand. She removed her shoes, jerked the quilt over her, and submerged into dreamless sleep. The last thing she heard was the cedar bough rubbing against the side of the house.

For a week, Aurora cleaned, scrubbing and polishing until her knees and wrists ached. She washed all the bedding in the copper tub outside the kitchen door, hanging the clothes on the line that ran in front of the lilac hedge. With a scythe, she cleared the yard, hacking away at the wild blackberry and raspberry thickets that were crowding the flower bed and grassy space around the porch. In the late afternoons she picked several bushels from the apple trees Ethan had planted. The one pear tree did not look well; a few spotted, stricken pears hung on their stems like misshapen teardrops. She threw them into the bushel baskets of apple drops she had collected for the neighbors' pigs.

The couple who had bought Clyde Kleckner's farm were young, with a baby. They had been feeding Aurora's animals, getting milk from the cow and transportation from the horse in return. Aurora loaded a bushel of apples into the wheelbarrow and headed across the road, stopping several times to put her burden down. Her arms were aching by the time she reached the broad slanting front porch of the farmhouse. She introduced herself to the young wife, not much more than a teenager, who had a baby straddling one hip.

"Little Tom," we call him. "There's Big Tom," she laughed, as the husband came over from the barn.

It looked as though Aurora's hopes, false hopes, for her future with Martin were now being lived out across the road from Starrvation Corner. "Thank you for caring for the livestock. I need the horse and wagon for a few days, but I'd like to arrange for them to stay here—indefinitely. I'll be in Grand Bay City for some time." She was grateful that the couple were either too polite, or too uninterested, to ask questions. "These apples will be good for pies. And I'll bring over some for your pigs. Pat told me you had pigs," she added.

As she returned to the house, she marveled at the geometry of haystacks decorating the fields along Sawyersville Road. Though she knew about their construction, the final product never ceased to amaze her. Other farmers must have benefited from the instructions for building a properly ventilated haystack in Uncle Ethan's farm manual:

> *Stacks of hay, corn-stalks, etc., may be ventilated by making a hole perpendicularly through the [center], with apertures through the base and top or sides of the stack to admit a current of air. The orifice should be constructed when the stack is being built, which can easily be done by filling a bag of the requisite size with hay or straw, placing it upright in the center of the stack, drawing it upward according as the stack rises. In this way a chimney will be*

formed in the center of the stack, which will carry off steam, if the hay or corn-stalks should ferment, and by admitting air will prevent damage from mold. The top of the air tunnel should be protected by a roof to keep out rain.

Aurora recalled the heat and dust in the September air of last year when haying had consumed her life.

" " " "

At mid-day Aurora took sandwiches and lemonade out to the fields. School would not start for another week because many students were also out working in their families' hay fields. Pat jumped off the wagon, and he and the others came towards the huge oak where Aurora laid the lunch on a blue-checked cloth. Two buckets of water stood in the shade, a ladle resting in one. Although the morning had been cool, the temperature had climbed and the men were bare-chested, their skin slick with sweat that held chaff and longer pieces of hay. Clyde Kleckner had reddish curly hair sprinkled with renegade white ones covering his chest and shoulders. The others, including Pat, were hairless, all of them tanned a rich deep brown by the summer's work. Pat wore a mantle of freckles across his neck and shoulders. Aurora thought of the hides tanning in the huge vats down at the leather company. That disruptive, horrible thought was banished by the solacing smell of sweat and timothy hay. How secure she felt. She loved to pass closely to Martin when he came in from working outside. Something quickened within her, then spread peacefully through her body. She let herself luxuriate in the aroma until she became self-conscious of being surrounded by four half-naked men. She backed away from the assembly. "Help yourselves. I forgot something back at the house." The dog, who had been lounging in the shade, reluctantly followed her. Marble knew his duties.

She retreated, dizzy with longing to touch a man's, no, not any man's, Martin's bare skin. Although she knew he could never have worked outside in the sun without a shirt, his back would have been red and blistered, Aurora sank into imagining Martin's sweaty chest pressed against her own exposed breasts in the bedroom, cool from the shade of the cedar tree.

Like his great uncle, Martin rented out forty acres to Kleckner and forty to a man who worked at the sawmill. Martin had neither the skin nor temperament for a farmer's life, and he especially disliked haying. He'd had his fill working for Uncle Ethan, the stiff stalks cutting his hands and causing an itchy rash on his exposed skin. However, he did not mind the physical work involved in following a dream. His letter, arriving at the Blackbird Post Office in a mud-smeared, ripped envelope, had taken nearly three months to reach her. She considered it a minor miracle. Martin sounded different, as if he'd gone through some initiation and was changed, a bit foreign from the husband who had left last February.

June 5

Dear Rory,

I picture you out in the yard cutting lilacs. You are wearing your wide-brimmed hat and have your sleeves rolled up. How is the haying proceeding? It's on my mind because a few days ago we crossed the Hay River. This morning we reached a meadow where a party driving some cattle had camped. We ate one of the steers this evening; the poor beast was near death. Uncle Ethan's saying "Do by your cows as you would like to be done by yourself" haunts me here. The animals are treated shamefully. They lead wretched lives on this expedition, and then wretched deaths. The only ones who show compassion to the animals are the Cree. Of course, they kill wild animals for food, they must in this wilderness. But it is careful, necessary killing, and they respect their prey as a living thing that is worthy to feed them. It seems the longer I am on this journey, the more I understand the Indian thinking, and less the white man's way. There is no one in my party, including Frank, who I feel free to discuss these matters with. I know you understand this connection between man and beast, although I doubt you would be shouldering a rifle and killing beaver, geese and a cow moose, as I have done. I give thanks to the animal and treat the carcass in a respectful manner. The meat from the wild game has saved our lives and kept us going.

You will be relieved to hear that Frank and I have left Mac and his Philadelphians. We joined forces with three others, who were also fed up with Mac's questionable ethics. There is Harry, a butcher from Brooklyn, New York, who brought along the tools of his trade—many fine, sharp knives, which have come in handy when we are dividing up fresh meat. He also gives haircuts! And Jim, a quiet fellow from Wisconsin, was so perturbed with Mac that he called him a "madman" to his face. That may have been unwise because I feel Mac used that insult as justification for cutting back on our fair share of provisions. But we have no way to prove it because Mac holds the reins for every aspect of the operation. The third man is Ulrich, a German from a county outside Philadelphia. He is boisterous and cheerful, making us laugh when things are grim.

When I am at a low point, I think of you and feel sure you will be all right at Starrvation Corner, with the rent for the fields coming in, and money from the hemlock bark, too. Of course, there is your teacher's pay, which I hope will be paid to you on time this year. Let me know what you planted in the garden this summer. I'd trade a couple of beavers to taste a real garden vegetable about now.

So we continue, working our way towards the Liard, where surely we will start to find paying gold. We've heard there's plenty to be had all along this river, so before the arctic winter sets in, I may have some new-found wealth to bring home.

With all my love and hope,
Martin, your husband

If he did not find gold along the Liard, what then? Would he keep going? Would he come home, defeated but alive? In the parlor, she tacked a map of Canada and Alaska to the wall. With her finger, she traced Martin's route, amazed at how much longer it was taking him than the promotional pamphlets had promised. When he first told her about his idea of joining his boyhood friend to go search for gold, she was angry. It seemed like a childish escapade. But she read the literature that Martin sent away for and allowed herself to be persuaded that it might be a worthwhile trip. The brochures claimed that men of "good physical constitutions and undaunted determination" could travel from Edmonton to Dawson in ninety days. The Klondike gold fields were in the Yukon Territory near the border with Alaska. The Klondike River, explained Martin, was really just a spur off the Yukon River. He had heard that Klondike was the white miners' mispronunciation of the Indian name of the Yukon River. Even here, north of Blackbird, Michigan, Aurora and Martin had heard of the Klondike Stampede, which started back in July of 1897. When two ships carrying successful miners docked in Seattle and San Francisco, along with over two tons in gold, the big rush was on. Aurora did not know that Frank had written to Martin last summer, urging him to leave for the Klondike then.

"Ninety days," she snorted. She measured the distance from Edmonton to the Hay River using her thumb and forefinger. It had taken Martin over ninety days to go that distance. She looked at what was ahead. He had gone less than half the distance! She thought it a cruel trick for the map to look so harmless. The white spaces between the thin, delicate squiggles of rivers gave no hint of menace or difficulty. *Martin, I won't think any less of you if you turn around now.* A desperate longing for him overcame her, and she fell into the rocker, moving herself back and forth in the chair, comforting herself the way her mother had comforted her when she was small, rocking her, not talking, just rocking.

Checking on her second seeding of carrots and beets, she saw that the dog had been helping himself to the carrots again. Half a row was dug up and a pile of carrot tops, their lacy greens wilted, lay in the dirt. Marble was nowhere in sight. Aurora harvested the rest of the row, carrying the small orange spears into the kitchen. The second planting of carrots was mainly for the horse; they'd stay in the ground (if Marble did not dig them up) until late fall or even early winter so they'd grow larger. She could not get angry at Marble; he loved carrots, and she had to admire how clever he was to dig them up for himself. She rinsed the dirt off a carrot and bit down into a sweetness that tasted to her of soap. The men's voices carried from the fields.

She wondered if Pat would be too tired to come for his lesson that evening. They had long ago finished *Kidnapped* and now were nearly through *The Red Badge of Courage*. He was moving quickly through the math text she lent him, her own from when she was a student. He was insatiable for knowledge and wanted to continue. Now the state's compulsory attendance law said that all children between eight and fourteen had to attend school for at least four months of the year. Most of her students stopped their education at fourteen, just when Pat's was beginning. The attendance rule allowed exceptions for "mental or physical weakness," like the ten year-old boy whose leg had been amputated below the knee. He fell off the wagon driven by his father, when the right front wheel hit a huge rabbit hole. While he was recovering, Aurora made house calls, delivering the day's lessons and going over them with him.

"He's got no interest in anything. Just looks out at the window," said his mother, the first time Aurora stopped by. The boy, Wilbur, was on a bed in the front room, a quilt drawn up to his waist. He did not look up when Aurora entered the room.

"I'm sorry about your accident, Wilbur. The other students are anxious to have you back." She sat on the edge of the bed, resisting the urge to cover his hand with hers.

"I'm a cripple," he said. "My leg's not about to grow back." He sounded like an old man resigned to his fate.

"No. But you will keep growing, and you will learn to walk with a crutch. It will take a while to get used to this, and when you do, others will too."

She placed a get-well card from the class on his lap. "Your mind needs to keep growing, too. So I brought you some assignments to do while you're home. That way you won't have missed much when you come back." Aurora stood up.

The boy looked down at the packet on the bed, then up at his teacher. "The others are going to laugh at me."

"Wilbur, there are always ignorant people, and they can be cruel. I hope none of your classmates are like that. If one of them does make a mean comment, you're smart enough to know what to say." This time she did reach out and cover his hand. "I'm counting on you to do this work." He nodded his head, his forelock brushing his eyes, reminding Aurora of an acquiescent pony.

And now she heard he was coming back to school this fall. Sometimes Aurora wondered if she would be tutoring Pat, would be keeping up Wilbur with the rest of the class, would be making calls to the Bohemian woman who lived in her girlhood house, if Martin were at home. She missed him, but her life seemed rich and blessed to her, when she wasn't feeling sorry for herself. Those moments of resenting Martin and his quest, of despairing over her lack of children, those moments occurred less frequently. If her husband were here, her attention would be more on him and perhaps she wouldn't miss the connections she had with these others who filled her life. Perhaps.

The Bohemian woman's name was Marisa Bartek, and Aurora had grown fond of her in the short time they had been acquainted. After refusing Marisa's first invitation to come into the house, Aurora returned the next week. She brought along her mother's curtain tiebacks. Blue and white, shaped like clamshells, they had been used to secure the net curtains where they dipped in a curve against the scrolled woodwork in the parlor. Aurora felt these items belonged back in their original room. Her own parlor windows were decorated with practical damask. Returning these small items to their former home would be a memorial to her mother.

Marisa scrunched up her round face in pleasure at Aurora's present. "They are so beautiful. And your mother's? But you should keep them. Something of your mother's."

"They seem to belong here," said Aurora, then feeling foolish as she looked around at the curtainless windows.

Marisa slipped the drawstring bag containing the clamshell tiebacks into her apron pocket. "Come to the *kitshen* and sit. I'm just finishing up with these *shickens*." Marisa, barely five feet, raised up on her toes to lift a chicken by its feet from a pot of boiling water on the range. Three plucked birds were already lined up on the counter. The evil smell of hot, wet feathers filled the kitchen. Aurora moved her chair a bit closer to the open window.

"This is the last one. Phew! Such stinky work," she pulled off the big easy feathers, then went at the pinfeathers with tweezers. The bird's naked, pimpled skin gave Aurora the chills, though the summer day was warm and close.

Aurora watched her, marveling at Marisa's cheerful, exuberant spirits. She was like a plump, energetic little hen, darting here and there, always busy. Aurora had come thinking she'd ask Marisa if she could walk through the house, just to see the rooms again. But now that she was here, she had no desire to. The house was no longer hers. Though clean, it had a sparse, utilitarian look. The floorboards were scrubbed white, the furniture was plain wood. There were none of the colorful objects of her mother's time, no flowers in a jug on the table, no woven runner down the center of the table. She felt certain there would be no books in the parlor, much less a piano. Still there was a feeling of family here, of closeness and cooperation, especially as the two youngest girls, twins she learned, but not identical, threw open the screen door and entered sideways, carrying a bucket between them. Water sloshed onto the floor.

"What are you two rascals up to? More frogs? Go get the floor rag and wipe up that water. Then say hello to Mrs. Starr." Marisa slapped the last chicken down beside the others.

"Hello, Mrs. Starr," they said more or less in unison. The smaller of the twins was bouncing around in the spilled water. "Mama, you should see all the frogs in the creek. I think all the frogs in the world live there."

Aurora laughed. "I used to love to catch frogs when I was your age. I had a dress with big puffy sleeves, which I wasn't supposed to wear down by the creek. One day I was down there, in my dress, and started to catch frogs. Since I had no bucket with me, I stuffed them in my sleeves."

She had the twins' attention; they were staring at her open-mouthed. "Those frogs tickled my arms," she continued. "I tried getting them into a bucket on our porch, but my mother came out of the house just then and saw my sleeves jumping all over the place."

"Did your mama whip you?" asked the taller, more sedate twin.

"No, but she was angry. I had to first wash my dress, then go to my room," said Aurora, remembering standing at her bedroom window and watching her dress dry on the clothesline, the puffy sleeves inflating with the breeze. "But later, she told me she had taken the frogs back down to the creek, because if my father saw them, he would want to cook them."

"Papa likes to eat frogs," said the smaller twin.

"Yes, I know many people do. I wanted to keep the frogs as pets." Aurora avoided looking at the pail on the kitchen floor. She was sure its cargo was destined as food for the family, and how silly she must sound to them.

After the children went back outside, Marisa poured two glasses of cherry juice and set a plate of kolatches on the table. "Oh, my," said Aurora as the zing of fermentation flooded her throat then stomach. The rich round pastries were filled with prune, and Aurora unabashedly helped herself to two.

"Very nice, yes?" Marisa raised her eyebrows.

"Very nice," laughed Aurora. "Everything is very nice." She enjoyed being here with Marisa, though they had little in common from their backgrounds or present circumstances. Being around Marisa made her feel that life was to be enjoyed in spite of its difficulties. And as she sat there, she had no trouble seeing it as the Barteks' kitchen. Aurora had no need to dredge up the images of her mother's big copper kettle on the fire, the rag rugs in front of the sideboard, the pie safe with it fragrant, fruity contents. Those things had vanished; she could no longer live in this house. It was up to her to make new memories, to make a life apart from her parents.

Marisa gave Aurora six smooth, brown eggs from her chickens, packing them in straw in a basket. "You can return the basket next time you visit," she smiled as she put an arm around Aurora's waist. Since Martin had left, she no longer kept chickens. He had been able to kill them, but although she could chase them around the yard and catch one, swinging the clucking mass of feathers by the horny feet, she could not, would not, chop off its head. She'd heard of farmers who could wring the chickens' necks with one swift twist, but that was a skill she had no desire to acquire.

A dead animal smell assailed her nostrils as she walked across the porch, a smell that had not registered when she entered the house. A washtub filled with clothes, the surface coated with a gray, greasy scum and long hairs, was the source of the odor. "Is stinky, yes?" laughed Marisa. Those are Jory's clothes from work. I don't let him wear them in the house."

Jory worked at the tannery and was now most likely unloading the hides that had come by rail from Chicago, but had started out on the backs of cattle in the Argentine. The smell did not bother Marisa in the same way it bothered Aurora. To Marisa the smell meant income; she just didn't want it in her kitchen.

II II II II

News of Aurora's return from out west, without Martin Starr, was circulating. Two parents of students from last year had come out to see her, asking if she would be teaching. Was she unhappy at the school? She was also visited by the Methodist minister. She was hanging clothes on the line and saw his buggy turn into the drive from a space between the sheets. She ducked behind the hedge and into the smokehouse, the interior cool and rank with the odor of smoke-infused beef and pork from over thirty years. She heard Reverend Hartless knocking , calling her name (*Mrs. Starr, Aurora Starr*, then just *Aurora*), heard the creak of the front door as he went into her house. She stayed hidden, gazing up at the hooks where slabs of meat were hung to cure. When at last she heard the groaning of his wagon as it rolled onto Sawyersville Road, she emerged into the golden world, beech and maple leaves twirling in the breeze, some brushing against the clean clothes on the line as they made their descent.

It was during a vigorous cleaning of the bedroom, after sorting through Martin's clothes and finding few appropriate garments for his time in the hospital, that she discovered a short loosened floorboard near the window. She pressed on one end, and the other popped up. Several paper-wrapped bundles rested in the space between the floor and the ceiling of the kitchen below. The first musty-smelling package contained several little flannel blankets edged with sturdy tatting. The next held pairs of knit booties, and then a tiny christening gown, its once innocent, spotless white now dotted with black specks of mildew. Aurora suspected that these items had been made by Lenora. Why had she hidden them? Perhaps she could not bear to throw them away after the baby's death, but wanted them out of sight, so hid them here. How had Ethan reacted to the baby's death? It must have been a blow to him, awaiting an heir after all that time. Aurora felt protective of Lenora, but having found the baby clothes, she could not leave them there, in this room where she slept. She rewrapped the packages, carried them with her, stopping in the barn for a spade. Beside the *Infant S.* grave, she dug a hole, placing the packages of clothes, tenderly. She didn't think Lenora would mind. Aurora knew this grave of baby things was for her, too, for she was burying the hope of a child with Martin. This was the grave of her unborn child.

So far only the Barteks and Pat knew of Martin's condition. She couldn't keep the secret much longer. It was a small community, and Grand Bay City was only eighty miles south. Someone would eventually learn that Martin was a patient at the asylum. She had signed the papers in Dr. Shelby's office, and then gone shopping for the required clothes.

3 new shirts
1 new coat and vest
2 pairs pantaloons
3 pairs socks
2 pairs drawers
2 undershirts
1 hat
1 cravat
3 collars
6 handkerchiefs
1 pair shoes or boots
1 pair slippers
1 overcoat

She added one pair of gloves to this fresh wardrobe, which was more formal than what his previous life had required. Surely Martin had never worn a cravat, but the hospital schedule included "little social gatherings," which required nicer clothing.

Aurora had no idea what had happened to all of Martin's possessions. When they left Dease Lake with the pack train, Martin possessed almost nothing, like a saint who had renounced all earthly goods. Even his watch, with her hairwork woven into the chain, was missing. Of course he had left his everyday farm clothes at home. They hung, useless and dejected, from hooks in their bedroom. Downstairs by the kitchen door, Martin's brown farmcoat, which he wore in the barn, reminded Aurora of a side of pork dangling in the smokehouse. She took it out to the barn, where she wouldn't have to look at it.

The board of trustees, which oversaw four school districts, persuaded a young man from the U.P. to come down and be a permanent substitute for Aurora's position. They had received no word from her about the coming school year. Now she wrote to the board, informing them that Martin was "in Grand Bay City, recovering from his time in Canada." She regretted she could not be more certain of her commitment to teaching at the Sawyersville School. She missed her students, but needed to be near her husband.

And then, the day before she was to return to Grand Bay City, she received a blessing. That was how she regarded it—something unforeseen and positive developing from the tragedy that was now their life. She was in Blackbird to collect her mail and have her rental contract notarized. Her new tenant was a widower who wanted, not to farm but to live in the country, having just come to the area from Chicago. He was cheerful and handsome for his age, somewhere in the late sixties, she guessed. He had been out to look over the farmhouse. "It will suit me fine," he said, signing the contract on the kitchen table. She agreed to rent until the spring. By then, she would know if Martin was recovering, if she could plan for them to be together, or if . . . right now she couldn't think of the alternatives.

Standing at the counter in the post office, she stared at the envelope bearing a Brooklyn, New York postmark. "Must be important if it's from so far away," observed the postmaster. His nose was nearly twitching with curiosity.

"I don't know anyone in Brooklyn," she said, more to herself than to the postmaster as she moved out of the way for a woman waiting behind her. It was a letter from Harry, whom she had never met but who seemed to know about Martin's state of mind when he was still at Dease Lake. Perhaps Mr. Woolsworth had contacted him. Several men, including a Jim and an Ulrich, who had traveled with Martin, as well as others from the cripple camp, had sent her a bank draft for $500! "Oh my," she exhaled, causing the postmaster's head to bob in her direction.

"Is everything all right, Mrs. Starr?"

"Oh, yes. Quite all right." So Martin's journey had resulted in some riches after all, she thought. It was his money, although her name was on the paper. Because the asylum was a public institution, she would not have to pay for Martin's care. However, his clothing and any other personal, and allowable, possessions would be her responsibility. And she would have to find a place to live near the hospital. Then there were maintenance projects for the farm: the barn roof, which leaked over one of the stalls; the siding on the west side of the house was buckling. Her new tenant's rent would hardly cover these costs. True, there was some money from the farmers who leased the Starr fields. But there was no nest egg, no feeling of security that the money from her parents had given her. Now that was gone.

A cold rain began during the night. She woke to the drumming on the roof with a lingering dream of Martin running through the asylum grounds in his nightshirt. She lit the lamp to help dispel the image, reminding herself that Dr. Shelby had said that women patients were much more likely to run away. Martin was in the receiving ward, where he could acclimate to the new environment and where the attendants could observe him. When the image of her running husband had faded, she was assaulted by self-recrimination: was she putting Martin away because he no longer showed her any affection?

Was she getting even with him? She'd heard of family members, usually men, who had their wives arrested for minor offenses (selling furniture or espousing the suffragist cause) and then declared insane. Usually the men wanted their wives' property or wanted to take up with another woman. Would anyone in Blackbird accuse her of committing Martin so that she could have the farm to herself?

She let herself imagine Martin returning to Starrvation Corner, assuming his former routine. But try as she might, she could not see him here, moving through these rooms, walking to the barn, tending the apple trees. She could only envision him sitting in a ladder-back chair, staring out the window.

Chapter Twenty-two

November 1899

Sore Throat—Clergyman's

A peculiar condition of the throat and larynx, the effect of prolonged use of the voice and straining of the vocal chords. Characterized by hoarseness and catarrh of the mucous membrane, the voice loses its normal tone and not infrequently disappears altogether. It is generally associated with a rheumatic constitution. The proper treatment is rest, and repeated inhalations of creosote, eucalyptus, or pumuline in the vapor of steam. The general system should at the same time receive tonic treatment. The application of electricity to the throat has also proved of immense service. The best internal remedy is the glycerite of tar, combined with minute doses of arsenic.

Martin's parents arrived in Grand Bay City the night before and were staying at the Park Hotel. It would not help matters, thought Aurora, to have their first impression of the town and hospital be one of lifeless gray and cold, not softened by the autumn colors. The leaves had long since fallen from the trees and a threadbare blanket of snow lay on the ground. From the porch of the house where she rented a room, within walking distance of the institution, she watched smoke rise in dark vertical smudges from the asylum's many chimneys. It resembled a fortress—or a huge factory.

Aurora met them in the hotel's dining room for breakfast. At her approach, they rose from their chairs, appearing to her smaller, frailer versions of the in-laws she remembered.

"Oh, our poor boy. How can this be happening?" sobbed Mrs. Starr as she grasped Aurora's hands in her own, gripping them until Aurora winced.

Mr. Starr moved in to embrace Aurora, patting her on the back. "How are you holding up, Aurora? Sit down and have something to eat." A rack of toast and a large pot of oatmeal sat on the table. Mrs. Starr removed several paper packets from her purse, emptying them into her china bowl. They looked to Aurora like assorted grains, in a raw state. One of her mother-in-law's nutritional regimens, no doubt. Martin had told how his mother and two other women had formed the Pelican Nutrition and Culture Club. For a brief period, they experimented with drinking their own urine in order to boost the body's healing powers, a method advocated by Dr. Murphy in his monthly newsletter mailed from Battle Creek. Dr. Murphy had also run a "clinic" out of his home. After he was closed down for lewd and lascivious behavior with his female patients, Mrs. Starr never mentioned Dr. Murphy or his methods again.

A waiter in a white jacket brought a pot of tea with a dish of lemon wedges. He poured a cup for Aurora and Mr. Starr, but Mrs. Starr declined. When he retreated, she withdrew a bottle from her resourceful purse.

"Carrot juice," she announced. Then with a deep breath, she fixed her eyes, a lighter version of Martin's color, on Aurora. "I need to know why you did not consider bringing Martin to Pelican. I could care for him. He must be suffering from a vitamin deficiency. He didn't have proper nutrition on that expedition, and it has affected his mind."

Aurora watched her own hand tremble as she placed the cup in its saucer, creating a fluttering tinkle. "I think when you see Martin for yourselves, you will better understand that he needs profession-al help. He is suffering from more than a physical malady. Frank's death, the amputation of a companion's toes, and continual hard-ships took a toll on him. He needs the care of many people right now.

Neither of us has the strength to carry that out." Aurora only wished Martin could be made right with some vitamins and potions from his mother.

"We know you did what you thought best," said Mr. Starr, forcibly including his wife in this declaration as he focused his gaze on her. "We want to talk to the doctor who admitted him."

"Dr. Shelby. I could not see taking him back to the farm, so I came here directly. I first had to get a judge here to declare Martin incompetent. Then I had to commit him . . . to the asylum." Her voice trembled. "He's been busy. He has things to do," she offered. "He's being well taken care of."

Mrs. Starr ignored this. "There's never been mental disease in our family," she protested, as if some stray gene from the Gray family had infected her son. "None of our relatives has ever been in a mad-house."

Both Mr. Starr and Aurora flinched. "Perhaps none of them had ever been on the Edmonton Trail for months, with death and starvation all around," countered Aurora, defending her husband's right to be insane. She took a breath. "I know he'll be happy to see you; it will be a comfort to him," she softened, though she couldn't be sure it was true. "I have some news. I'll be living here for a while. Dr. Shelby has employed me as a teacher at the hospital. I'll be close to Martin, although the doctor has advised me that it is best if I do not see him every day. I'll be teaching English to some of the foreign patients."

"And the farm?" asked Mr. Starr, tentatively.

"I have a tenant until the spring. I couldn't leave it sitting empty."

"No, no, of course not," Mr. Starr agreed.

"Aurora, did you never think of asking us to come and stay at the farm?" Mrs. Starr, pushed a soggy brown lump around the cereal bowl with a silver spoon with PH stamped on the handle, but did not raise her eyes to look at her daughter-in-law.

"Why, no," she said, startled at the suggestion. "It never occurred to me." Was the woman actually thinking of leaving Pelican to be closer to her son?

"I'm not sure that would be a good idea," said Mr. Starr, sounding as if the idea was one they had never discussed. Aurora gave him a grateful glance, which was intercepted by Mrs. Starr, as she looked up from the vitamin-packed remains of her breakfast.

She did not tell them that when she visited Martin once a week in the dayroom, she had to force herself to see him as a patient, to put no expectations on him to act as her spouse. Martin was vaguely polite to her. When he did talk, it was about his outdoor work and the weather conditions. He was obsessed with any changes in climate, and now as the November storms raged on the Great Lakes, he was agitated by the news of a Canadian passenger and freight steamer which had gone down in Lake Michigan the week before. The reports of survivors were still sketchy, but there were more dead than living. The rumor was that only two children had survived.

She accompanied her in-laws to the hospital and directed them to Dr. Shelby's office, under the scrutiny of Flora. Then with nervous anticipation, a feeling that always took hold of her at the start of each school year, she made her way to the women's receiving ward to meet with two of her students: Greta Herrmann, a young German; and Wanda Jankowski, a middle-aged Polish woman. She knew little about them except that neither had ever been violent. She wondered if the Polish patient was related to Harold Jankowski, her harmonica-playing student back in Sawyersville. The two women would have their lessons in a little sitting room off the women's receiving ward, a more private space. On the way she passed the women's dining room, where the tables were set precisely, as if even the arrangement of cutlery and dishes was an aspect of the order that Dr. Shelby had outlined. She gazed in at the tripod of butter knife, fork and spoon, balanced on their handles at the head of each plate. The ends of the knife and spoon were inserted into the tines of the fork, creating a trinity. Each table was set for six, with a place setting consisting of a metal plate, really a shallow bowl; a cup with no handle; and the curious cutlery display. The tables were bare of coverings or napkins, only salt and pepper shakers in the center. Tiny tiles covered the floor, similar to those in the main entrance, where she and Martin had stood weeks ago. Though clean and orderly, the bareness, the lack of those items that soften and enhance daily life—pictures, books, rugs—seemed a cruel aspect of life in the asylum.

Next she paused at the open door of a room where a nurse attendant made beds, the cone-shaped cap perched on her head with dark wings of hair sweeping out on either side. The beds had white iron bed frames and were being covered with textured bedspreads, one green, one peach. In the coming weeks, Aurora would learn that the patients never saw these bedspreads, which were placed over their coarse brown blankets when the women went to the dayroom or to do chores after breakfast. The patient rooms were locked during the day, removing the opportunity to nap. The bedspreads were removed before the supper hour, before the women went back to their rooms in the evening. Aurora thought of locked, empty rooms softened by the coverings on the beds. It seemed mean-spirited, if economical, to Aurora. She wondered why they even bothered with the bedspreads. Who would see them, other than the attendants who put them on and took them off the beds?

Her two students were already in the little room, its space overwhelmed by urns of maidenhair fern. They looked up at her like two creatures taking refuge in a woody glade. "Good morning. I am Aurora Starr," she began, dispensing with the Mrs. The two women stared at her. The younger of the two was thin, her clavicles in relief beneath the wool material of her dress. Her pale skin dramatized a port wine stain, the birthmark starting far back on her left cheekbone, continuing down her neck and disappearing under the tatting of her collar. Aurora in trying to not stare at it too long thought of the Michigan mitten, the shape of the state's lower peninsula. The older woman, perhaps in her fifties, rather frightened Aurora with her angry eyes and clenched fists which were wrapped in an apron she wore over her dress. "Good morning," she repeated. Then she pointed at her new students, followed by a sweeping motion of her arm back to herself. Since Aurora knew neither German nor Polish, translating their language into English was not an option. She would have to use the imitation method of students mimicking the teacher and learning to associate words and phrases with specific situations, plus a lot of gesturing.

"Gut Morgen," whispered the thin one.

"Good morning," said Aurora, nodding in approval, grateful for a response. The other woman remained silent, glaring at Aurora. She decided to concentrate on the younger and let the angry woman (the mad woman, Aurora said to herself) listen. She pulled a cane-back rocker closer to the German woman.

"My name is Aurora," she said. She emphasized Aurora by pressing her palm against her chest.

"Greta," said the German, splaying a long bony hand on her meager bosom.

"Good morning, Greta."

"Gut morning, Aurora." She smiled, revealing a charming gap between the upper front teeth.

The Polish woman muttered something, twisting her hands in her apron. All around her chair were crumpled, torn fronds from the nearest fern. Aurora locked her gaze with the woman's, now a look less of anger than of panic. She managed to smile at the poor creature, who began muttering again.

In the coming weeks, as the staff grew used to seeing Aurora on the wards, some became more friendly. She learned Greta's story from a chatty nurse attendant. Greta had been sent for by relatives who had settled in Bethel County as part of a financial arrangement with a neighboring farmer—an arranged marriage, with financial strings. She sailed over from Germany to be wed, but when her intended saw the birthmark, he backed out of the deal. Her cruel relations rented her out as hired help, and she eventually became destitute when they refused to have anything to do with her, other than have her committed to the asylum. The fact that she knew no English made the situation more dire. Aurora wondered how many women here had been sane when they entered. Surely being abandoned and committed by those closest to you would drive you mad.

Late that afternoon, she met with her subdued in-laws in the hotel lobby. They were huddled together on a long upholstered davenport, the only people in the lobby, other than the desk clerk. The resort season was long since over, and the hotel had an abandoned air. Her father-in-law's distress was manifest in the constant patting of his wife's hand. She, red-eyed, looked bereft, perplexed by the man so unlike the son she had last seen in February of 1898 when he and Frank King had set off like excited schoolboys to find their fortune.

Edith Starr looked up at Aurora, as if she could provide the answer. "Why does he treat me like a stranger? All he talked about was the asylum orchard and the new varieties he wants to grow." She dabbed her nose and the corners of her eyes with a lace-edged hankie. "And he spoke in a hoarse voice, rather rushed. The nurse said he had been yelling most of the night about someone called Wiggins. I told that nurse that Martin should have applications of eucalyptus vapor for his throat."

"Now dear," said Samuel Starr, as he resumed the hand-patting, "try to keep in mind what Dr. Shelby said."

"Yes, yes, too many stresses. His guilt over Frank and the other men. I told Martin that Mr. and Mrs. King do not hold him responsible. Goodness, it was Frank's idea to go on that awful expedition."

Martin's parents stayed one more day for a final visit with their son, then headed back to Pelican, where winter was already firmly entrenched. Aurora waved to them from the depot platform, standing back from the hissing train as it carried away her in-laws on the icy rails. Wet, biting snow stung her skin and tore at her eyes. She promised Edith she would write on a regular basis to report Martin's condition. She felt utterly alone, without prospect of solace from another human. Martin had deserted her. She was a widow.

She had read Martin's notebook, several times by now, without coming across any mention of Wiggins. Her husband must have stopped writing in it, decided to burn it, before he encountered the man.

Chapter Twenty-three

Thanksgiving 1899

Turkeys—Charcoal for

A recent experiment has been tried in feeding charcoal for fattening turkeys. Two lots of four each were treated alike, except for one lot finely pulverized coal was mixed with mashed potatoes and meal, on which they were fed, and broken pieces of coal also plentifully supplied. The difference in weight was one and a half pounds each in favor of the fowls supplied with coal, and the flesh was superior in tenderness and flavor.

The weak November light leaked through the tall windows of the sunroom. Aurora did not see Martin when she first entered the room. An older man with stains on his vest moved back and forth determinedly in a rocking chair, as if urging it to take him somewhere. He didn't look up as Aurora passed him. The sunroom was full of rocking chairs, and Martin sat motionless in one beside a huge potted palm. His hands rested on his thighs, and his feet were encased in thick socks stuffed into slippers. *He* looks like an old man, too, she thought, noticing the white in his moustache.

"Hello, Martin." She placed her hand over his as she sat down next to him in a rocker with a calico cushion. "What are you going to do today?" She resisted any reference to their life together, or to his time as a Klondiker. She would like to talk to him about his notebook, to let him know she shared a knowledge of what he had been through. But Dr. Shelby had advised that she focus on the present and see Martin in his environment, thus helping her husband to heal through the stability of a regular routine.

Martin looked up, welcome and avoidance warring on his countenance. "Hello." This in a dull, raspy voice. Then, "Hello, Aurora." He lifted his face toward the windows. "There are thirty panes in each window. Five windows in this south-facing wall, and three floors in this wing. That makes 450 panes of glass. So much glass." He looked down at his hands, as if they too were a cause for amazement.

Her mouth formed a slight, sad smile. "It is a lot of glass. Are you working in the greenhouse today?"

"Yes." He sat up straighter, more business-like. "I'll be putting together arrangements for the chapel and for the dining rooms. For Thanksgiving." He stood up quickly, startling Aurora. "I need to get ready." With that, he shuffled jerkily in his thick footwear out of the sunroom and down the long, linoleum hallway to his room on the ward.

Aurora stayed, tears running down her face and pooling near the corners of the mouth. She tasted their salt as she rocked. A handkerchief, a red bandana really, appeared before her face. "You keep this, dear," said the old man, who had ceased his constant rocking to comfort her.

"Thank you," she said to his retreating back. He lowered himself and resumed his back and forth rhythm.

She allowed Martin some time to change in his room and leave the ward, and then she headed down the hall to his room. Unlike the women's wards where the rooms were locked during the day, Martin seemed to have access to his. His name and that of his roommate were posted in a card slot on the door. She knocked softly and turned the knob. The room was empty. Too empty, though the slippers were lined up near the side of the bed, toes pointed out ready for feet. His bureau held the few toiletries she had purchased for him. Razors were kept by the attendants. She opened one of the small top drawers. The cravat and collars laid there, seemingly unworn, untouched by

Martin. The corner of a crumpled envelope caught her eye, and she slipped it out from under the unused accessories. Leaning against the oak bureau, she read Frank's final words to his parents and to the woman he loved in Pelican. She moved the paper so her falling tears would not blur the ink. Hearing voices in the hall, Aurora returned the envelope to its place in the drawer. Martin was still carrying out his obligation to Frank, in the only way he could. She was sure the notes were meant to reach Pelican. Aurora decided to not mention her discovery to Martin, not yet.

The chatty nurse attendant, named Clara, invited Aurora to her home for Thanksgiving. Aurora suspected pity to be the motivating factor. Everyone on the staff knew of Aurora's situation. However, she was so hungry for the diversion of talk and laughter, so eager to escape the hopeless, deadened smells of the asylum, and the confines of her small, if comfy, room that she readily accepted the invitation.

Clara's whole family was employed, or had been employed, at the asylum. Her father, a mason, had been one of hundreds to construct the buildings. "That job gave me three years of work, from '82 to '85," he told Clara, as he distributed turkey, turnips and potatoes on each plate. He continued to explain that the bricks he laid started as local "blond" clay, and had been made at the brickyard just south of Grand Bay City. "And this turkey, he's local, too. From the asylum's own turkey yard. We get a free one each Thanksgiving." The man's pride in his association with the asylum made Aurora uneasy. It was as if he saw it only as a collection of buildings, a generator of employment for the locals, not a place where people who had once lived in the "real" world were kept apart, and sometimes forgotten. That was what she would never do, no matter Martin's mental condition—she would never erase him from her memory or sever contact with him.

"It's delicious," Aurora said, raising her eyebrows in approval towards Clara's mother. Actually the meat was a bit dry, cooked too long.

"Yes, the asylum's been good to us. Our Clara has a steady job. The wife works in the laundry, and Chadwick here," he pointed his fork towards his sullen, pimply son, "he's working in the carriage barns. It was a great day for Grand Bay City when that institution opened."

Aurora managed a weak smile.

"Sorry, Aurora," said Clara. "Dad didn't mean that the way it sounded." She shot her father a stern look.

"I'm sorry for your misfortune, Mrs. Starr. I just meant it gave the folks here jobs other than lumbering or working at the brickyard."

"I know. It's all right. Martin's getting good care there. He's not unhappy," she put down her forkful of cool, lumpy turnips, "I think."

"Your husband is on a good ward. Be thankful he's well enough to stay off the most-disturbed ward, and doesn't have to wear a muff," said Clara.

"A muff?" Aurora wondered if this was because of unheated rooms.

"It's a device that some patients wear so they won't harm themselves, or others. It looks like a pair of leather mittens with steel buckles and a chain. The patient's hands are held together."

"But how do these patients eat, or . . ." She paused thinking of all the personal things one needed hands for.

"Well, the attendants feed them and take care of bodily functions. An attendant on that ward, she started working at the asylum the same time as I did, grew fond of a woman who wore the muff. The woman promised she would behave, so the naive thing took off the contrivance. Quick as a blink, the patient attacked her. Left gouges from her fingernails on the poor girl's face and bites on her arms. That attendant left her job immediately. I've heard she's working in a dress shop now."

If Clara had intended to ease Aurora's mind, she had done the opposite. She was Job's comforter, an expression her mother had used, meaning someone who while supposedly helping only heaped more worry on the beleaguered person. Was Martin aware of the most-disturbed ward? What if a violent patient attacked Martin? Her stomach knotted and against the protestations of Clara's mother, she declined the dark, dense mincemeat pie.

Large, wet flakes were falling when she left Clara's house. The cold air was intoxicating after the overheated interior that smelled of the asylum. The whole family must have absorbed the odors of their workplace into their skins and clothes. Aurora experienced this. When she returned from the hospital, she seemed to carry with her a smell that brought to mind dried drool and lye soap. She immediately removed her clothes and washed her face and forearms in the basin in her room. Still when she turned her head, she caught a whiff of the institution, insinuated into her hair.

Clara's house was even nearer to the hospital than the house where Aurora lodged. She looked over her shoulder to where the lighted, steaming gothic grouping of buildings seemed to rise and hover in the falling snow, like a mysterious empire, a phantom city.

The next day she met with her men students for the first time. All three knew more English than Greta or Wanda. Aurora supposed that was so because men were out in the world more often than women, dealing with others outside the home. This group consisted of one German and two Bohemians. They were past the "Hello, how are you?" stage.

She missed her students back home, but not the incessant noise from the sawmill, less than half a mile from the school, which was a constant distraction. Her new teaching setting would be peaceful in comparison. In the little school building, students stuffed paper in their ears when the whine of the blades reached an uncomfortably high pitch. Then she stopped whatever lessons the students were on, and they all sang at the top of their lungs. The Jankowski boy carried a harmonica in his pocket and was always ready to play it. Then they'd sing "When the Birds Go North Again" or "The Boy Guessed Right." Aurora had them write out the lyrics as part of handwriting class, and then they all memorized the words.

Her critic teacher in Mt. Pleasant, the slab-faced Mr. Malcolm, who avoided all contact with children declared, "If you don't love children, consider another occupation." Well, Aurora soon discovered she did not love children *all* the time, and furthermore she did not love all children. Some could be cruel and spiteful. Aurora felt she was effective at hiding her personal feelings; in fact, she tried harder to engage the difficult students, to let them experience self-worth, at least within the walls of the school.

Until now, she had associated teaching with the screaming of saws and the smell of sawdust, which left a fine film on the desktops, the globe and blackboard. Even the pages of books had a layer of grit waiting for the readers' fingers. Her two youngest students sneezed and wheezed during school. Aurora knew the sawmill was not good for their health. But then their fathers worked there, so she was unsure of how to approach their parents about her concerns.

This teaching job would be a plum. She looked forward to dealing with grownups. That day she went through names for clothing and furniture in the sunroom, where the men students sat in a circle of rocking chairs. She had stiff paper and a thick pencil for making signs for common objects: *vest, slippers, trousers, rocking chair, carpet, window.* Her method was the one she used with her young students back in Sawyersville. Now she placed the signs on corresponding objects, pronouncing each word twice, then having the patients say the word twice. The next meeting she would give each man several signs and have them place them around the room on the matching object Perhaps this was beneath their dignity, but she couldn't think of a better way to teach basic vocabulary. Energized with being a teacher again, she planned for a future lesson where her students would use short sentences incorporating the familiar nouns.

"I'll see you next week," she said to the group as the hour ended.

"Gif me your hant," said the youngest, about twenty-two, she thought, a handsome man except for his huge ears, which flapped out from his skull, and who obviously knew more English than he was letting on.

Aurora extended her hand towards the patient, who grasped it softly at the wrist, bowed and kissed the back. The other two chuckled, and so did she until she noticed a shape in the doorway. Martin looked in on the group, then turned abruptly, hitting the doorframe with his shoulder as he headed down the hall. Did he think she was betraying him? Was he turning away from her for good? Or could it be a good sign? She told herself this reaction could speak of a growing response to her as his wife, an awareness of their connection.

At the old prospector's cabin

Chapter Twenty-four

December 1899

To Clean Knives and Forks

Wash the blades in warm (but not hot) water, and afterwards rub them lightly over with powdered rottenstone mixed to a paste with a little cold water; then polish them with a clean cloth.

*A*urora quickly finished her letter to Martin's parents. At least she could report that *his yelling has ceased and his voice has returned to normal. He is engrossed in preserving buds and forcing bulbs for winter blooming. His life here revolves around horticulture.*

She was meeting Greta in the women's dining room, where Greta set the tables. Aurora had found teaching in the little plant-packed alcove too constricting. The learning of a new language should be active. Greta needed to learn English that she could use immediately in her daily routine. The other woman, Wanda, had grown less hostile but still spent most of the time mumbling to herself in Polish. Aurora told Dr. Shelby she wanted to concentrate on Greta for now, and received permission to accompany Greta on her activities.

She arrived to find Greta arranging the silverware in the curious tripod arrangement she had noted before. "Hello, Greta."

Greta was intent, the birthmark accentuated by the starched white coverall over her dress. She turned to face Aurora, causing the mark to appear as a shadow on the left side of her face. "Hello, Aurora." She paused, recalling the appropriate phrase, "Please to be seated. Ya?"

"Yes, that's good. Please be seated," she corrected gently.

"Please be seated."

Aurora pulled out a chair and watched as Greta moved efficiently from table to table getting ready for the noon meal. The smells of turkey soup and fresh bread, delivered from the bakery in the basement, signaled her stomach, which growled in anticipation. The institution incorporated a working farm, which included a calf barn, bull pens, horse barn and milk depot. It even boasted several silos built of Cyprus wood. It was a town within a town, sealing in the patients from the "outside," only a short walk from the front gate. Aurora wondered if this was good, especially for patients like Greta, who needed to be in touch with the outside world, so they would be ready to move into it. She did not belong here. But where would she go? Here she was fed, housed, protected. In the few weeks that Aurora had known the young German woman, her English vocabulary had increased by leaps and bounds.

"Why do you place the silverware that way?" she called across the dining room. Aurora joined her and tried her hand at configuring a set of utensils.

When they tipped and clattered to the table, Greta laughed. "Watch me," she said, glorying in her role as teacher.

When Aurora saw how the pieces were interlocked, she managed to help Greta finish the last table. "Where did you learn to do this?"

Greta looked puzzled. Aurora repeated the question pointing to the tripod.

"I learn it myself. Me," she said, tapping her sternum and smiling.

The women filed in, moving to their assigned tables. Aurora sat down next to Greta. Soon three other women joined them.

"Hello, dear, are you the new patient?" inquired a woman whose mouth caved in. Although she appeared no more than forty, Aurora could see she had not a tooth in her head.

"No, you toothless idiot, she's not a patient," snapped her neighbor, a woman with skittering black eyes and sausage-like gray curls.

"You're a teacher, aren't you sweetie?" she asked, giving Aurora a brilliant, if rather threatening, grin. "Her husband is a patient here," she said, giving the toothless woman a withering look.

"Yes, that's right," Aurora said. How amazing that even this patient knew of her situation. Another woman brought a tureen to the table. Greta began ladling the soup into the bowls. The other woman assigned to this table was still praying, her hands clenched so tightly the knuckles were turning white. Two nurse attendants stood in the doorway watching. Did the patients find this reassuring, or annoying? All the work seemed to be done by the patients. She saw one of the attendants nod towards her table and whisper something to the other. At that moment, Aurora felt herself more allied with the patients than with the nurses. The still warm loaf of bread was passed, and she cut off a piece, coating it with butter. Aurora caught Greta's eye and nodded, encouraging her to use English with the other women.

"Please pass the salt," she blurted out.

The praying woman unclenched her hands and handed the salt shaker to the toothless woman, who handed it to Greta and said, "You can talk English real nice. Can't she?" She looked around the table, her head bobbing. The praying woman leaned forward to smile at Greta. Sausage Curls was not as impressed. "You'll have to learn more than pass the salt if you want to get out of this nuthouse," she snarled.

Aurora, fighting to control her tongue, was about to reply. Even though this woman was a patient, she had no right to berate poor Greta. But she was saved from responding, for at that moment the disagreeable woman let out a *whoop* as she dredged up a small feather encased in a glob of fat from her soup. She flung the disgusting surprise over her shoulder, where it landed in the hair of a woman at the table behind her. This patient in turn shrieked as the warm fat ran down her neck. The woman next to the stricken one jumped up overturning her chair. Suddenly the room was electric; the attendants moved swiftly, like ships under full sail, one to the fat-thrower, the other to the recipient. "Come Evelyn. You cannot behave that way during meal time," said the attendant, a burly woman from whom Evelyn shrank. Aurora felt a bit sorry for her as she was hustled out of the dining room. The other woman, crying loudly, was dealt with in a more soothing manner. "Let's get you cleaned up, shall we?" said the attendant in a brisk, chirpy voice.

"Intermediate ward for Evelyn," said the toothless woman, a broad smile exposing her gums.

"She should get the muff," said the other woman, who had blessed her food so thoroughly.

Peace descended on the dining room again. Aurora saw that Greta was upset, her hand trembling as she lifted the spoon to her mouth. The port-wine stain was on the side away from Aurora. In profile, away from the distraction of the birthmark, Greta was a pretty young woman, with regular features, artistically arching eyebrows. Aurora thought back to Eleanor in Wrangell and her disfigurement. At least Eleanor had an advocate in Astrid; who does Greta have? She has me, thought Aurora.

After the meal, Aurora marched to Center Hall. She stood in front of Flora's desk, watching the woman's fingers assault the typewriter keys. The receptionist could not help but be aware of her presence, yet she made no acknowledgement. Aurora moved past her desk toward Dr. Shelby's office.

"Mrs. Starr, you cannot just barge in. You do not have an appointment." She puffed as she pushed herself away from the desk to rescue Dr. Shelby from the intruder.

Aurora knocked on the solid door, heard a faint "yes?" from within and entered just as Flora's bulk closed in on her. She closed the door firmly behind her. Dr. Shelby quickly brushed off his desktop, where it appeared he had been paring his nails. "Mrs. Starr." He appeared flustered, then pleased to see Aurora before him. "Is everything all right?"

"I've come about Greta Herrmann. She needs to be out more, doing things other than setting tables. You can't think her insane." Indignation built and carried her. "Surely, speaking German does not qualify one for the asylum."

"No, no, of course not. Miss Herrmann was exhibiting signs of withdrawal from society, even of paranoia." Dr. Shelby was the epitome of the calm doctor.

"Who could blame her after what she has been through!" Aurora felt she was talking to a simpleton, rather than a medical doctor. "For that matter, my husband, too. Don't you think any of us might be here if we were subjected to the trials they have gone through?"

"That is precisely why they need to be here, in a refuge where their tortured minds can heal," he said, with more force than before, as the rash colored his cheeks.

"But I don't think Greta, unlike Martin, has a tortured mind. She has been manipulated, treated like a piece of furniture, and then abandoned. She is bright, capable of making her own way in the world. She cannot rot here!"

"So what are you proposing, Mrs. Starr?" Dr. Shelby seemed interested. It was not often someone from outside the institution took such an interest in a patient, and that included their own relatives.

"I would like to take Greta out for some fun, perhaps going to a restaurant, a concert, or just walking along the bay. She needs these experiences. Consider it part of her language instruction if you need to justify it on paper."

Dr. Shelby took a deep breath and lifted his pen from the inkwell. "I'll have Flora type up something for you to sign, saying you take responsibility for Miss Herrmann, or I should say 'Fraulein Herrmann,' " he said, giving a guttural pass at the title.

"That's fine," she said, as she extending her hand. "Thank you."

"I should thank you," he said, holding her eyes in gratitude. As her hand was resting on the ceramic doorknob, he said, "You didn't ask about your husband."

"No, I didn't think there was any reason. Has there been a change in his manner? Have you talked to him?"

"Only to see if he liked his chores in the greenhouse. He told me the nightmares of his ill-fated trip are not occurring as often, so he's sleeping better. He seems quite content," said the doctor, proud of Martin's adjustment.

"Perhaps he's found a life that suits him," she offered sadly.

Three days later she met Greta at the entrance. They walked into town to the stores on Front Street, the leather of their boots turning dark from the slush. The scant snow of November had long ago melted, and everyone was commenting on the prospect of a "green Christmas." Aurora thought this an odd phrase; the only green was in the far-off line of spruce trees behind the asylum barns and in the occasional pine or cedar trees on town lots. More likely a gray and brown Christmas. Only the yellow bricks of the Great Lakes Asylum stood out, their color enhanced by the muted landscape.

As they entered a dry goods store, Greta gasped at the shelves loaded with bolts of cloth, the drawers of thread and buttons. "I must shop here," she insisted.

"Then you must deal with the clerk on your own," said Aurora.

"Deal with?"

"Talk to. Ask for things."

"I can do that," said Greta, smiling in her new way, a way that released her from past mistreatment. The wine-red cap and scarf, which she had knitted herself, made the birthmark a part of her ensemble. Aurora thought it extraordinary that she had been so brave to do such a thing.

Then four days before Christmas, the winter solstice, it began to snow. Aurora was meeting with her male patients, all of whom were progressing with their English. The light in the sunroom changed, as if soft gauze had been dropped over the building—a darkening brightness, if such a thing were possible, thought Aurora. They were all drawn as one body to the windows, and stood transfixed as the snowflakes danced tentatively, then gained resolve and joined forces to become a solid curtain of white. She hoped Martin was as entranced over in the greenhouses where he was working.

The snow accumulated. Sometimes there would be several hours when it ceased, but then the air would grow full of the smell, the feel of snow, and the solid presence of white would return, muffling all sounds of wagons, buggies, horses. Aurora wondered how her tenant was faring at Starrvation Corner. There was probably more snow further north. She was glad to be in a city now, where the snow could not isolate her, where the chores of staying alive and keeping the animals tended could be set aside.

On December 23, she ate with Greta in the dining room, and then the two left the asylum for Aurora's lodgings. Behind the house, a gentle hill covered with two-days worth of snow sloped down to a meadow. The landlady lent them a sled, one her children had used to make countless boisterous, thrilling runs down that very hill. Aurora sat in front, her feet on the steering mechanism, the rope clenched in her mittened hands. Behind her, Greta wrapped her arms and legs around Aurora after pushing off. The runners engaged and they went plowing through the snow, the sled lurching in the wet heaviness. They reached the bottom, both covered in snow, which worked its way down the tops of their boots and mittens.

"So, we do it again," said Greta, grabbing the rope and dragging the sled back to the top. This time the ride down was faster, and their involuntary *whoops* exhilarated them even more. After they had made eight runs, taking turns at steering, they were thoroughly soaked and chilled. As they climbed the hill for the final run, Greta looked beyond the house and the city blocks to where the venting towers of the asylum rose like hazy apparitions through the screen of snow.

"I do not want to go back," she said.

"Only for a short time. I promise, I will help you to leave." Aurora wasn't sure how, but she knew she would.

Greta, eyes shining with tears, embraced her. "You are my only friend."

The landlady, who had been watching from the kitchen window, helped them spread out their wet wool garments near the stove and urged them to the table for hot cocoa. She gave them glycerin and rosewater for their chapped cheeks and wrists, which were circled with bracelets of raw, red skin. Aurora observed Greta's rosy face and damp curls where her hair had escaped from her cap and thought, *this is the friend I have longed for.* The contentment of the moment was overcome by the sad realization: *I have lost a husband but gained a friend.*

Chapter Twenty-five

Christmas Eve to New Year's Eve 1899

Flowers—To Obtain from Bulbous Roots in Three Weeks

Put quicklime into a flower-pot till it is rather more than half full; fill up with good earth; plant your bulbs in the usual manner; keep the earth slightly damp. The heat given out by the lime will rise through the earth, which will temper its fierceness; and in this manner beautiful flowers may be obtained at any season.

*T*he city's sidewalks disappeared. There was no longer any pretense of trying to keep them clear. All the streets were reduced to a one-vehicle width. When the snowplows came through, pedestrians scrambled up on the banks; other conveyances pulled into side streets to make way. The plow drivers were accorded a respect usually reserved for undertakers as they drove two teams of horses in a tandem hitch. With hoots and hollers they urged the huge farm horses to drag the plows, triangular devices made from wood planks, through the streets of Grand Bay City.

On Christmas Eve Aurora attended a service at her landlady's Swedish Lutheran Church. This woman was not Swedish, but her deceased husband had been. She explained that Santa Lucia Day was really December 13, but the church decided to celebrate it this year in combination with their Christmas Eve service. Aurora held her breath as a young woman in a long white gown bound with a red sash, her blond hair braided and coiled on her head, walked down the aisle of the dimly lit sanctuary wearing a crown of blazing white candles. Half the hymns were sung in Swedish, but Aurora recognized the melodies to *Silent Night, Joy to the World* and *O Come, O Come Emmanuel* and sang along in English. Afterwards there were cookies and hot cider. Aurora immersed herself in the buzz of conversation, in the warmth of the church heated by a ceramic stove at the rear and by the wool-bound bodies of the believers. Martin would probably be back on the ward now after attending a service in the chapel, whose front and sides were lined with pots of poinsettias, plants Martin had been nurturing for weeks.

Around ten o'clock on Christmas Day, Aurora walked to the asylum along the roadway, moving up against the bank each time a wagon or sleigh passed. The packed-down snow provided a firmer foundation than the ridged sandy roadbed of the other seasons. A sleigh whizzed by, its runners zinging over the compacted surface, the driver happily ignoring the 12 miles an hour speed limit. *Merry Christmas* floated back as the blur of horses, sleigh and passengers receded. "Merry Christmas," she yelled back. The words sounded so precise, as if they were carved out of ice, each letter seeming to hang suspended in the air above her head. A joy seized her, rattled her, so that she yelled it out again. "Merry Christmas!" She hugged the presents to her chest more tightly—a bottle of glycerin and rosewater for Greta, combs for Clara, who would be working today because she had drawn Thanksgiving as her "off holiday"—and for Martin, a hair wreath for his room. She had incorporated as many different flower designs as possible, using a flower identification book her landlady had lent her. She had worked on it every night before going to bed, wrapping the thin wire with brush leavings saved over many years, which she stored in a powder box of her mother's, twisting it into flower shapes until her eyes could no longer focus and her fingers cramped. What had happened to the watch chain woven with her hair? She was sure Martin would treasure it forever. Both watch and chain were gone, perhaps in some muskeg in British Columbia.

The sleigh that speeded past her on the street was one of many conveyances crowded around the Center Hall entrance. Steam rose in a rich, warm cloud from the horses' bodies. Aurora knew that on Christmas Day the city officials, including the mayor, came to serve a Christmas dinner to the residents.

The aroma of roasting turkey and ham overpowered, but did not completely eliminate, the asylum's smell. Tables covered in red cloths were arranged in orderly rows in Center Hall, where Aurora and Martin had stood, both overwhelmed by the intimidating space, just last September. Her eyes scanned the huge area, looking for Martin among the mixture of patients and staff who were setting up. Greta's face broke into a brilliant smile when she saw Aurora. She was setting the tables, but this time the silverware rested proper and flat beside the plates. Clara was bringing in chairs from the dining rooms. Then Martin appeared, bearing an armful of cedar and pine boughs, which he jammed into a huge urn near the stairway. The air was spiked with the scent of resin and snow. Martin wore a bulky coat, not one she had bought for him, and oversize boots that left puddles of melting snow on the tile floor as he clomped back outside for more greens. She weaved through the tables and caught up with him.

"Martin, I've come to have dinner. I guess Dr. Shelby considers me a staff member," she said, laying her hand on his sleeve.

He turned, his face flushed from the cold, his nose running a bit. His smile shocked her, made her wary. When was the last time Martin had smiled at her?

"Merry Christmas, Rory. I have something to give you, after the dinner," he said turning, his startling blue eyes pinning hers. Then he was moving purposely down the hallway.

Her spirits soared. A miracle. He had called her *Rory*. For the first time since Martin had come to the asylum, she allowed herself the luxury of hope that he would return to her.

At noon all the patients, except those from the *most disturbed* wards, filed in and found their name cards. Aurora's name card was at the end of a table; Dr. Shelby's was to her left. Martin was seated several rows over—at the same table as Greta. She noticed that at least one staff member was assigned to each table. A local priest, young and handsome, and the Lutheran minister, stern and grizzled, had come over to the asylum after their Christmas morning services. They each offered a prayer for the bounty of food. Aurora much preferred the young priest's simple prayer. The Lutheran's words made her cringe as he droned on and on about "the poor benighted souls" being "God's children, too." As if there were any question of that, she thought, lifting her head from its bow to glare at his fierce countenance. Several, including Martin and Greta, had not bowed their heads. And, perhaps it was her buoyant attitude at the moment, but she was sure she detected a slight smile directed at her, just before he averted his gaze, as if she and Martin were again sharing a joke.

"I know you are not having office hours now, but tell me, don't you think Martin seems to be more," she paused for the right word, "more *aware* of others, less isolated in his own mind?" She turned to face Dr. Shelby, so she could read his expression. A member of one of the Ladies Aids Societies placed a platter of turkey and ham—white, brown and pink slices—at the head of the table. She nodded at Dr. Shelby, but avoided Aurora's eyes. Most likely she assumed that Aurora was a patient, a "poor benighted soul," ready to spring from her chair and assault the meat-bearing matron.

"Yes, he does. He's been more communicative with his fellow workers in the greenhouses. I guess you know he's quite talented with plants. It seems to give him a purpose," said the doctor, spooning creamed corn onto his plate.

A shriek and the ring of china smashing on the tiles brought all conversation to a halt. All heads turned as two attendants half-escorted, half-carried a thrashing Evelyn, her face contorted with rictus and rolling eyes. One fist made contact with the cheek of the attendant on the right. "God damn Father Christmas," were Evelyn's parting words to the assembly. Aurora suppressed a smile.

Dr. Shelby sighed. "I think we'll have to move her to another ward. She begged to come, but I fear she's going to injure someone seriously one of these days."

At the next table, the tearful woman Aurora remembered from her first meal with Greta in the women's dining room commenced weeping, shaking her head as a rotund man wearing a red vest, the mayor she learned from Dr. Shelby, offered her steaming Parker House rolls from a basket.

After raisin cake and apple pie, the town's children's choir arranged themselves on the grand stairway. The older ones looked nervous and wary of being inside the asylum, for already, barely fifteen years after its opening, the institution was fertile ground for stories and legends, usually told by those who had little knowledge of it. The younger children were wide-eyed with curiosity at being in such a cavernous space. Their bell-like voices pushed the Christmas melodies up and out towards the patients, many joining in spontaneously, their faces transformed for the moment. In that brief time, Aurora could see them as happy people with families and livelihoods. But then the music ended and they were again patients, dulled by the routine of the institution as they returned to their wards.

Aurora, now a familiar figure here, blended into the group of women heading for the convalescence ward. She handed Clara her present.

"Oh, Aurora, I have no gift for you," she said.

"Your kindness at Thanksgiving, that was a gift."

Aurora found Greta in the plain room she shared with the woman she and Martin had seen on their first day, the woman carrying the doll. She laid her gift for Greta on the scratchy surface of a brown blanket that covered the bed. It seemed that they could have left the bedspreads on, just this one special day. Greta went to the plain wood dresser, its top bare of any female luxuries, and opened the top drawer. She turned and lifted Aurora's right hand and placed a small box in her open palm.

"Do not keep me suspended. Open it now," Greta urged her.

"Keep me in suspense," said Aurora, always on duty as a teacher.

"However is correct." She could barely contain herself, and her accent grew thicker, more German.

"Oh, my, they're beautiful," she said, though Aurora's first unbidden impression as she lifted the lid of the box, one she would try to dispel, was of little black shiny corpses laid in their satin-lined coffins. Jet earrings. Tapered ebony shaped like long teardrops.

"They look very pretty with your hair," said Greta as Aurora put them on. She needed no mirror to know she was instantly elegant; she could see it reflected in the eyes of her friend. "And one more," she said, pulling a soft tissue-wrapped square from the drawer.

Aurora took a deep breath and laid back the tissue, gasping at the soft moss-colored scarf which Greta had knitted. "Where did you ever find such a color? Maybe it's made from moss."

"Yes, I thought it looked like it was picked right from the woods. You must wear it today. Right now," she said, draping the material around Aurora's neck.

Aurora kissed Greta on the cheek, the stained one. "I have never felt more beautiful." There were tears in her eyes. "Now open yours."

"Lovely, for my chaps," said Greta, as she poured a bit of the lotion into her palm and rubbed it into her reddened, rough hands.

"My baby needs some on her poor skin," whined Greta's roommate, from her perch on her bed, rocking the doll in its red nightgown.

Greta went to the woman and poured a glob of lotion into her outstretched hand.

"I told her not to go out in the cold today," fussed the woman, her straight gray hair cut like a schoolgirl's, chin length with bangs.

"Martin spoke to me during our meal. The first time," said Greta.

"How did he seem?"

"Well, I do not know him from before the asylum, but he seems to me frightened."

"Frightened of what?"

"Of himself."

Martin was in the sunroom, pacing back and forth and still wearing the too-big galoshes, looking like a boy dressing up in his father's clothes. When he saw her he bent and retrieved something behind a potted palm. He held it out to her, an offering. She took the terra-cotta container from him, breathing in the sweet fragrance of the miniature white narcissi, bobbing on their slender green stems. It seemed a freak of nature, an anomaly, to be holding them on Christmas Day. How long could they last?

"You've worked a miracle, Martin. Thank you." She bent to kiss his cheek and saw him staring at the earrings. "But if I take them home, I mean back to the lodging house, won't they die from the cold? Maybe I should leave them here, so I can enjoy them when I come to see you."

"No. They must go with you. We'll put a gunny sack over them. If you can ride, rather than walk, they should be all right." He sounded assertive, knowledgeable, like the old Martin.

"This is for you," she said, handing him his present wrapped in a remnant of flocked wallpaper, a donation from her landlady.

He removed the wrapping carefully and drew out the hair wreath, then brought it to his face. "It smells like you."

A knot in the pit of her stomach loosened. This was her husband. "It seems we both thought of flowers."

That day, that brief time in the sunroom, and before in the hallway downstairs, was a brightening in the bleak landscape of her future. Martin's awareness, his attention to her allowed her to dare think about returning to Starrvation Corner in the spring, with him. As the time grew closer, she would broach the subject of Greta coming, too.

# # # # #

The snow was amazing in its constancy; it continued to fall, smothering the whole city in a slow, deliberate, soft manner. No one could remember what the city looked like without high banks lining the streets and white mounds pressing against the houses and public buildings. It was piled up to the windowsills on the first floor of the house where Aurora stayed; it pressed against the front porch railing.

New Year's Eve in Grand Bay City was silent and hushed. Few horses or people were out on the streets. The telephone poles, which had been erected in haste during the fall to meet the demand for now affordable telephone service, were plastered white on one side, and the lines sagged with a heavy layer of snow. Many thought the poles unsightly, and in the white landscape they looked like shorn trees, which in fact, they were. Most of the town's residents were indoors with their families, content to be in familiar surroundings as the nineteenth century wound down. The only revelry was at the Park Hotel, site of the Pioneer Society party. Tomorrow, Aurora had read on the placards in store windows, businesses would be open to make the most of the first day of 1900. There were all kinds of "new century" sales and specials, like 15¢ for a shave at Allen's Barber Shop and half-price for gloves and hats at Beatrice's Ladies Store.

Wrapped snugly in a shawl, Aurora stepped onto the porch, lifting her face to the snow, the jet earrings swinging against her cheek, their mineral bodies chilled and smooth. By squinting she could make out the vague outline of the asylum and the blobs of light from its solid windows. She had been there in the morning to visit Greta and Martin. The institution was having no festivities this evening, so she was sharing cider and popcorn with her landlady, who was at the moment making more popcorn in the iron pot on the range. She tried to persuade Greta to come out for the evening, but she had shaken her head at the invitation. "It is too sad to haf to come back. It is better for me to stay here tonight."

Aurora stared into the house through the parlor window, as if into a museum display, feeling disconnected, an observer with no knowledge of this place. The snow had blown a scalloped design at the bottom of the panes. The delicate narcissi leaned toward the glass from their position on a piecrust table. Her landlady was only too happy to have flowers in her parlor—*Just think to have bulbs blooming in this snowy winter!* On Christmas night, Aurora had placed the plant beside her bed, longing for this part of Martin to be close to her as she slept. But the light, cloying fragrance would not let her sleep, so she got up, the cold floor boards shocking her bare feet, and carried the plant to the other side of the room and settled it on the little desk, where Martin's brown notebook resided. The golden eyes of the perfect white flowers followed her as she climbed back into bed. Still the funereal scent disturbed her, threatened to crush the tiny seed of happiness that had been planted, that was buried deep in her, under her layers of clothes as she rode home in a sleigh, courtesy of Dr. Shelby, balancing Martin's gift under its gunnysack hood on her lap. The next day she removed the flowers from her room.

Now as she stared at the narcissi, one fragile stem, the head too heavy, leaned out from the community of its fellows, its green stalk creased, then buckled, the petals brushing the table's surface. Inside the phone rang, reluctantly, as if the newly strung wires found carrying the weight of human voices too much under the burden of snow. Aurora stepped into the entryway to see her landlady hanging up the receiver on the wall.

"A sleigh is coming from the asylum. There's been an accident." Her landlady moved toward her and swallowed, then placed a hand on Aurora's forearm.

She asked no questions. She needed to conserve her strength so she could bear the answers when they came. A dull humming throbbed in her veins. Her mouth was dry; her hands icy. "Well, I guess I'll need my coat," she said, thinking it a stupid thing to say as her kind landlady removed the shawl from her shoulders.

Tahltan Canyon, Indian graves and salmon-drying racks

Chapter Twenty-six

April, May 1900

Embalming—French Method

The following is M. Gannal's mixture for injecting the carotid artery, whereby all the purposes of embalming are attained:—Take dry sulphate of alumine, 1 kilogramme (equal 2 lbs. 3 oz. 5 drs. avoirdupois) dissolved in half a litre (a little less than a pint) of warm water, and marking 32° of the acrometer. Three or four litres of this mixture will be sufficient to inject all the vessels of the human body, and will preserve it in the summer; in the winter, from one to two litres will be enough.

From the kitchen door, Aurora watches a mother phoebe traverse the territory between woods and the overhang above her. This is an established site for a nest, and Aurora looks forward to the friendly birds sharing her house. Trout lilies carpet the area to the right, beside the path to the barn, where Pat is attending to the animals. There is Marble sitting in the reluctant warmth of the northern sun. A foot away the cat is licking its paws, which just a few hours before were clearing out the winter's mice population in the barn. The animals' quick readjustment to being back home makes her wonder if her time away from Starrvation Corner, over a year, was a dream. Perhaps she is still that sheltered domestic woman tending to her daily routine. But no. There is the rectangle of disturbed sod in the graveyard, the ground still looking startled, to remind her. Martin's body was kept in the asylum's icehouse until the ground thawed. Last week it arrived by train. She and her new family—now she is legal guardian to both Pat and Greta—went into Blackbird, to bring her husband home. Sam Agawisso and Jory Bartek met them at the depot to unload the plain coffin from the train and onto the wagon, then out to the farm to dig the hole and place the box in the earth as the season's first robins strutted nearby. Reverend Hartless was at the depot, too, ready with the arrangements to conduct a funeral at the church. Aurora declined. She, Pat and Greta had a private ceremony as snowflakes scurried about. April in northern Michigan was cruel, promising spring one day and yielding to winter the next. In June, Martin's parents would come from Pelican for a proper memorial service. Aurora planned to invite all those who had known Martin and Ethan. She would be ready to share Martin with the community by then.

He had been returning to her, she was sure. He would have regained his sanity, his desire to live a life with her. He was on his way home. This is her comfort. When she saw him drained, motionless and cold in the infirmary at the asylum, she knew he had not given up. She forced herself to look at the slash down the side of his face and through the neck where the pane of glass had fallen at a lethal angle. The man who supervised the greenhouses was so upset he could not look at Aurora. He looked down at his wet boots, sobbing.

"He had gone down to check on the oil heaters in the one greenhouse we're using now. It was the snow. We should have cleared off the snow, you know," he appealed, looking at Dr. Shelby, who had been in the sleigh when it arrived at Aurora's door. "The last two days it piled up and the roof just caved in."

The supervisor and another patient who worked in the greenhouses went to look for Martin when he had been gone for over an hour. Already the snow had filled in his boot prints. They found him, where he fell, his blood on the dirt floor, broken pots which toppled from the closest shelves, all sprinkled with a layer of fresh snow. The flowers still upright on the table were witnesses, forced early from their bulbous bodies, gasping at the cold and shock of the outside world as it swooped in through the broken panes.

Like the flowers, Aurora went into shock. After bending to kiss his icy cheek, she could not move from her position beside Martin's body. Finally, Dr. Shelby cupped her elbow with a firm hand. "It's time to go," he said as he guided her from the infirmary to his office, instructing Flora to make "orange pekoe tea, strong."

She was given her own room in the women's ward so she wouldn't be alone. Her landlady's feelings were a bit hurt that Aurora chose to sleep at the asylum. Dr. Shelby had fetched some of her belongings, including Martin's notebook, which remained on the chest-of-drawers, unopened. The hair wreath, her last gift to Martin, hung from a nail on the wall. Martin's few belongings, including the notes from Frank, were given to her in a canvas bag. She donated his clothing to the men patients. The hospital allowed her liberties not afforded the patients, even so far as to leave a bedspread in her room. She took long walks to the barns and outbuildings, though she avoided the path that passed close to the greenhouses. At first she took meals in her room. Often Greta, with red-rimmed eyes, brought the tray. She had started reading books in English and would pull one from her coverall pocket, pointing to words for Aurora to explain and pronounce.

Aurora found the most solace in the dayroom, where she sat in the rocker beside the potted plant, rocking and counting the panes in the tall windows as Martin had done. The men shuffled in and out, being especially quiet. The old man who had comforted her before brought her little gifts— a peppermint one day, a crow feather the next. In the rocking chair, she started to form an understanding of Martin's detachment, of the shock life had dealt him. How painful it must have been for him, to be numb and unable to respond to her. She was indifferent to her future. Perhaps she would spend the rest of her days here at the asylum.

After two weeks, the numbness receded, and anxieties moved in. What was she to do? She couldn't return to Starrvation Corner. The tenant was still there. Even if no one was there, she had made no preparations to make it through the next few months of winter on a farm. She did not seriously consider making the long trip to Minnesota to stay with her in-laws.

She started eating in the dining room and moved back to her lodgings. Dr. Shelby asked her to resume English lessons with the male patients. It seemed natural that she would. She was comfortable within the hospital's walls. The routine stabilized her; it was something to shape her days. And she was a woman who had not abandoned or forgotten her husband, who had not been ashamed of his condition. Now her bereavement brought her closer to those inside. Even Evelyn became subdued when she saw Aurora approaching. "Please accept my condolences," she mumbled at the dining room table.

"Thank you, Evelyn."

Her guardianship of Greta came more easily than she'd expected, the relatives having no objections. Greta was released from the asylum and moved into Aurora's lodgings until spring. Then, like birds pulled north by the dictates of the season, the two women headed for Starrvation Corner.

Now as Aurora watches the frenetic activity of the phoebe, she foresees the quickened pace of her own life in the days ahead. She has been approached by a school board member. Would she consider stepping into the principal's position at the Blackbird school? She is qualified educationally, though lacking in experience of managing others. She is considering, although it would require her to take lodgings in Blackbird during the tough weeks in winter. She has confidence that Greta and Pat could manage the farm.

And Greta—the young woman seemed to have been reborn when she met Aurora—now exhibits a confidence in herself that is astonishing. Aurora cannot imagine from what well Greta draws her strength and zest for life. Already she has been roaming the woods and fields looking for madder root, black walnut trees, familiar growing things from her girlhood in Germany. She is going to dye wool (already she's in contact with a farmer with a flock of sheep) in colors no one in Blackbird, or Grand Bay City, for that matter, has seen before, and then knit sweaters, hats and gloves to sell. An old galvanized tub she found in the barn will be used for dye preparation. But that is not all. "I must pay my path," she told Aurora with resolution.

"Pay my way," Aurora corrected, and listened to Greta's plan for extensive flower gardens on the south side—gladioli, sweet peas, daisies—which they could sell at the depot as resorters arrived on the Grand Rapids and Indiana line for their summer in paradise.

Greta is a relentless entrepreneur. Her first two projects are dependent on nature, but a third is a business they can start in May. During Aurora's absence, the lumber train has developed another role as an "observation train," which transports summer picnickers, both local and resort people, out of town on the narrow-gauge railway through fields of blackberry, ox-eye daisies and buttercups to secluded spots on creek banks and in stands of pines. Aurora was seized with enthusiasm immediately at Greta's idea to sell picnic boxes to the passengers. It will mean income right away

Pat will stay on the farm another year and then he wants to go to university in Ann Arbor and become a lawyer. It makes her breathless to think he is growing up and ready to move out into the larger world.

"He should do that so he can keep people from being thrown into asylums," Greta declared. She regards Pat as a younger brother and promises him he will go off to college with the most beautiful woolens ever.

Martin's death has not made the world stop. She has not had time to settle into grief. Her widow's weeds were worn in Grand Bay City for a month, and then packed away. No doubt her mother-in-law assumes she walks the boardwalks of Blackbird in bombazine. Aurora has not yet decided what she will wear when it is time for Martin's memorial service, but it will not be black. She likes to think he would be pleased and excited by all these plans. In his own way, he had been moved forward by his dreams.

On May Day, a faint trace of green laces the trees. It will be a few weeks before the leaves open fully, but in the woods and scattered in the open meadows, morels thrust their pitted heads through the decay of fallen leaves and rotting logs. The lilacs, bushes of lavender, dark purple and white varieties, are full of promise, but won't offer full revelation until the beginning of June. She still has her mother's secateurs, with which she'll cut armfuls of lilacs to put in vases throughout the house for Martin's memorial service. When she and Martin married in the front room, the air was seductive with their scent. And during the early days of that first June when Martin was on the Edmonton Trail, she kept lilacs in the bedroom to keep him close.

Aurora stops at Bartek's on her way into town for provisions. The youngest member of the family, nearly three months in the world, is crying, his face clenched like a red fist. After first asking Aurora, Marisa and Jory named their new son Martin, and asked her to be godmother.

"How is my godson today?" Aurora asks, taking the solid infant from Marisa's shoulder. The little fellow quiets, and Aurora feels his body mold itself into her own topography.

"You look good with a baby there," says Marisa, who has lost weight, too much Aurora thinks, after the birth of Martin. She looks drawn, tired. "You are still a young woman, Aurora. Remember that."

Aurora's life has taken on momentum since her husband's death. She has little desire or time to think about remarriage or motherhood. Her life with Greta and Pat is enough. Still she cannot entirely banish such considerations. "I know, Marisa. For now, I'll enjoy my godson." She has trouble calling the baby *Martin*.

She finds herself up on the bluff at the Methodist church. She had not planned to come up here, but her mind drifted and unconsciously she guided the horse to this spot. She glances over at the parsonage, hoping she has not been noticed by Reverend Hartless or his wife.

The church is larger with its new addition. Inside, the air retains a hint of cold ashes, Methodist incense, she thinks. Climbing the stairs to the choir loft, she feels the ghosts of her parents and Martin ascending with her. The children's stool is no longer beneath the round window. Of course, she has no need of it, in fact she must crouch a bit to get an unobstructed view. It makes her sad that this object from her childhood has disappeared.

The noises of that centennial celebration, when she was six, float up from the meadow: the shouts of the Johnson boys, the singing clang of a ringer in the horseshoe pit, her mother's laughter as she hops down the course, one leg in a gunny sack. These sounds recede as she gazes down at the town laid out on the edge of the harbor. Stillness. How full of curiosity she had been about the world and her place in it. Today she carries that child within her; she still has much to teach it.

Aurora stays at the window, not registering the scenery, but reviewing the last decade of her life. Ten summers ago she first met Martin Starr. Six summers ago she was a new teacher with a certificate and five, only five, though it seems a hundred, she was a new bride. She still struggles to put in order the events since Martin left for the Klondike. Sometimes it is too much and she diverts her thoughts with chores. But here she is at thirty, a woman who has been *beyond*. She thought her life with Martin was safe and secure, but how much can be certain when someone that close to you has dreams that take them beyond the familiar yard, the quiet town? She is learning that security is tenuous, and has to be continually refashioned. Martin had found a new security at the asylum greenhouse. She can imagine herself being grateful one day for what Martin has done for her, in forcing her to leave the nest and try her wings. At odd moments she finds herself shaky and weepy, but more and more she is content just to be with people she cares about.

Out on the big lake, a steamer rides the line where water meets sky. The lake has not changed in a decade. From her position in the choir loft, it is difficult to tell if the ship is moving, but she knows progress is sometimes hard to gauge from afar. The whistle of the train coming north from Grand Bay City pierces the quiet of her sanctuary, reminding her that she needs to return to earth and get to business.

When Martin's parents come in the summer, she will go back to Pelican with them for a visit. She will carry with her the notes Frank wrote to his parents and the woman he loved—Eunice, Aurora has learned. She will deliver them in Martin's place, making sure they understand he was on his way.

Acknowledgements

Thank you to Bobbi Stinchcombe and Jan Worth for their careful reading and feedback on the whole book. Also to Judith Hitz and Christina Rajala for their suggestions over wine and cheese. And to Craig Holden at the Ludington Conference on the Novel for his recommendations on organizing the narrative.

Western Canada and Alaska

Books and Articles Consulted

Barton, David W. *Kegomic, The Forgotten Village of the Michigan Tannery and Extract Company 1885-1952.* 1999. (self-published)

Berton, Pierre. *Klondike: The Last Great Gold Rush 1896-1899.* rev. ed. Anchor Canada/Random House of Canada Ltd., 2001.

Cole, E.L. "The Deadly Edmonton Trail." *Alaska Sportsman.* March, April, May, 1955.

Geller, Jeffrey L. and Maxine Harris. *Women of the Asylum: Voices from Behind the Walls 1840-1945.* New York: Doubleday, 1994.

Greenwood, Barbara. *Gold Rush Fever: A Story of the Klondike, 1898.* Toronto and Tonawanda, NY: Kids Can Press, 2001.

Haskell, William B. *Two Years in the Klondike and Alaskan Gold Fields 1896-1898.* Fairbanks: University of Alaska Press, 1998. (originally published 1898)

Johnson, Heidi. *Angels in the Architecture: A Photographic Elegy to an American Asylum.* Detroit: Wayne State University Press, 2001.

May, Marge and John Hall (ed.). *Memories of Little Traverse Bay.* Petoskey, MI: Little Traverse Historical Society, 1989.

Morgan, Lael. *Good Time Girls of the Alaska-Yukon Gold Rush.* Fairbanks and Seattle: Epicenter Press, 1998.

Morley, Jan (ed.). *Harbor Springs: A Collection of Historical Essays.* Harbor Springs, MI: Harbor Springs Historical Commission, 1981.

Rosen, George. *Madness in Society: Chapters in the Historical Sociology of Mental Illness.* New York: Harper & Row Publishers, 1969.

Steele, Earle E. and Kristen Hains. *Beauty is Therapy: Memories of the Traverse City State Hospital.* Traverse City, MI: Denali and Co., 2001.

Wheeler, Keith. *The Old West: The Railroaders.* Alexandria, VA: Time-Life Books, 1973.

Books Quoted (epigraphs on some chapters)

Yaggy, L.W. *How To Do: A Consulting Library for Every Want.* Chicago: Powers, Higley & Co., 1902.

About the Author

Marla Kay Houghteling lives north of Harbor Springs, Michigan. She is a graduate of Vermont College's MFA in Writing program. Arts councils in both Pennsylvania and Michigan awarded her fiction-writing grants. She has also been active in the Writers-in-Schools programs in both those states.

Her two books of poetry are *The Blue House* and *Assisted Living*.

CPSIA information can be obtained
at www.ICGtesting.com
Printed in the USA
LVHW101003070522
718029LV00018B/944